'You're a ..'

'You're beautiful when you're wearing those plain dresses. And when your hair is pulled back...' If he could give her nothing else, Jake resolved, he would give her this.

Katya began to tremble. 'Pride is a sin.'

'No,' he said fiercely. '*No*... Pride is nothing more than believing in yourself.'

'You don't have to say these things.'

'I'm saying it because I'm scared to death to *show* you.'

'You're never scared, Jacob,' she said, as she had once before. 'I want this *now*, Jacob. With you. While I have the chance.'

How the hell was he supposed to turn away from that?

Dear Reader,

It's summer. The days are long...hot and just right for romance. And in Sensation™ this month we can offer you a little of everything, from hot summer sun to winter in the Amish heartland of Pennsylvania.

Our HEARTBREAKER title this month is Suzanne Brockmann's *Love with the Proper Stranger*. Suzanne's moved on from all those luscious Navy SEAL's in TALL, DARK & DANGEROUS to the FBI and a hero who's so dedicated to his job that he's prepared to marry the woman he suspects of being a serial killer...

Next comes the second book in Beverly Bird's THE WEDDING RING trilogy, *Marrying Jake*, it's a glimpse at another way of life entirely and has all the drama you'd expect when a hunt for kidnapped toddlers and a really strong romance combine. *Wife, Mother...Lover?* also features kids, but this time the guy is the single parent and he's in need of his sister-in-law's help or he won't be able to keep his twin boys. How could she resist?

Marie Ferrarella is our final author this month and you should be getting familiar with her name by now as she's been very busy and prolific in the last couple of years. *The Amnesiac Bride* is the latest in the long line of her recent novels and it's one of her best!

As always, it's a *sensational* month. Enjoy!

The Editors

Marrying Jake

BEVERLY BIRD

*Silhouette, Silhouette Sensation and Colophon are
registered trademarks of Harlequin Books S.A., used under licence.*

*First published in Great Britain 1998
Silhouette Books, Eton House, 18-24 Paradise Road,
Richmond, Surrey TW9 1SR*

© Beverly Bird 1997

ISBN 0 373 07802 1

18-9808

*Printed and bound in Spain
by Litografía Rosés S.A., Barcelona*

BEVERLY BIRD

has lived in several places in the United States, but she is currently back where her roots began on an island in New Jersey. Her time is devoted to her family and her writing. She is the author of numerous romance novels, both contemporary and historical. Beverly loves to hear from readers. You can write to her at P.O. Box 350, Brigantine, NJ 08203, USA.

Other novels by Beverly Bird

Silhouette Sensation®

*A Man Without Love
*A Man Without a Haven
*A Man Without a Wife
The Marrying Kind
Compromising Positions
†Loving Mariah

Wounded Warriors
†*The Wedding Ring*

Silhouette Desire®

The Best Reasons
Fool's Gold
All the Marbles
To Love a Stranger

Prologue

It was a good country-and-western bar, and it had taken Jake Wallace several days to find it in the urban sprawl of Washington, D.C. He was offended at first that an area teeming with so many ethnic backgrounds seemed to have neglected the tastes of a good ol' boy from Texas, but once he was pointed in the direction of Clyde and Bob's Bull's-Eye Bar, he generously forgave the nation's capital.

The band was a little too twangy, but he could live with that in light of the genuine sawdust on the floor and the great little getups on the waitresses. They wore bright red bandannas in lieu of skirts, tied in convoluted knots at one hip. And cowboy boots, down there at the bottom of miles of legs. *That* was a nice touch, he thought approvingly. The smoke was thick enough that he could probably scoop a handful of it. There were shouts and laughter, but there hadn't been a fight all night—although if that woman in the painted-on purple jeans kept up with her gyrations on the mechanical bull, Jake thought there'd probably be one soon.

Not his problem, he decided, leaning one elbow back against the bar. He'd left his badge at home.

"There you are."

The voice came from behind him, and Jake's good mood vanished like a burst bubble. It was Albert Paisner, FBI wanna-be, his roommate for the week over at the Academy in Quantico.

Every once in a blue moon, Jake took a continuing education course with the federal government. Not that he'd ever leave the employ of the Dallas Police Department. The Bureau tried to enlist him every time he enrolled, and they had consistently failed to do so. Jake just loved information. He got a kick out of collecting it. You never knew when some odd scrap of knowledge might come in handy.

Paisner, on the other hand, wanted to grow up to be an agent so badly he fairly drooled with it. He was fortyish, a tad overweight, bald, and had the suit-and-tie routine down pat. He'd said—proudly—that he worked with the New York Transit Police. The FBI had not yet offered him a job, though Jake suspected Paisner would be perfectly willing to sweep the floors of their hallowed halls just to get an in.

Jake had spent as little time as possible in their shared room this week. Paisner grated on his nerves.

"Hey, Albie," he said mildly, turning to face the man. "Fancy meeting you here."

Paisner looked around the crowded bar with an expression that said he smelled something foul. "Figured I'd find you somewhere like this."

"Doesn't seem like your kind of joint," Jake admitted. "You know what it is, Albie? It's that tie. You need to lose it." He reached for it. Paisner jumped back, out of reach.

"I'm not staying," he said quickly.

"Too bad. They've got great waitresses."

"I'm married."

"I'm sorry."

Paisner's face started mottling. He reached into his suit jacket pocket and came up with several pink slips of paper. "Leonard Houghton sent me."

Houghton had recommended Clyde and Bob's. He was a

good guy. He was also the director of the continuing education department.

Jake took the phone messages. "Earn any brownie points?"

"Go to hell," Albert Paisner answered, his face growing redder still.

"Been there. Done that." Jake sighed. "You need to lighten up, Albie. Life's too short. And it's ugly enough without looking for things to make yourself frown."

"I take my responsibilities and commitments seriously."

"Well, good for you." Jake started fanning through the messages, then he stiffened. "When did these come in?"

Paisner scowled even more. "All week. Two last night. I've got to go. I don't know how you breathe in this place."

"Deeply, through your mouth, if you're an ex-smoker and still feel the yearning now and again," Jake answered absently. He stuck the messages in the pocket of his sport coat. No coat and tie for him. He wore a T-shirt beneath the jacket, and jeans. No one at the Academy had complained. Yet.

Now they wouldn't get the chance.

"Come on, I'll walk out with you."

"My lucky night," Paisner muttered.

Jake looked at the other man quickly. Then he flashed a real grin. "There you go, Albie. That's it. A wisecrack every now and then is good for the soul." But his heart wasn't in rattling the man anymore.

Seven messages had come in from his brother, Adam. That wasn't good. That couldn't be good at all.

Adam had spent the better part of the past month tracking down his lost son. His ex-wife had disappeared into thin air with the boy four years ago. Earlier in the month, Adam had finally located him, in an Amish settlement in the Pennsylvania heartland. He'd brought Bo home to Dallas two weeks ago, and it hadn't gone well. The boy had more or less been raised Amish. He didn't remember Adam, at least not cohesively. And he had been horrified and frightened by the dizzying rush of twentieth-century humanity and all its toys and trinkets. There'd been a couple of breakthroughs, but acclimating the kid to his old life was going to take some time.

Adam had reluctantly planned to take his son back to visit the settlement to ease the transition. That had been the same day Jake had flown east for the FBI classes, a little over a week ago now, and they hadn't spoken since. But something had gone wrong. Something *had* to be wrong for his brother to call him seven times.

A hollow sensation rolled over in Jake's belly. Had Bo disappeared again? He'd tried to run away from all of this upheaval once. Had he succeeded in staying lost for more than a few hours this time? Maybe as soon as his seven-year-old feet had hit Pennsylvania soil again, he'd bolted.

Jake went outside, where the light was better, and reread the seven messages in the flickering neon above his head. He swore colorfully enough to stop Paisner, who was several steps ahead of him.

"You have a cab waiting for you, by any chance?" Jake asked.

"Right over there. Do you need to go back with me?"

"I need you to drop me off at Washington National."

"The airport? But we still have classes—"

"There'll be classes long after I'm dead and gone," Jake interrupted. It wasn't as though he needed the completion certificate for any real reason. He'd just end up shoving it in a drawer with the others.

"Jake!" a female voice called out from behind him.

He turned to find one of the waitresses standing in the doorway. She was beautiful, with long dark hair in a soft swirl. Her skin was ivory and she had doe eyes and incredible legs. Jake felt a warm sweep of pleasure just looking at her.

It was followed immediately by a twitch of regret. "Sorry, Ilena. I've got to run."

"You forgot your hat." She held the Stetson out to him.

"God bless you," Jake said fervently. He would have hated to have lost it. He crossed back to the door to retrieve it.

"Are you coming back?" she asked.

Ah, hell, Jake thought, the regret growing. "Probably." It wouldn't be until the FBI made courses available again, and by then she would have a boyfriend, but he would almost certainly return to this place now that he had found it.

"Good." Her voice fairly hummed with anticipation. "I get off at midnight."

"Catch you later," he said, perpetuating the small white lie. Then he jogged for the waiting taxi.

"What about your clothes?" Paisner asked once they were inside. "You've left all your stuff back in our room."

Jake thought about it. There wasn't much—a few pairs of jeans, some shirts—just one small duffel bag's worth. "Send it to General Delivery, Lancaster, PA. I'll find it."

"Hey, I'm not your lackey!"

Jake muttered to himself and shifted his weight to dig in his jeans pocket for his wallet. He'd thought he had roughly fifty dollars in cash. He had less than thirty. "Here," he said, handing it to the other man.

Paisner reared back. "I didn't mean—"

"It's a family emergency, Albie. I appreciate your help, that's all. This ought to cover the shipping, and if there's anything left, you can buy some souvenir for the missus. Hey, those cute globes with the snow inside are only a couple of bucks, right?"

Paisner's face tightened again.

"Listen, I really do need some help here."

"An emergency?" Paisner repeated as the cab sped along neon-lit city streets.

"Yeah. I think so."

"That guy's been calling all week. Every night. You never came back to our room."

"You're not my type."

A smile almost got away from the man. Paisner finally took the money.

"You could talk a sky diver into giving up his parachute," he complained, but without bite. "You know, I've been leaving those messages on your bed all week. I thought you saw them when you came back to shower." By the time he finished, his voice had gone disapproving again. "Then Houghton finally said to just take them to you."

Jake was thinking that that was why the Bureau did not want Albert Paisner. It was why he had never gotten past entry-level courses. If he wasn't given directions, he just sort of hovered and waited for them. Then again, Jake reflected, that tended to be the kind of guy the FBI liked most. Why they had been trying to recruit *him* for so many years was still a mystery. He didn't take orders well.

"How come you don't call this Adam guy?" Paisner pressed.

That would take too much time and effort to explain, and they had nearly reached the airport.

"I just can't," he said simply.

The settlement didn't have telephones. The Amish people were convinced the contraptions disrupted the warm, simple lives they led. Jake had worked around it before, when he'd helped Adam unravel the mystery of how his son had ended up in an Amish village called Divinity. He'd do it again.

"Thanks," Jake said. "I really appreciate this."

Paisner sniffed, somewhat mollified. "Of course."

Jake went into the airport, thinking he'd bet his last buck that Paisner would buy his wife one of those little snow-filled globes. Except, of course, he had already given Paisner his last buck.

Ah, well, he thought. Easy come, easy go.

Chapter 1

Jake just barely caught a 10:40 p.m. flight direct from Washington to Philadelphia. He was encouraged that this sudden change of plans seemed to be going off without a hitch—until he actually got on the plane.

He'd used his credit card to purchase the only available seat on a DC-9. It was, of course, the seat no one else wanted—with good cause. It was the last one in the back, tucked against the engine wall, with no window. It involved a total of one, maybe two, square feet.

He was six foot three plus some change. The last time he'd been on a scale—admittedly before he'd spent a week eating government food—he'd weighed two hundred and twenty pounds. Uncle Sam had been real big on watching his cholesterol for him. He was grateful that he had probably dropped a few pounds since last Monday. Otherwise, he wasn't convinced he could have fitted into the tiny space.

As it was, when the woman in front of him put her seat back, it hit him squarely in the chest. Jake pushed his own back as far as it would go. The seat wasn't just uncomfortable.

It was downright painful. *Damn it, bro, this had better be important.*

All his instincts said it was. Adam knew him better than anyone alive. Their sister had disappeared ten years ago, their parents had each died not long after that, and the two of them were all they had now. Adam had never left seven demanding messages before in their lives.

Bo again, Jake thought. It had to be Bo. That was the only thing that made sense.

He looked up to see a flight attendant inching down the aisle with a beverage cart. When she glanced over at him, a question in her eyes, he grinned. "Got a beer in there somewhere? Any ol' brand will do."

She shook her head. "Sorry."

Jake was taken aback. "You want my ID? I swear, I turned thirty-seven last month. I'm of age and I can prove it."

She laughed. "And I'd give you one if I could. But we don't carry alcoholic beverages on board."

He looked around, mystified. "You're kidding."

"We're no-frills."

He definitely remembered the girl at the ticket counter mentioning something about that. Still...no *beer?*

"Something else?" she asked. "Coffee is a dollar, a soft drink is a dollar fifty."

He started to nod, then he remembered that he'd given Paisner all of his cash. He settled back again, swearing a little.

"My treat," the attendant offered. She handed him a cola with a little plastic cup full of ice.

"Thanks," he answered. "You're a doll."

She beamed and moved up to the next row. Even then, her gaze lingered. Jake's charm, his sometimes-easy, sometimes-smoldering grin, were things he had worked at perfecting over the years. He'd been forced at an early age to learn the knack of grinning his way out of almost anything.

He turned his attention to his tray. He couldn't lower it. There wasn't enough room. He scowled and balanced the can and the cup on his thighs.

Oh, yeah, bro, this better be good. There better be four kids in trouble to justify this.

Then, unaccountably and out of nowhere, he remembered something his mother used to say a long time ago, before she had started drinking, before she had taken to hiding from her husband behind a bottle. *Be careful what you wish for, Jake. You just might get it.*

He told himself that he felt edgy because she had then admitted that she'd once wished for his father.

He made it into Philadelphia without further aggravation and managed to snag a cheap rental car. Given that he was currently taking three weeks off from the Dallas P.D. without pay, Adam—or his company—would have to reimburse his expenses this time.

Assuming the company had any money left.

That was something Jake worried about a lot lately. Adam pretty much funded ChildSearch. Jake knew his brother's pockets were deep, but he also knew that every pit had a bottom. And damn it, he didn't want ChildSearch to go under.

It was a national network of mostly unpaid computer buffs he had put together four years ago to find Bo. Along the way, once he and Adam had perfected the network, they had also searched for other missing kids like Bo. There were forty-eight investigators on staff now—Jake was one of them—and they all donated their time. In the four years since the company's inception, ChildSearch had found roughly twenty percent of the children they had looked for—a pretty good record. But the company hadn't yet turned a profit because those parents who couldn't pay staggering sums to find their child were never charged.

Adam was a bleeding heart, Jake thought. Or maybe it was just those parents' nightmares had so closely mirrored his brother's own anguish over losing Bo. Either way, Adam had poured his heart and soul and income into the company for four years rather than force ChildSearch to stand on its own feet. And even with all the volunteer efforts, the setup was expensive to run.

Most of the company's queries and searches—both legal and those that fell into a gray area because they involved some hacking—centered on the mind-boggling network of databases a minor child might fall into. That was where the computer hackers came in—a bunch of good-hearted folks who tickled their keyboards for free. The legwork didn't start until the computer guys got a hit. Then the team of investigators kicked in. Jake had found at least one guy in every major city willing to donate his time. But although they didn't charge Child-Search, their travel expenses had to be covered. The pictures that ChildSearch put on mailers and milk cartons had to be paid for. The staff who handled the phones in the home office needed wages. Then there was the overhead on that office, dismal and dilapidated though it was. And their Web site on the Internet cost money, as well.

Jake swore aloud as he drove west out of Philly. As he had done more times than he could count these past few weeks, he wondered if Adam would be as willing—or even able—to keep funding the whole thing now that he had found his Bo.

Except Bo was quite possibly gone again.

That rattled the headache loose that had been lingering just behind Jake's eyes. It bloomed and sank in with claws. It was one-thirty in the morning. He was bone tired, but it was going to be a long night.

He drove into the city of Lancaster to drop off the rental car, ever mindful of the fact that ChildSearch's coffers could be at rock bottom. Adam would have rented a car, he thought. Why keep two? He took a cab back out to Route 30 by eking a few more bucks off his credit card in a cash machine.

Route 30 was one of three major east-west arteries that ran through Lancaster County. The routes offered what civilization the Amish heartland had to offer: restaurants, hotels, retail outlets, tourist traps. He'd already learned on his last visit here that they didn't constitute the real Pennsylvania Dutch country.

He had the cab drop him off at the motor inn Adam had stayed at the last time. He trudged wearily inside to the desk.

"What do you mean, he's not here?" he demanded five minutes later.

"He's not registered, sir," the desk clerk replied. "We have no Adam Wallace staying here."

"He's *got* to be here. Where else would he be?" An inkling came to him in answer to that, but he pushed it away because it seemed impossible. Last time, he had found Adam at Mariah's house. But Mariah Fisher had been tops on Adam's blacklist when his brother had left Texas a week ago.

"Would you like a room?" the clerk asked.

"Sure," Jake quipped. "One of your free ones." His credit card was close to maxed out.

The man didn't even crack a smile.

Jake turned away from the desk and went back outside to make sure he had the right place. He did. Loudspeakers still piped the sound of gulls over the parking lot, as they had the last time. The lobby area was still shaped like a ship landlocked in the Amish heartland, just as it had been three weeks ago when he had been here to help with Adam's search for Bo.

The temperature seemed to have plummeted ten degrees since he'd left Philadelphia. There, it had been a balmy twenty above zero. Now the wind cut across the street, all but shrieking at him. It hurt, biting whatever skin it could find—his cheeks, his hands, even the nape of his neck, where it then tunneled down into the collar of his sport jacket.

Even as he stood there, snow began falling. Again. Like last time.

"Well, hell," he muttered aloud. He didn't have enough cash left for another cab.

Adam must be at Mariah's, he realized. Apparently, they had kissed and made up. Jake didn't know if he felt smug or irritated. He'd given his brother a pretty impressive lecture on that subject while they'd still been in Texas. At that point, Adam hadn't even been able to speak her name without snarling.

Irritation finally won out. How the hell was Jake supposed to know to look for him at Mariah's house under the circumstances?

He started walking, turning left on the next side street. For

a while, civilization tried to cling. There were still telephone
poles, electrical lines. The touristy businesses gave way within
a couple of blocks to a residential area, but it was not Amish
country. These were mostly contemporary homes with automobiles in the driveway.

Jake's boots crunched down on the dirty, exhaust-laced
snow at the edges of the road. There were no sidewalks to
speak of. The fresh flakes began to build in momentum. He
tugged his collar up, but his face stung from the wind and the
whipping flakes, and his sport jacket had never been meant to
ward off the cold. He cursed his brother six ways to Sunday
for not mentioning his whereabouts in all those damned phone
messages.

Civilization began to give out. Somehow, impossibly, the
night got deeper, darker, colder. He was in the village of Divinity now, he realized, looking around. He had stepped over
an invisible boundary into a place where time had
just…wound down.

It had nearly enchanted him before, and he wasn't easy to
enchant. Not by things like simplicity and quiet, at any rate.
He preferred more raucous, lusty pleasures. But the pure honesty of the people he had met here had touched him a little,
and the village tried to work its magic on him again.

The houses became crowded, sitting close together in pockets—which meant, he remembered, that for the most part their
owners were all kin. Some of the homes were buffered from
the narrow road by sprawling trees, their limbs naked and
gnarled in February. Snow was beginning to clump on the bare
limbs—*clean* snow, almost painfully white in the darkness. He
could just make it out in the last glow of the streetlights now
behind him.

No electric lights here, he thought. Most of the residences
pressed close to the macadam, their windows all dark. They
were mostly white, with an occasional redbrick home threaded
in. The front portions of the dwellings were square, two-and-
a-half stories. On most of the backs, flatter one-story append-
ages were stuck on.

Keeping rooms, he remembered. They were the gathering

places for weddings, church services and big off-Sunday suppers, because the Amish only had services every other week. Jake hadn't consciously memorized that, either, but sometime during his other brief stay, someone had told him. Like all unusual tidbits of information, it had lodged in his brain.

The people who lived in the village were...well, outcasts and elderly. He remembered that, too. Ninety-five percent of the Amish population lived farther out, on the farms. Those dwelling in the village were mostly elderly; their children's farms would invariably spread out directly behind their *grossdawdy*—or grandfather—houses. The occasional single man and woman would live in the village, too—young people moving in from another settlement to court someone here, or, like Mariah Fisher, someone who was living under the *meidung,* the shunning punishment for a major transgression against the Amish way.

Every once in a while, the moon peeked out from behind the heavy cloud cover and it made ice glimmer on the homes, on mailboxes and hedges. It gave the whole sleeping village a fairy-tale effect. The night was utterly silent. Jake thought he could even hear the snow settling on the ground. He was very much aware of his own heartbeat.

He stopped a moment, just *feeling* the quiet. Then he moved again and stepped in something that didn't crunch. He went very still and closed his eyes, then smelled it before he actually tried to look at his boot heel. Horse manure.

"Son of a..." He trailed off because there was no one to hear him swear, which robbed some of the enjoyment from it. He hopped out onto the cleared macadam to rake his heel clean on the hard surface. When it didn't entirely work, he swore again anyway.

Headlights would have warned him that a vehicle was approaching. As it was, he didn't register the clop-clop-clopping sound he was hearing until it was almost too late. He was bent over, trying to inspect his boot heel in the cursory moonlight. The snow was getting heavier, obscuring his vision now. He straightened at the last moment, heard a shout and jumped clear. The horse reacted in fright to his sudden movement, skittering sideways. The buggy wheels screeched and rattled as they were dragged over the road in a direction wheels weren't meant to go.

"Whoa!" Jake shouted, not knowing what else to do.

"Whoa!" a young voice echoed. "Easy there, easy…"

Jake looked at the Amish buggy and tried to see the young driver inside. *Tell me this is somebody I met last time.* Damn, but he was cold.

"Sorry about that," he said, charmingly, he hoped. "Didn't hear you coming."

The young man gave a polite nod, peering at him out the side window. "Yes, sir."

"Guess you don't have horns on these things, huh?" Jake kept stomping his feet, partly to get rid of the last of the unwelcome stuff still stuck to his heel, partly to keep warm.

"Yes, sir, we do. But I didn't see you. I didn't expect any person to be in the middle of the road at this hour."

"Yeah, well, I am. Was." He stepped a bit aside, but not far enough to really let the boy pass. "Hey, maybe I could catch a ride with you? I'm Jake Wallace. I don't know if I met you before, but I was up here a few weeks ago…" He trailed off when the young man's expression didn't change. "Please," he said carefully, "I could really use a lift now."

"We haven't met, sir. Where are you going?"

"Uh…" He dredged his memory, and it served him well again. "Bachmantown Road."

"Well, there you go, sir. You're fine. It's right there."

The boy pointed. In the next moment, the horse sidestepped a little and the buggy moved on.

"Sir," Jake echoed distastefully. "For God's sake, I'm still a pup. Not even forty yet." He looked after the buggy as it disappeared into the darkness, the clopping of the horse's hooves fading into the night.

He started walking—without much hope—toward the side street the boy had pointed to. But the kid had been right. It was Bachmantown Road, where Mariah Fisher lived. A white shingle swung from a post on the corner. He remembered it from the last time he'd been forced to walk this way.

Her house was the third one down on the right. It was dark.
He had expected that. God knew it was late enough. Jake
jogged up onto the porch, and rammed a fist against the door,
relieved that this night was finally over.

"Let's go, bro. Enough already. I need some heat." He
stomped his feet again.

Nothing happened. No one answered his summons.

"Damn it, come *on*." He moved to the side of the porch
to peer in a window there. His jaw dropped, then he shook
his head slowly back and forth in denial.

The furniture was gone.

Gone?

There hadn't been a lot of furniture three weeks ago to begin
with. There'd been just a rocker, a wood-burning stove, a sofa,
and an armchair for reading. The living room had been tiny,
neat and pretty. He remembered some kind of hooked rug on
the floor and a lantern hanging on the wall nearest the door.
That was all gone now. There wasn't a stick of furniture inside. No lantern, no pretty rug. Nothing.

"What the hell?" he said aloud this time.

"Hey! You there!"

Jake jumped. He knew the voice. It came from behind him.
He dragged on his patience and slowly, carefully, turned
around. He held his hands up over his head. It was a cop, and
cops carried guns. It generally wasn't smart to alarm one un-
necessarily.

"It's me again. Chill out." He grinned at the officer, though
his grin was getting decidedly ragged around the edges by
now. "Langston, isn't it?"

The man stuck his face close to Jake's. "That's right.
You've got a good memory."

Jake lowered his hands. "I'm looking for my brother
again."

"Won't find him here."

"No kidding," Jake snapped, his irritation winning out.

The cop studied him. "Having a bad night, huh?"

He seemed pleased by that. Jake struggled to remember
what he might have said to offend him the last time and came

up with nothing. Admittedly, that hadn't been a real good night, either.

"Bad enough," he agreed. "Look, I really need to find my brother."

"Down the new spread."

Down the new spread. "Huh?" Jake stared at him and had a feeling this night was about to get a whole lot worse.

"Esbenshade Road. About nine miles from here, as the crow flies."

"The new spread," Jake repeated carefully.

"Yup. Went up two days ago." The cop turned away.

"Wait! We're not talking about the same guy here. I'm looking for Adam Wallace. Big, blond dude, blue eyes. An inch or two shorter than me, but he looks bigger."

"Yeah. Married Mariah Fisher. They put his new spread up on Tuesday."

The night went blacker.

For a moment, Jake couldn't even see the man. The darkness was too complete. He felt light-headed, unsteady, like a toddler who had just learned to walk. "No," he heard himself say, and he barely recognized his own voice.

"Thought you was coming in for the wedding and was late."

"No." It seemed the only word he was capable of. At least it was the only word that would get past his throat. There was a whole raging cacophony in his head.

Adam had left seven messages because he was getting married? But he wouldn't do that! He wouldn't even say her name last week. *He can't marry her, can't do that. He's all I've got.*

It was irrational, it was wild, but his palms started sweating in the biting cold.

"He wouldn't get married," he said aloud, his breath puffing white. No matter that Jake himself often disappeared for days on end, without warning. Adam was predictable. Adam was in a rut.

Adam was the only small scrap of Wallace kin that remained in the universe as far as Jake knew, and in that moment he hated Mariah Fisher with her soft voice and her serene eyes because, damn her, Jake needed Adam more, even if he would die before he admitted it.

The feeling passed in a heartbeat, but he realized his hands were still shaking. Cold. It was just the cold.

"He wouldn't get married," he said again.

"Yeah, well, he did."

"To an *Amish* woman?"

"Yup."

"Can they do that?"

"Guess so. Justice of the peace will marry anybody. Don't know about the Amish deacons, though. She was one of those shunned folks, but they let her back in."

Mariah Fisher had committed the grievous sin of educating herself, and her settlement had spent several long years treating her as an outcast. So the cop had the right woman. He was definitely talking about Adam's Mariah.

Adam had gotten married.

"Can you...uh...give me a lift?" he asked, eyeing the guy's cruiser, and his voice was hoarse.

"Sorry. It's against regulations."

"Bull—" He broke off just in time as the cop's brows lowered. "Look, I'm a cop in Dallas. It's no big deal, Langston. I'll sit in the back, all proper-like."

"Guess things are different in Texas. We don't do that here."

All right, Jake thought. Okay. So this guy wasn't a friend. He could accept that. "How would a non-crow get to this...new spread?" he asked hoarsely. There was real desperation in his tone now. Jake hated it, but the cop answered more kindly.

"That main road you just came in on is Ronks. Take it south about four miles to Paradise Lane, go east until you get to Cherry Hill, then loop around west again on Esbenshade. It's just below Sugar Joe Lapp's place. Used to be his acres."

He'd been to Sugar Joe Lapp's place. "Couldn't I just cut across a field or something?"

That pleased look came back to the cop's face again. "You could, but I reckon Joe's got his bull out tonight and those buggers get amorous come the full moon. I wouldn't want to be mistaken for a cow, if I was you."

Jake shot a glance skyward. Damned if there wasn't almost a full moon peeking through the clouds. He watched the guy get in his cruiser and drive away.

Married. Adam had gotten married.

Surely Jannel, Adam's first wife, had taught him the unholiness of the union—especially after the harsh lessons their parents, Emma and Edward Wallace, had imparted first. Married? Married. With responsibilities that couldn't possibly be met, needs that could never be realistically fulfilled. Married. And then the irrational thought came back into Jake's head again: *Gone to me.*

Gone to a woman. Gone to a marriage. Gone to another family.

Jake finally started walking because the only thing that would find him at Mariah Fisher's old house this time was the dawn. And if it was anything like this night had been, it was going to be rotten and wretched.

Chapter 2

Katya Essler had forgotten how to sleep.

It had begun ten years ago, stealthily, a little bit at a time, after she had first married Frank. She had learned to listen for his approach up the stairs, for the heavy, staggering thump of his footsteps that would tell her he had been out behind the barn again, getting drunk. She had learned to hold herself so incredibly still then, scarcely breathing, that her bones would literally ache. She had learned not to make a sound, a twitch, the slightest movement, because then, if she was lucky, he would just forget she was there and he would pass out.

Those were the good times.

She had escaped Frank, with Mariah's help, almost a month ago. But Katya still wasn't quite able to let sleep take her completely. She knew, in her heart, that it would be a very, very long time before she relearned how.

Suddenly her throat burned. It felt as though a line of fire came up from her chest, where her heart was, and she was ashamed enough of that that hot tears scalded the corners of her eyes, too. She should have been grateful, to Mariah, to her new husband, Adam Wallace, for saving and protecting her. And she was, oh, God, she was.

But Katya would never really be free, and for that she wept. *That* was why her chest burned with a fury she could scarcely bring herself to acknowledge. She should be grateful, and she was, but she also felt more hopeless than she had even when she had been married to Frank.

By some miracle of a true and loving God, the vast majority of her *gemeide*—her church district—had chosen the same time to break off from their old church elders. They had done it mostly because the outside world had begun touching them in hideous ways, and the people disagreed with their deacons as to how to handle it. Someone was stealing their babies, and the old deacons had proclaimed that they should let the little ones go. They would not allow the parents to search for them because nonresistance to trouble was the Amish way. They said it was God's will that the babies had vanished. God wanted it that way. He had a better plan.

Too many people had been unable to tolerate that. So, as had happened a few times before throughout history, a hundred or so families had split off, forming their own *gemeide*. And they had changed things, important things, though they were still Old Order, the most strict and old-fashioned of the Amish and Mennonite faiths. The new *gemeide* had sought the help of the FBI to find their babies. They had lifted Mariah's *meidung*—the shunning that she had been subjected to since returning from college because the old *gemeide* had considered it a sin to educate oneself past the eighth grade. Education was still a sin, but the new deacons said that Mariah had repented enough with her devout behavior since then. And they had thrown the *meidung* on Frank Essler for his sins against his wife and children.

Frank was shunned and he no longer existed to the community. He was invisible to them. Should Frank ever choose to walk among the people in this new *gemeide,* they would turn their backs upon him. He was not welcome at their tables, and joyous, ample meals were the cornerstone of their ways. He could not spoon food from the same bowls they used, and his wife certainly could not have any sort of relations with him.

Frank was gone. Yet Katya lay in the dark of Adam and Mariah's new home, trembling with fury because she would always and forever be his wife. There was no such concept as divorce among her people.

There was no hope left. She would be twenty-nine years old next month, she thought, and these days of loneliness would stretch out forever. Unless Frank repented and somehow worked his way back into the fold—and she prayed to God that he did not—she would never again enjoy married life. She would never love, be loved.

Through no fault of her own.

That was what enraged her the most, what made her throat close and her eyes burn and her heart pound. She had wed Frank Essler in good faith. Perhaps she had never loved him, not in the way Sarah Lapp loved her Joe, but few Amish women ever experienced that kind of joy. Holding out for love was considered "silly," at least to hear the deacons tell it.

But she had respected Frank—at first. She had liked him. She had believed they would have a good life together and she had tried hard to make one. *He* had betrayed his vows. *He* had sinned. And *she* was trapped. Forever.

Her freedom should have been enough. The health of her children should have been enough. Her skin burned with shame in the darkness because, in one small, secret place in her heart, they were not. She wanted to know she might someday have hope again. And she needed desperately to stop depending on Adam and Mariah—or anyone else, for that matter—to support her and her children. She *hated* being pitied, dependent upon the charity of others, but what else could she do?

Those words echoed in her head again and again. *What else?* She had an eighth-grade education from an Amish parochial school. The settlement was her *life*, all she had ever known. She couldn't leave, dared not leave. Yet here, in the Amish heartland, she was not permitted to work. Or, at least, there were precious few ways for her to earn a living that were

acceptable to the *ordnung,* the Amish rules of faith. Here, in
the Amish heartland, she was permitted to do, to feel, virtually
nothing.

Her hands curled into fists at her sides. She forced herself
to breathe—aloud this night—evenly, strongly, getting control
of her emotions. And then, beneath the sound of her own exhalation, she heard a footstep from somewhere below.

Her body reacted first. If a moment before her heart had
been chugging in silent anger, now it erupted in terror. *He had
come for her.* Frank would get to her anyway, even here, even
with Mariah and Adam, because he respected no laws.

She sat bolt upright in the narrow bed, her hands still fisted,
listening, trying hard to hear over the roar of her heart. *Outside.* The movement seemed to be coming from outside, on
the porch below her window.

If it had been inside, she would have relaxed, maybe even
felt foolish. The new house, constructed only a few days ago,
was full to the brim. In addition to her and her four little ones,
there was Adam and Mariah and Adam's son, Bo. And Bo's
best friend, the boy he had been raised with here in the settlement before Adam had found him, was sleeping over also.

There were nine people in the three bedrooms. But someone
was outside. No one should be outside, she thought. It wasn't
even dawn yet.

Katya felt the cool, hard wood of the floor beneath her bare
feet before she even realized she was standing. *No, no, no, not
anymore.* It was a litany in her head, pounding, hurting. She
crept to the window, looking down, but she could see nothing.
The porch overhang was in the way.

She tiptoed to the hall door, stepping over Rachel, her oldest, and Delilah, her four-year-old, who shared a corn husk
mattress on the floor. She skirted around the makeshift crib
that held her youngest boy, eighteen-month-old Sam. *No, no,
no,* she thought again. She moved down the stairs like a wisp
of smoke, barely disturbing the air. She had learned to do that,
too, while she had been married to Frank, to move with a
minimum of motion so as not to call his attention to herself.

It had broken her heart when she had noticed Rachel moving that way also, at only ten years old.

No, no more.

She reached the bottom of the stairs and stepped into the living room. She hovered a moment, trembling, holding her breath. And then she saw him through the window on the front porch.

The sky was still dark. The sun did not yet show on the horizon, but the air had taken on that odd, almost glowing hue that came just before sunrise. It threw the man outside— *Frank, who else?*—into deep silhouette. Her eyes riveted on his hat, the broad-brimmed head covering that all Amishmen wore.

No more. She was shaking hard now. But her fear was gone. She was furious again.

It had to be his brother's house, Jake decided. And if it wasn't, he was too tired and cold to care.

It was new enough that the pungent smell of fresh plywood seemed to hang about it. And there was a section over on the right side where they hadn't finished putting up the siding yet. The wood there was still yellow golden, new. The small barn in the back was unpainted. The chicken coop beside it was all shiny new wire.

The *chicken coop?* Adam?

Jake took one more stealthy, quiet trip around the house, just to convince himself. He hesitated in the back a moment, studying the place, and felt something warm, large and alive push between his legs from behind. He jumped out of his skin and came around, his fists up and ready.

He'd been expecting the bull that Officer Langston had mentioned and had wondered how he was going to argue with it. But it was only a horse.

Jake took a quick dip sideways to ascertain that it was a male, a gelding. He had a little experience with horses, though not much. Once, as a boy, he'd thought maybe he'd be a real cowboy. One of the last of a dying breed. The legend and the mystique had appealed to him until his father had put an end to such daydreams. Edward Wallace had beaten him within an inch of his life for taking on a low-paying summer job on a ranch outside of Dallas. Edward rarely worked. It fell to the kids to help bring in his beer money. Admittedly, most of Jake's earnings that summer—before he had quit—had gone into cab fare, getting back and forth to the Flying Bar.

He closed his palm over this horse's nose. "Tell you what, buddy," he said in an undertone. "You've just gone where no man has gone before. Keep it to yourself, and we'll forget about it."

The beast snorted at him, studied him, then apparently decided he was bored with what he saw. He tossed his head, jerked his nose free of Jake's hand and trotted off again into the darkness.

Animals running loose. Well, hell, Jake thought.

Enough was enough. He was going inside. He was so cold now he could barely feel his extremities, although, thank God, the snow had at least stopped falling. But his hair was frozen with it, or at least the ends were, where they stuck out in the back beneath his beloved cowboy hat. He didn't want to know what the snow had done to the soft gray suede. He'd kept the hat on only because he knew he needed to trap his body heat beneath it. What little body heat he had left.

He ambled around to the front of the house again and tried the front door. He was moderately amazed to find it unlocked, then he was gratified. He could see no sense in knocking, in waking everyone up. There wasn't a chance in hell that he was going to talk to anyone about anything right now anyway. He'd been awake for nearly twenty-four hours. He didn't want to talk about his brother's marriage. He didn't want to exchange niceties with Mariah *Wallace*. He didn't even want to talk about Bo. He needed sleep, even if it was just an hour's worth before the sun demanded his awareness again.

He stepped into a living room and was immensely gratified to recognize the sofa, the wood-burning stove, the hooked rug on the floor, from Mariah's old house. He glanced around at all of it, but the sofa drew him.

Just an hour's sleep, he thought longingly. However long

he could steal until the sun came up and the house began bustling. He started toward it.

As Katya stared, her pulse slamming, Frank came inside. *Inside.* But then, she had known he would.

She slipped reflexively to her left, through the door there, into the kitchen. She hid from him as she always had, before rage consumed her completely. Her gaze began flying about wildly, looking for something, anything, some sort of weapon. He would not strike her this time. He would not hurt her. She would no longer allow it. She'd had enough.

Her eyes fell upon the solution. Mariah hadn't finished unpacking the kitchen things. "Thank you, God," she whispered aloud. Hot tears were scalding her cheeks now. She could no longer contain them. She tiptoed to the first box and hunkered down, and a rolling pin was right there, right on top of the clutter. She prayed again, gave thanks again and hefted it.

She crept back into the living room. He was still just standing there with his back to her. She had yet to see his face, but she didn't need to. He turned and headed in the direction of the sofa.

Katya screamed and ran for him.

She had the rolling pin in both hands and she wielded it like a baseball bat, putting all her strength into the blow, though admittedly it wasn't much because she couldn't even remember the last time she'd kept a whole meal down. Still, adrenaline and fear were on her side and it connected with a satisfying thud that reverberated up her arms. His hat came off and went sailing. And Frank went down.

Katya dropped the rolling pin with a clatter onto the hardwood floor and simply stood, sobbing. *"No more."* She whispered the chant aloud now. *"No, no, no. No more."*

Pandemonium erupted at the scream she'd given. Footsteps seemed to thunder on the stairs, then Adam was shouting something and all the kids were creating their own unique brand of bedlam. Katya turned to them quickly, still crying, but her children had been her reason for surviving for too long to count now, and she didn't want them to see their father this way. It helped her to move, to function, after what she had done. *Nonresistance. You're not supposed to resist.* She gave a tense, fractured laugh at that.

She had to get the children back to their rooms.

She glanced up at Adam as she tried to step past him on the stairs. But Adam wasn't even looking at her, and that made her pause. He was staring over her shoulder at Frank. Mariah had crowded up behind him. One hand was plastered to her mouth, and with the other she held a lantern high. Her eyes were wide...and aghast.

Mariah, of all people, should have understood.

"What?" Katya asked shakily. She turned around, even as Sam and Levi crowded against her, clutching her nightgown. Only Rachel remained farther up on the stairs, holding little Sam. "What?" she said again.

And then she looked into the living room, where Adam had lit another lantern. She saw that it wasn't Frank she had struck.

Katya felt her blood almost literally drain out of her. She swayed, and she knew she would probably have fallen if her children hadn't been bolstering her. "Oh, my!" she gasped, then she, too, clapped a hand to her mouth.

"Okay," Adam said hoarsely. "Everybody calm down. It's all right."

Katya saw one of the man's boots move as though his leg had twitched. Cows did that when they died. She had killed him!

"Who is he?" she cried. "Who *is* that?"

"My brother. Although what the hell—*heck*," Adam snapped quickly as his son shot him a dirty look, "what the heck he's doing creeping in here in the middle of the night is anybody's guess." He knelt beside his brother. "Come on, cowboy," he muttered. "Roll over. You're all right. Ever hear of knocking and letting people know you're coming in?"

Katya stared at the man, her hand still clapped to her mouth. What had she done? Despite his light words, Katya heard real concern in Adam's voice. She closed her eyes, feeling faint. Surely Adam would throw her and her children out for this. *His brother?*

Then what he had just said about the man rolling over finally registered. She cried out again, pulled away from her children and rushed over to kneel beside them.

"No," she managed, her voice choked.

Adam looked up at her, startled. "What?"

"Don't roll him over. I m-might have..." *Oh, God!* "I might have cracked his skull. I...let me check first."

Behind her, one of the little ones started crying. Probably Delilah. If Rachel had learned to move like smoke, then Delilah cried at the drop of a hat. Another legacy from Frank.

But this wasn't Frank.

Her hands trembling, she ran her fingers over the back of the man's head in the general area where she thought she had connected with the rolling pin. She closed her eyes to concentrate, to follow her touch, as her grandmother, a respected Amish healer, had instructed her. Then her eyes flew open again.

His hair was dark, almost black, and straight. It was long. Not by Amish standards certainly, but by those of the *anner Satt Leit,* the other sort of people who lived outside the Amish settlements. People like Adam, the first non-Amishman Katya had ever had any real dealings with.

This man's hair covered the collar of his dark blue jacket. It was soft, thick, and the ends were going damp with melted snow. It felt like cool water sliding between her fingers, and suddenly, for a reason she could neither dwell on nor understand, it made her skin pull into goose bumps.

"No," she whispered, snatching her hand back. "I...didn't—I didn't crack his skull. He's fine." Except he was still out cold, she thought, flinching.

Adam rolled him over. Katya gasped, her eyes widened, and she pushed back to her feet again fast. The man she had nearly killed had the most fascinating face she had ever seen in her life, and she could only stare at him.

Part of it was that all Amishmen wore beards. It was part of their Old Order *ordnung,* their rules, that once a man was to be married, he allowed his facial hair to grow. And most Amishmen married in their early twenties. The only man of any age whose whole face she was used to seeing was Adam's, and even he was growing a beard now.

Adam's face had never affected her like this.

Even in repose, his brother looked...arrogant. He had dark brows and strong cheekbones and a long, straight nose. But more than anything, his mouth struck her. It looked so...well, soft in contrast to everything else. His features were unapologetically male and that frightened her, even as something about him made her pulse quicken in an odd sort of way. He wore a white T-shirt under the open blue coat. He was not even remotely dressed for Lancaster County's cold. She prayed that that was why his lips were blue, that he wasn't dying.

"Turn his head to the side," she said, not even aware she'd spoken aloud until Adam did as she instructed. "He might...he could get sick. It's a normal reaction to...to such trauma."

"Good point," Adam said. "Come *on*, Jake." He slapped him a little. Not hard, Katya thought, but not gently, either.

The man called Jake started to wake up. His eyelids fluttered. Katya let out a harsh breath of relief and kneeled beside him again.

For the longest time, whole seconds, Jake hadn't a clue where he was. Then his eyes focused. He recognized his brother's face—Adam was wearing an interesting scowl. Jake's gaze slid to his brother's right, and that was when he knew he was dead.

That damned bull must have butted him clear to heaven because there was an angel leaning over him. Her eyes were cornflower blue. Her features were perfect, her pale brows delicately arched. And her hair...dear God, he thought, her *hair*. He saw Mariah standing just behind her, holding a lantern. It spilled light over the woman, making her hair seem to glow. It was long but somehow...wispy and the color of wheat after the hot summer months. Strands of it curled forward underneath her jaw, shorter than the rest.

"Could have sworn..." He paused for breath. His tongue

felt thick and heavy in his mouth, slurring his words. "Thought I'd go the other way." He struggled to sit up.

"Oh, no!" she cried. "No, sir, please. You must lie back."

"Sir?" Bits and pieces of memory started clicking in. "I keep telling you guys. I'm not even forty."

Katya exchanged a quick, panicked glance with Adam. Adam shrugged.

"Well, he's not," Adam said finally. "He's a year younger than I am."

"Are you in much pain?" she asked the man.

Jake found her face again. "Hell, no. Not anymore." He watched her face go from parchment pale to a soft, rosy blush. Then Jake realized that she was crying silently. Her cheeks were wet. "What's wrong?" he demanded.

"I'm so sorry," she whispered.

"What for?"

"Well, for hitting you."

"You hit me?" His eyes coasted downward.

She wore a white cotton nightgown, and the light behind her illuminated her body beneath it—no details, not quite, just gentle curves and swells and shadows. He felt something quick and randy stir inside him even as he registered that she couldn't weigh more than a hundred pounds. She packed a hell of a punch for a hundred pounds.

He gave a short bark of laughter. "You hit me," he said again. *"Why?"*

"I thought you were my husband."

Every delightful fantasy he'd just begun to spin shattered into pieces.

Jake groaned. He struggled to sit up again, waving his brother's hands off, and actually managed to get upright this time. "I hate when this happens," he muttered, resting his elbows on his thighs. He covered his face with his hands, scrubbing it wearily.

"When someone hits you?" Her eyes widened. "Does this happen often?"

"No. When—" Jake broke off, more out of instinct than

anything else. *When a great-looking woman turns out to be married.*

There was something almost innocent about her, he realized, though he had finally come to the conclusion that she wasn't an angel. He was still on earth, sordid and ugly though earth could be. And he felt uncomfortable—uncharacteristically uncomfortable—explaining to this particular woman that while he observed few rules, not messing around with married women was one that kept him saluting and at attention at all times.

He got to his feet, swayed a little with brief dizziness, while Katya hovered, half of her wanting to rush to his aid, the rest of her instinctively staying clear of him. He stared at her, scowling a little, and she felt her heart cavorting all over again.

Mariah—bless her—broke the moment. "The sun's coming up," she said softly but efficiently. "I'll put some coffee on."

Jake looked sharply over his shoulder at the window. "Damn it." So much for sleep.

Adam shook his head. "You'll need to watch your language around here," he warned. "Otherwise you'll tend to get an elbow or two in your thigh."

Jake looked at him blankly.

"Upstairs, children," Mariah went on. "The excitement is over. It's time to get dressed for school. Matt, you need to go home and help your father with his farm chores. Bo, perhaps you could go with him just this one morning. I think we can spare you around here. I'll relieve the hens of their eggs myself."

"Did he tell you I was a lunatic?" Jake asked because she seemed nervous. "That I'm as likely to brawl with the dudes I arrest as throw handcuffs on them?"

Mariah flushed. "Well…yes." In fact, that was exactly what Adam had said.

Jake seemed to think about it, then he nodded. "Fair enough."

Katya continued to stare at him, and she felt her heart hitch at the surprising response. She didn't know if she was amazed that he'd admit such a thing…or more frightened than she had been yet in what seemed like a lifetime full of fears. Of all the men she could have clobbered! She watched bemusedly as he, Adam and Mariah went into the kitchen.

It wasn't just his looks that were fascinating, she realized. It was everything about him. The air about him almost...crackled with something just a little bit dangerous, something amazing, even perplexing. And he hadn't hurt her when she'd hurt him. It hadn't even seemed to cross his mind. He hadn't been horrified, either, at the way she had so blatantly broken the *ordnung* by fighting back. He'd just seemed...amused.

He had *laughed*.

She knew, after less than twenty minutes in his company, that she had never met a man like him before in her life.

Chapter 3

Jake didn't watch her, but he was aware of every move she made. She lingered in the living room while the rest of them trooped into the kitchen. She reminded him of a hummingbird, hovering there. In the blink of an eye, at the slightest provocation, she could be gone again.

She was.

He glanced back just in time to see her look down at herself, at her thin nightgown. She gave a tiny gasp and clapped her hands to her cheeks. No matter that when Mariah had carried the lantern into the kitchen, the living room was pitched into relative darkness again. No matter that the nightgown revealed really very little. She scurried away up the stairs, all blushing modesty.

Maybe that was what made him stare after her long after she was gone. He hadn't encountered that kind of attitude in…well, ever, he realized. He wondered where her husband was and why she would want to flatten him with a rolling pin.

Mariah hung the lantern on the wall, put a pot of coffee on the wood-burning stove, then excused herself. Adam sat at the table. Jake paced. The kitchen was homey enough that it got his hackles up.

The floor was dark wood, the walls white. A hutch sat against one wall; country-pretty plates showed through the glass-fronted cabinets. Jake scowled at the light hanging over the table and saw a low flame flickering there. There was a grandfather clock in one corner, tick-tocking audibly and steadily, and a pile of wooden toys in another. Boxes were everywhere. There was a hanging plant in another corner, green and lush.

It was the kind of place where things grew.

"Who is she?" he asked finally, because the woman who had knocked him silly seemed like the safest subject at hand. At least, she was the only subject he trusted himself with. A sense of betrayal over what the cop had told him still sat low in his stomach, making it feel sour. Worse, Jake had seen Bo, plain as day, standing there on the stairs. Bo was okay.

Adam hesitated a heartbeat. "Her name is Katya Essler. She's a childhood friend of Mariah's."

"She's *living* here?"

"She's had some trouble. She'll be staying with us for a while."

"What kind of trouble?"

This time Adam was quiet. "Husband trouble," he finally replied.

Jake rubbed the bump growing on the back of his head. That made sense.

"It's a long story," Adam went on. "But she's not for you, Jake."

Jake moved to the window, to the table, back to the window again. He gave a grunt of acknowledgment. No sense in arguing that one. She was married. She blushed. That alone put her well out of his usual repertoire.

Still, there was something captivating about her. Something almost...otherworldly. Something that made the hairs on his nape stand up with a sort of wary alarm. He needed to know more about her just to be able to put it all into perspective, but Adam changed the subject.

"Where have you been?" he asked. "I've been trying to reach you all week."

Jake waved a negligent hand. "Here and there. I just got your messages last night."

More silence fell. Adam waited. When Jake made no move to break it himself, he asked, "Want some coffee?"

"Make it a double."

The pot was burbling. Adam got up and went to it, then poured two mugs.

"What the *hell* have you done?" Jake burst out. *"Married?"*

Adam handed him a mug. Jake's hands remained fisted. When he didn't take it, Adam set it on the counter. "You told me to take a stab at believing," he said calmly. "I'm doing it."

"I said we both had a problem trusting in things that seemed too good! I told you to let go of hope and be done with it!"

"You've got a selective memory."

"The hell I do!"

"You told me I needed a woman."

"For a night! Maybe two! I was talking on a temporary basis, bro. I didn't mean you should *keep* one, for God Almighty's sake!"

Adam didn't answer.

"What's happened to you? What the hell has happened to you inside of one lousy week? You got religion, didn't you?" Jake whipped around, raking a hand through his hair, pacing again. "Oh, man, I told you this would happen. I *knew* it. I smelled it coming."

"No," Adam said quietly, "I haven't gotten religion. Yet. I'm sort of hanging here on the outskirts, keeping an eye on it, though. Thinking about it."

Jake made a strangled sound. "God gave up on us Wallaces a long time ago."

"Maybe not."

"Talk about a selective memory," Jake snarled, looking at his brother again.

Adam only shrugged.

"Jannel took your kid and relieved you of a couple million dollars. You remember that, don't you?" Jake demanded. "That's what 'married' does to you."

"That was an entirely different situation."

"You're scaring me, bro."

"Yeah, well, I thought I might."

"Is this why you left all those messages?" Jake still hadn't touched his coffee. He had adrenaline enough of his own at the moment. "You wanted me to come here and play best man? What happened? She wouldn't sleep with you until you said 'I do'? That is *really* a bad reason to get hitched, bro. Man, she must really have you wrapped around her finger."

Adam swung his fist.

It took both of them off guard, despite the fact that they'd pretty much scrapped their way through thirty-plus years together. Adam connected with Jake's jaw, then stared down, stunned, at his own hand. Jake dodged at the last possible moment so the blow wasn't quite as bad as it could have been. It grazed rather than impacted. Still, it sent him reeling back a few steps, trying to catch his balance.

"Good shot," he allowed, rubbing the sore spot.

"She's my wife," Adam answered levelly. "Watch your mouth."

Jake nodded. "Fair enough." There were lines he could cross and lines he couldn't. Whether he was happy with this situation or not, he was smart enough to know that he had just come up against the latter.

Adam met his eyes. "I didn't call you here for the wedding. I would have married her with or without your approval. I need her."

It all rushed in on him again then, the betrayal, the fear, and this time Jake knew it wasn't irrational. *I would have married her with or without your approval.* Because his approval, his opinion, didn't matter anymore. Because Adam had a wife, a family of his own.

And then there was one. One Wallace, Jake thought. Marriage didn't change Adam's blood, but it sure as hell changed the fundamental heart of the man. It changed what he was, changed what God had taught the Wallaces to be. Marriage hadn't changed his brother the first time around, but Adam had never slugged him on Jannel's behalf, either. Mariah was different. He thought of the other one, her friend, the one who had fled, blushing, up the stairs.

"I'm out of here," Jake said curtly, swinging toward the back door. Suddenly, the sensation that filled his gut felt almost like panic.

"Wait." Adam's voice was still calm.

Jake looked back at him, one hand on the knob. "I can't tell you congratulations," he said honestly. "I *do* wish you well, but I just don't see it happening." Or maybe he did, he thought, and that was what had him running scared. Maybe that was what he couldn't tolerate.

"I need your help with something else," Adam explained.

Jake's eyes narrowed warily as he looked back at him. "Yeah? What?" *I didn't call you here for the wedding.* He hadn't called him because of Bo, either. And Jake couldn't figure out what else his brother could possibly need him for.

"Someone is stealing the settlement's babies."

Jake went still and stared at him.

"The FBI is making a mess of it. I need you to look into it," Adam went on.

The words seemed to hang in the air a moment. Jake wanted to fight them. To pretend he hadn't heard them. He needed to do that because he didn't want to stay here where he'd have to watch what was happening to his brother. He couldn't stand here on the outside of Adam's world, looking in.

As though he had a choice. *Someone is stealing the settlement's babies.*

"Damn you, bro," he said quietly. Adam knew what punches to land and which to pull. He knew how to reel him in. "What's wrong with the Bureau?"

"The Amish culture isn't in their rule book."

Jake snorted. "No. It wouldn't be."

"It's a roadblock," Adam went on, "and those guys keep running into it, then they just mill around in confusion. They have no...compassion. They tried to interrupt church services to interview everyone. Said it was an ideal time, what with everyone gathered together that way."

Jake looked at him disbelievingly. "And you think *I* have compassion?"

"You've got heart, or you wouldn't have worked Child-Search these past four years without getting paid for it."

"We were looking for Bo."

"No. *I* was looking for Bo. You were the pit bull out there snarling over every other tip that came in concerning other kids. You went to Phoenix yourself, paid your own expenses and collected Amber Calabrese." The little girl's father had stolen her while Adam had been here in the settlement trying to reestablish his relationship with Bo. One of their L.A.P.D. contacts had been trying to handle the situation and had run into some problems. Jake had charged in like a white knight.

On a black horse.

Adam was under no illusions regarding his brother's darker side. Jake was irreverent, vaguely irresponsible and more than a little happy-go-lucky. He had a tendency to get into sticky situations. Often. He didn't have to go looking for fights and trouble. Both seemed to hang right over his head, just waiting for an excuse to explode. Adam couldn't remember his brother ever dating the same woman more than two or three times.

But…he was a walking encyclopedia. He was shrewd and he was bright, and he got outraged whenever anyone hurt one of life's weaklings. Like their mother. Or their sister.

"We need help here," Adam said again.

"I ran out of my annual leave with the department a while back," Jake hedged. "I had to take this last week without pay. I don't get any more vacation and sick time until the end of March."

"I've been thinking about that, too," Adam said quietly.

Jake's eyes narrowed again. "Yeah? How so?"

"ChildSearch."

Jake's heart thumped. He felt more bad news coming on. "What about it?"

"It's yours, if you want it. I'll fund it for six more months.

With you at the helm instead of me, it should be turning a profit by then.''

"You want me to take it over?" Jake looked at him as though he had grown horns. No matter what he had expected, this hit him out of the blue. "No."

"Think about it." Adam knew that that was the best he could hope for. He also knew that his brother wanted ChildSearch so badly it hurt. Jake cared about it. Jake cared about the kids, somewhere beneath that cocky, irreverent exterior.

But Jake never, ever risked being too happy.

He never got involved with anything he really loved, Adam thought, which was probably why he never dated anyone too long. He knew just when and where to draw the line. Give up, give out, before it gets too good. Before it hurts.

"We'll talk about ChildSearch later," Adam went on. "In the meantime, can you sniff around a little on this thing now?"

"I've got to get back to work," Jake said again. He didn't want to stay here. God knew, he didn't want to stay here. It wasn't just Adam and Mariah. It was the whole damned settlement. It was that woman upstairs, though why he should feel so inexplicably threatened by her was beyond him.

Adam went on as though he hadn't heard him. "There have been four of them now. Four babies. Just gone."

Jake felt something almost pained shift inside him. *Be careful what you wish for, Jake. You just might get it.* "Four," he repeated roughly.

"Lizzie Stoltzfus was the last. Before that, it was Michael Miller. Back in the fall, it was Lukas Eitner and Amalie Byler. They were—are—all not quite two years old. They all have brothers and sisters enough to fill Noah's ark, but for some reason they were each caught on their own just that one time, and then they just...disappeared."

Jake shook his head, but it wasn't a gesture of denial this time. It looked more like an effort to clear it. "I'm tired, bro," he said finally. "Bone tired. I've been up since 6:00 a.m. yesterday. And I didn't sleep much the night before that, either."

Two hours, to be exact. That was the night he had found Clyde and Bob's Bull's-Eye Bar.

A lifetime ago.

"I can't make sense of this right now," he went on.

"The house will be quiet all day. Take a bed. Crash. We'll talk more when you wake up." *Just don't leave,* Adam added silently. As long as he could keep his brother from leaving the settlement, Jake would come around. He knew him that well.

"Yeah," Jake said finally. "Damn it," he said again, but without bite this time.

"Our room is the last one at the end of the hall," Adam said. "The big one. That would be best. There are just bunks in the boys' room." And he sure as the devil wasn't going to point Jake in Katya's direction.

Adam had become fiercely protective of the woman since he had come back, since he had learned that his new wife would come to him encumbered by her friend and her children. Maybe it was because Katya reminded him a little bit of his mother. Except Katya had done something about her situation, at least as much as she was able. She had protected her children.

Adam pushed that thought away uncomfortably.

Jake moved almost numbly up the stairs. His headache was crashing around in his skull now, all the little shoots of hurt emanating from that spot at the back of his skull where Katya had clobbered him.

He encountered her on the stairs. For a moment, his feet went still, and he stared at her.

Everything had changed. The angel was…well, not gone, he allowed. Just hidden now. Her hair was parted in the middle and pulled straight back. There was a small white hat-like thing perched on the back of her head. The nightgown had been oddly alluring, virginal though it had been. Now she wore azure blue, a dress that came almost down to her knees. It had long, straight sleeves. A plain neckline barely revealed the hollow of her throat. A black apron was cinched tightly around her impossibly tiny waist. And for all that, he felt something odd happen in the center of his chest. Something that felt like an animal scurrying.

She avoided his eyes.

The sound of a door cracking shut came to him from the landing above, and Mariah appeared there, dressed just the same as Katya. He knew the Amish all dressed the same so that no one of them would stand out. Vanity and pride were sins. But this time, somehow this time, it really hit him. The kids were all dressed alike, too, and it felt as though he were seeing triple, even quadruple.

God, he was tired.

"Excuse me," he said to Katya with excruciating politeness. He started to step by her.

"Do you feel well?" she asked quickly.

"I've got a headache. I'm tired."

He was acutely aware of her watching after him as he finally reached the upstairs landing and went in search of the bedroom. He closed the door carefully behind him and began peeling his clothing off almost in the same moment. The room was chilly, cold even, despite another wood-burning stove in the corner. He didn't care. He dropped facedown on the bed and was asleep almost before he closed his eyes.

Chapter 4

By four o'clock, Katya was truly frightened.

I've got a headache. I'm tired. Jake's words kept bouncing around in her head. At first they had just pestered her because she couldn't banish them. Now they seemed to echo as they grew more and more insistent.

Headache. Tired. Both, she knew, were signs of serious head injury. She had learned that from her grandma, who had been one of the settlement's most sought-after healers back in the days when the Old Order had been even stricter than it was now. Back then, folks had rarely gone to doctors. Even now, they tended to be reluctant to do so. God was the ultimate healer after all.

Jake Wallace probably needed a doctor, but she did not think he would go to one. It was just a feeling she had.

She hovered at Mariah and Adam's closed bedroom door, as she had done several times now, and listened. She heard nothing from the other side of the door. Not a stir, no rustle of bedclothes as he rolled over. Her heart rate picked up a little more, edging into panic now. She twisted her hands together.

He had been sleeping for nine solid hours. He had come up here just before seven. At first she hadn't been concerned. But as time ticked by, she became more and more convinced that something was wrong.

What if he had died?

Katya pressed a trembling hand to her mouth. If Jacob Wallace died, she would almost certainly go to jail, she realized. The deacons, the church elders, would not be able to protect her from the law. Jake was *anner Satt Leit,* an outsider. And the outside government would become involved. If she went to jail, her children would be sent back to Frank. And Frank would destroy them.

And God? What of God? She began trembling harder as she thought of Him. What would God do if she showed up at heaven's door with a rolling pin in her hand? Resistance was a sin. And she had certainly been resisting the horrors of the man she'd thought was Frank when she had cracked him.

She had to check on him. Maybe it wasn't too late. Maybe if he was just on the verge of dying, she could still help him in time. There had to be any number of things she might be able to do. Her grandma had taught her well; the old woman had passed on everything she knew. But she couldn't do anything from this side of the door.

Katya turned the knob soundlessly. She eased the door open. She would just peek in, she decided, would just make sure his chest rose and fell normally, and if it didn't...well, then, she would deal with that if and when it happened. One step at a time, she told herself.

She leaned forward. She looked, then she gasped and jerked the door closed again. She backed up, both hands held to her burning face.

He was naked in there.

Jake opened one eye when the door shut again with a sharp crack. He angled his gaze that way without moving his head, watching it, scowling. It didn't open again.

He was reasonably sure that it had been Katya, although he

had looked too late to be sure. She'd moved without a sound, and then there had been that gasp—her voice.

His curiosity got the better of him, overriding his common sense. He decided to make this easier for her. He wanted to know what she was up to. He rolled over, pulling the blanket with him so that it covered his hips.

He waited, wondering just what she would do next.

Katya groaned aloud. *Now* what was she to do? She couldn't just…just waltz in with him in that condition. But the brief peek she had taken had told her nothing. She had not even looked at his chest to see if it moved.

She had seen many other things, but not his chest.

She hugged herself, close to tears now. He was sleeping. He would never know if she went in there or not. Although, she admitted, modesty didn't seem to be high on his list of concerns anyway. Not with the way he was lying in there, sprawled on his back. Actually, she didn't even have to go in, she realized. She could just peer around the door again and look in the right place this time.

She couldn't bring herself to do it.

She got angry with herself. She was a married woman, for heaven's sake! Well, she *had* been. For ten years. It wasn't as though she had never seen a naked man before.

She'd seen *one* naked man, she realized, her skin burning even hotter. Precisely one. And Frank Essler had not looked at all like Jacob Wallace.

Why in heaven's name had he felt compelled to take all his clothing off in the middle of the day? He certainly seemed crazy, she thought. She remembered what he had said to Mariah. *Did he tell you I was a lunatic? That I'm as likely to brawl with the dudes I arrest as throw handcuffs on them?* And what, for heaven's sake, was a *dude?*

It didn't matter. None of that mattered. She had to do something. While she was standing out here waffling, he could very well be dying in there.

She put her hand back to the knob, bracing herself. In contrast to her face, her fingers were fumbling and ice-cold now.

She eased the door open again very gently, holding her breath, peering in…and let out a shaky, relieved sigh.

He'd rolled over, dragging the quilt over his hips as he went.

She eased a little farther into the room, her eyes trained directly on his chest this time. But she couldn't see anything. He lay on his side—his left side. His left arm was stretched forward, his hand extending past the edge of the mattress. His right hand was curled up, tucked under his jaw. That arm hid any and all evidence as to whether or not he was breathing. But he had to be breathing. He'd moved. But people could move reflexively in a coma.

She took another silent step and stopped again. His chest, his shoulders looked so big, so…so solid. She thought his body would probably feel hard and unyielding to the touch. And his skin was surprisingly smooth, she realized, mesmerized. Frank had been covered with so much hair. She inched a little bit closer and saw a spattering of freckles there, trailing downward onto his back.

But she couldn't tell whether or not he was breathing normally. He was so *still.*

But he had just moved, hadn't he? The first time she'd looked, he'd been flat on his back. She sorted through her mind to think if there were any after-death reflexes that could make a body turn all the way over. There were twitches, yes, certainly. Spasms. But no, a body couldn't turn all the way over. She was very nearly sure of it.

He was fine, then. But his breath must be awfully shallow because she still couldn't hear it. He didn't snore as Frank had done.

Her gaze slid down his torso, to the blanket curled over his hip like the arm of a lover. *Where had that come from?* She would have run then and there, she was that shocked by her own embarrassing thoughts. But she was…fascinated by him.

She remembered a time when she had been very little, probably no more than six. She and her mother and all her brothers and sisters had gone into the city, into Lancaster, for some reason. In fact, it was the only time in twenty-eight years she had ever gone there. Nearly everything the people needed was to be found on their own farms or in the village. But something odd had happened, she remembered, and her mother had said that that trip had been necessary. So they'd called an *anner Satt Leit* taxi to take them there.

It had been December. And there, on the street corner, ringing a bell over a metal kettle hanging from a post, was Santa Claus.

Now, more than twenty years later, Katya was aware of who Santa Claus was, but he had no place in Amish Christmas celebrations. Her people exchanged cards and gifts and they decorated their homes with greens on their mantels and in the windows, but Christmas Day itself was a somber religious observation, and the day after, called Second Christmas, was a time of quiet family activities. The Amish did not have decorated trees and special lights and mistletoe. They most certainly did not have Santa Claus.

She had never seen that jolly red-garbed man before that day. Katya remembered being in the back seat, scrambling around quickly onto her knees, staring out the rear window at the spectacle, amazed. And she had felt just as she did now, enthralled, captivated, enchanted. The sight of that Santa Claus had made her heart trip and her mouth open wide.

Sort of like her heart was doing now. She clapped a hand to her mouth. This, she thought, was much better than Santa Claus.

Jake's legs were so long. And bare. One knee was cocked up. Unlike his shoulder, his legs wore a faint, dark hue of hair that looked soft. She inched even closer and reached a hand out as though to touch it, the way she had longed to touch that Santa's red velvet tunic. She realized what she was doing and jerked it quickly back to her side.

She had to do what she had come in here for and get it over with. If anyone came home and caught her at this, if there *wasn't* anything wrong with him, she thought she would probably die of embarrassment.

She crossed the remaining distance to the bed. At least she had thought to take her shoes off earlier so her footsteps downstairs wouldn't disturb him. Now she moved silently and finally held a trembling hand just in front of his face. She caught her breath, waiting to see if she would feel his exhalation.

His own hand moved so quickly she was stunned. The one dangling over the edge of the mattress shot up and his hard fingers lashed around her wrist with an iron grip. She was so startled she wasn't even able to cry out.

He rolled onto his back again, pulling her along effortlessly. The blanket slipped away. Katya was appalled. She gave a little cry as she lost her footing and tumbled on top of him. "Oh, my!"

Then her heart exploded into a rhythm so hard, so fierce, it hurt. She stared into his eyes for that one terrible second—they were a deep, dark blue. Then he moved again. This time he rolled so that she spilled onto the mattress beside him, and—oh, God help her—his thigh came up over hers and pinned her there.

"Never, ever, sneak up on a sleeping cop."

His voice was a sleepy, unperturbed rasp. Oh God, was he laughing at her or chastising her? Finally, too late, it occurred to her that if he *wasn't* laughing, he would probably hurt her. No matter that he hadn't earlier, when she'd knocked the rolling pin against his head. This time she could have bothered him once too often. And he was big—much bigger than Frank—so he could hurt her badly.

Katya screamed.

She struggled against him helplessly and realized that not only were her legs pinned under his thigh, but he had her arms over her head, holding both her wrists in one hand. But at the sound of her voice, he reeled back and let her go. For one wild, incredible moment, she thought *he* looked frightened.

Katya scrambled off the bed and pressed her back against the wall, trembling. *The blanket.* Oh God, the blanket had fallen away again!

"What in the hell is wrong with you?" he demanded, almost shouting.

Her throat worked, but Katya couldn't find her voice to answer.

Jake watched her face as a million transformations took place there. Her skin was pale enough to be nearly translucent, but twin spots of bright color had appeared high on her cheeks. Whatever trouble she'd had that had brought her to Adam's home had left subtle shadows beneath her eyes. That silly Amish cap had come off in their struggle. Her hair was still pulled back, but those shorter wisps had come free to curl around her jaw.

It struck him anew how really beautiful she was. And how genuinely terrified. He'd thought...but no. Jake shook his head at his own stupidity. He'd started to think that the existence of a husband bothered her a whole lot less than it bothered him and that she had shown up to make more personal amends for clobbering him.

"I've done a lot of things that will probably damn my soul to hell for eternity," he said finally, roughly, "but I've never hurt a woman in my life. You can relax."

"The blanket," she squeaked.

"What?" His eyes narrowed. Then they followed her gaze. "Oh hell."

He grabbed it and hastily dragged it up over his hips. He got to his feet, taking it with him. He tripped on the edges and felt like a fool, so he swore again.

Her breasts rose and fell with every agitated breath. They were small, but her nipples were hard against the thin fabric of her dress. She squirmed a little, and her gaze whipped to a place to his left, staring there determinedly.

Well, hell, he thought uncomfortably. "Okay. Okay. I'm dressed. Sort of. Calm down. What the hell were you *doing?*" he burst out.

His skin had been so warm, she thought, shuddering a little. She recalled the sensation of it through her dress where he had been pressed against her side. His nipples were flat and his chest was so broad, and suddenly her mouth went dry as ash though she refused to allow herself to look a second time. God help her, all sensation, all her blood even, still seemed to be sluicing toward those places where they had had contact. The side of her breast, where his chest had pressed against her. The tops of her thighs, where his own had lain across them.

Even with the blanket wadded around him, all lumpy and twisted, he was the most beautiful man she had ever seen in her whole life.

"If you didn't come in here to roll around with me, then what the hell were you doing?" he repeated harshly, dragging her attention back.

Roll around with him? "Oh. *Oh.*" Katya crossed her arms carefully across her waist to still her trembling, her face flaming. "No. No, I didn't want...I mean, I wanted to see if you were all right," she whispered.

"You couldn't knock?" he demanded. What the *hell* was happening here?

"I didn't want to wake you."

"Why not? That would have given you your answer in a hurry."

"You weren't...uh, clothed," she managed, mortified.

"So you just wanted to creep in and take a look without me knowing about it?" He stared at her incredulously. "What's your story, woman?"

"Yes—I mean, *no!* Not—I didn't want to *look!* Not exactly. I mean, I wanted to see if you were *breathing!*"

"Breathing."

"Alive!"

"Why wouldn't I be?"

"Because I almost killed you!" she wailed.

She was serious, he realized. He stared at her, stunned all over again. "Honey, I take worse blows than that in barroom brawls, and I always walk out upright."

Katya knew in that moment that she was out of her depth here. She had no way of even conversing with this man. *Dangerous*, she thought again. Her eyes fell to his big hands, and she imagined them fisted, raining blows. They would be even more horrible than Frank's fists...but Jacob had said he had never used his on a woman. Still, she did not think they'd know how to be gentle.

"I'll go now," she gasped and began circling the bed, giv-

ing him a wide berth. He caught her arm anyway, just above
the elbow. She cried out. And once more, she could feel the
heat of his grip clear through to her soul.

He dropped his hand after he had stopped her. She gingerly
rubbed the spot he had touched.

"Where's Adam?" he asked roughly.

"Adam?"

"My *brother.*"

"Oh, yes. Yes, of course. He's helping the men put up
another new school," she blurted. "He should be back right
after sundown." He hadn't asked where Mariah was, but she
rushed on, telling him anyway. "Mariah is teaching, and she
should be home any time now. My children also."

"That whole brood was *yours?*" He looked appalled.

"Oh, no. Bo is Adam's." She flushed and closed her eyes,
mortified all over again. Of course he knew who Bo was! She
was so *stupid,* just as Frank had always said.

"And Matt is a Lapp," she went on tremulously, unable to
look at him now. "He belongs to Sarah and Sugar Joe. He
was just sleeping over."

He wasn't sure *what* he'd thought all those kids were doing
here. He'd been too tired to make sense of it. "Dear God."
He looked away from her, then back, still frowning. "*Four* of
them? You have *four?*"

She nodded. "I'll take you to Adam, if you like."

"No," he said too quickly, too instinctively, for comfort.

He wanted to say, *Keep your distance. Just stay right there.*
It was on the tip of his tongue. And he had no inkling why it
seemed so important. Women were a dime a dozen—soft ones,
hard ones, thin ones, round ones, all with their own unique
virtues. He could enjoy them fully and walk away just as easily. They could come close or they could stay away. Neither
reaction bothered him particularly.

But this one really had him rattled. He needed to keep far
afield of her. That instinctive necessity made his skin feel too
tight for his body. Maybe it was her blushes. Maybe it was
her innocence. Four kids or not, he could scarcely believe how
innocent she seemed. If she had stood there and told him that

she had found them all in cabbage patches, he'd probably believe her.

"You don't want to hang around with me too much," he finally said hoarsely, and he felt like a fool again.

She brought her chin up a notch. "No, sir. I don't. But I...owe you."

"Don't call me sir!"

She lowered her eyes. "I'm sorry."

"You know, that just really sets me off."

"Yes," she whispered.

"I'm not that damned old."

"No."

"And you don't *owe* me anything, for God's sake. Are we back to that knock on the head again?"

"Yes." She gave a small nod in the direction of her toes.

He had already learned that these people were long on virtue. This woman had a palpable goodness to her that was the first thing a man noticed about her. He'd thought she was an angel.

"Look," he said, "I'll tell you what. Just point me in the right direction to find Adam, and we'll call ourselves even."

She hesitated, then finally looked up again. "That would be fine."

"Okay." He waited. She didn't move. "Katya."

"What?"

"I'm going to drop this blanket now so I can shower and get dressed."

"Oh!" She bolted for the door.

"Wait!" he called out as something else occurred to him. No electricity, he recalled. No phones. No running water? "There *is* a shower, right?"

She had stopped cold in the hall and looked back at him. "Of course. We're not heathens."

"I never thought that."

She hesitated, then gave a little nod. "The men dug a well late last night. Everything's working fine."

Thank God. Splashing around in the horse trough would have been a little bit more than he could stand.

"Okay," he muttered. Still, she hovered. "Go on—get out." He waved a hand at her. This time she vanished like smoke.

He stared at the door where she had been, feeling a little bemused, which was not an emotion he'd ever experienced before in his life. It was almost impossible to believe that less than twenty-four hours ago, he'd been in a country-western bar in Washington, in a really good mood and enjoying the hell out of himself.

Chapter 5

Jake found Adam with a minimum of fuss. Katya's directions were excellent. Unfortunately, he had to walk. Several more tours of his brother's property had not turned up a rental car anywhere. That worried him as much as anything had yet.

The sun was starting to set and the crew was just finishing up when he strolled into the new school yard. Six men hammered and nailed away, and Jake stood back, unobserved for a couple of minutes. He gathered from their conversation that they'd been rotating all day so that no one man would have to remove himself from his farm for more than two hours. That would have slowed them down. Adam, apparently, had been here since morning. Adam didn't have a farm, and Jake devoutly hoped he never took it into his head to get one.

"We didn't arrange for anyone to be here in the morning," one man called out as he scrambled down from the roof.

"Thought for sure we'd get done today," someone else remarked.

"Fresh snowfall bollixed us up."

"I can finish up by myself tomorrow," Adam offered.

"Shouldn't be necessary," Jake said.

They all turned to look at him. Jake was hard-pressed to tell them apart. They all wore beards ranging from black to blond to gray. They all wore broad-brimmed hats. There were six pairs of black broadfall pants, black boots, colored shirts—mostly blue—and black suspenders.

All except Adam. But suddenly Jake realized that it didn't look as though Adam had shaved in several days, either. Something else he needed to worry about.

"You can finish in half an hour," he observed. "Give or take. Why quit now?"

"Supper's on. Cows need to come in and get hayed. Horses need to be settled down for the night. And it's getting too dark to see," someone responded. "We didn't bring lanterns."

"And there's a whole section of shingles to put on up there," another guy said, pointing to the roof.

"Give me that hammer," Jake returned.

A man dutifully turned it over.

"Come with me, bro. You guys start handing the shingles up. Who's got the tar? Okay, we need to rig that bucket with a pulley, then the rest of you can go. We can take it from here."

He worked because it was easier than what he had to discuss with his brother. He worked because three years ago, he'd been temporarily suspended from the D.P.D. when a female witness had charged him with sexual misconduct. He had never touched her and had never even implied that he'd like to. Work was work, and pleasure was pleasure. He always drew the line. Still, it had taken Internal Affairs a few months to reach that conclusion.

In the meantime, Jake had hired on with a construction crew. He enjoyed it, baking in the Texas sun, straining muscles that had gone softer than he would have liked since he'd left the police academy. It wasn't quite as good as playing cowboy, but it had felt just fine. He'd learned his share of nifty shortcuts, a few of which wouldn't put the quality of the building at risk. Like everything else, those shortcuts had nestled in the back of his brain, waiting for a time when they were needed.

Like now.

They were finished with the roof within twenty minutes, although he realized that the chimney bricks still needed to be laid in. Jake climbed down from the roof again, his bare hands nearly frozen. Most of the men had stayed anyway. One of them tossed him a pair of gloves. Jake caught them in the air, frowning.

"I'm going home to supper," the man said. "I won't need them. You're going to hang around and finish up. Am I right?"

Jake looked at the chimney again. More than it needed him, he needed it. He wasn't sure why he felt this compulsion to keep moving, but it was there. He thought of Katya's innocence again. Of her terror. Presumably she was still back there at Adam's house. "Might as well," he answered.

He pulled the gloves on. The last of the men drifted off to various buggies, hitching the horses up to the vehicles again. It took a surprisingly short amount of time, but then Jake figured they had been doing the task all their lives and could probably accomplish it with their eyes closed by now.

Adam shoved his own gloved hands into his coat pockets and watched him climb back onto the roof. "So?" Adam prompted finally.

"You have any mortar mixed?" Jake asked.

"'Round the corner here. I'll get it."

He was going to stay, Adam realized. He let himself grin once, briefly. Mostly he was relieved for the sake of the missing babies, but a part of his heart was solely centered on Jake. Although his brother didn't know it, he needed this settlement, Adam thought. It was a good place to unwind, to calm down and take stock.

"How long?" Adam called up to him. "How long will you stay?"

"Start shoving those bricks up here," Jake answered.

Adam loaded half of them into a new basket and used the pulley to send them up. He climbed the ladder himself and perched at the edge of the roof, smearing them with the mortar, handing them over to Jake.

"I need to get to a phone tonight," Jake said after a while. "I've got to call into the department and make sure they don't need me."

"There's one at the end of the lane."

Jake looked in that direction, surprised.

"Another slight change with this new *gemeide*," Adam explained. "The people have always been permitted to borrow *anner Satt Leit* phones in the event of an emergency. So Sugar Joe Lapp and the new deacons have had three public phones installed in those areas closest to the village, where the service lines still reach. See that little wooden thing way down there?" He pointed.

Jake looked into the gathering darkness. He could just make it out now, but he had noticed it before. "Yeah. I thought it was an outhouse."

"Phone booth."

"Good thing I didn't try to use it."

"Yeah." Adam chuckled. "The Amish aren't against civilization. They're against civilization breaking up the strength and solidarity of their families. As long as the phones aren't actually in their homes, disrupting family time, they're okay. And these are pay phones. The deacons collect the money and use their share for people suffering hard times."

Jake gave him a strange look. "You sound like a damned travel brochure."

Adam shrugged. "Sorry. You just always liked to know the why of things, so I thought I'd tell you."

"Yeah," Jake said grumpily, working again. He was quiet for a long time. "If the department will spare me, I'll hang around for a week," he said finally. "I'll see what I can get started. I should be able to learn enough in that time to finish things off out of the ChildSearch office back home."

"That's what I was thinking," Adam said mildly.

"Okay, then," Jake said.

"Okay," Adam agreed.

"You've got no room for me in that house, do you?" And inside Jake's head, a voice pleaded, *Tell me no, tell me you'll put me up in a motel.* A motel where innocent women with wide blue eyes wouldn't creep up to his bedside.

"We'll make room," Adam answered.

"Great," Jake bit out.

"Give her a chance, Jake," his brother said quietly. "Please."

Jake looked at him sharply, something thumping him squarely in the breastbone. "This morning you were telling me she wasn't for me!" he snapped.

Adam scowled. "I was talking about Mariah."

Jake's breath shot out of him. "Oh. Sure."

Adam began making his way down the ladder again. Jake followed him and they packed up the remaining bits and pieces of the construction site. That was when Jake noticed there was still one buggy left and one horse grazing. And damned if it didn't look like the one he'd made intimate acquaintance with early this morning.

"No way," Jake muttered. "Uh-uh. I'll walk."

"It's got to be five miles back to the house."

"I made it here on foot, didn't I?"

Adam looked at him oddly. "What's the point here? You've ridden before, cowboy."

"*On* them. Not behind them, and it's been a real long time regardless."

Adam waited.

"Look, I just don't want to get all sucked up in this quaint way of life, okay?" Jake said finally, defensively. And he wondered why he felt such a strong, instinctive aversion toward it. Sort of like the strong, instinctive need he felt to steer clear of Katya Essler.

Adam shrugged, knowing better than to push him. "Whatever. Catch you back at the house."

Jake only stood staring at the buggy. He thought of piles of horse manure invisible in the darkness. He thought of marauding buggies without horns. And the damned ever-present cold that was seeping back into his bones now that he wasn't working, moving, staving it off. "Damn it," he snapped.

Adam was waiting for him. He'd gotten the horse hitched

up with a lot more difficulty than the other guys had had. Jake walked around to the front of it and looked the horse in the eye.

"Not a word," he warned in an undertone. "I'll be holding the whip." Then he went around to the passenger side and levered himself up onto the seat. "We don't belong here, you know," he said at last. "We can't step back in time and be like them."

Adam said nothing. They clop-clopped onto the road in silence. Then, finally, he shrugged. "Probably not. But I want to."

Jake decided to ignore that. It made his heart kick with something too much like real fear. "So what's her story?" he asked after a moment.

Adam felt a wary feeling roll over in his gut. He knew whom his brother was talking about this time, and it wasn't Mariah.

"Leave her alone, Jake."

"There's more to it than a hard time," Jake went on as though his brother hadn't spoken. "That woman didn't just come off a hard time. She's like a rabbit caught in headlights. She's terrified. She jumps if someone says boo."

"Yeah." Adam scowled. He didn't want to tell him.

Adam knew there were two things in the whole world that consistently lit a fire under Jake Wallace. He'd tell anyone who cared to listen that he didn't like kids. But let someone, anyone, snatch a kid away against his will, hurt him, threaten him, and Jake was right there, ready to set things straight.

He was the same way with battered women. They'd both watched their own mother get smacked more times than they could count. Their little sister, too. Their mother, Emma, had let it happen to all of them. And if Jake was right there when a child needed him, well, then... Adam had once seen him nearly kill a man who'd had the unfortunate timing of swatting his girlfriend on the same street Jake was traveling. Jake had jumped out of his car in the middle of traffic to do it, causing gridlock for two blocks in each direction.

If he told Jake about Katya Essler, Adam knew that one of

two things would happen. Frank Essler would be in danger of becoming a dead man. Or Jake would use that rakish charm to endear himself to Katya, to get close to her and watch over her, to keep her safe. Then he would leave again, and Katya's heart would be broken once more. No, she definitely didn't need Jake Wallace in her life.

"He smacked her around," Jake said, and it wasn't a question. "Her husband smacked her around, right? Does he drink?"

Adam let out a breath as he drove the horse onward. "Yeah," he said finally. It was pointless to argue.

"What about all those kids?" Jake demanded. "Did he hurt the kids, too?"

"It's past, Jake. You can't do anything about it now."

"I'm just asking a question," he said angrily.

Adam sighed. "Only the oldest. He slugged the oldest girl. And only once. The night before Mariah...helped her get away." It still bothered Adam to think about the danger she'd put herself in. "She used to check in on Katya every morning—they'd meet in the barn. One day after I'd left for Texas, Katya didn't show up. Mariah barged into the house and boarded them up in Katya's bedroom. She tied the sheets together and they used them to work their way down from the second-floor window." And if Frank had caught them at it, Adam knew the man would have killed both of them. Adam's heart spasmed, though the incident was nearly a month behind them now.

Jake whistled tunelessly. "Good for her." He felt a surge of respect for Adam's wife. "So what's Mrs. Essler going to do now?" Emphasis on the *Mrs.*, he thought.

"I don't know," Adam answered. "She needs to figure out a way to support herself, then I guess we'll all build her a little house close to ours. Until then, she can stay with us."

Jake nodded. "What are the odds that she's one of those who'll go back for more?"

"Given what she did to you this morning, I'd say nil. She fought back, and that's against her religion."

"If she leaves your place, this guy can get to her. If she's living alone, she has virtually no protection. Guys like this don't give up, bro, no matter what the woman wants or how hard she tries to stay clear. They just follow."

"Yeah," Adam agreed unhappily. "I know."

"Well, hell. Guess this sort of thing happens all over the place, huh? Even here in God's little Divinity."

"I guess it does." But here it was harder—almost impossible—for a victim to escape, he thought.

They had stopped in front of Adam's house. Adam got out, but Jake only sat, staring at the place. Houses looked different at night without electricity, he realized. Homier. Warmer. Light didn't glare out the windows; it glowed. Softly. It had almost a golden hue.

"Go on in," he told Adam. "I'll take care of the beast."

Adam raised a brow. "Do you know how?"

"Nope."

Adam shrugged. Jake would figure it out.

Jake watched his brother go inside, but he didn't move. He watched Katya pass by one of the windows. She did it quickly, but her movements were all smooth as velvet. Or drifting smoke, he thought again.

He recalled the way she had trembled beneath his leg earlier, probably, he realized, in sheer terror. But then there had been the way her breasts had risen and fallen. Despite her understandable fear at what he had done to her, she hadn't quailed and succumbed. She had fought him, had struggled away.

Jake swore aloud.

She was afraid of him. He wanted her to be, he told himself once more. He wanted her to stay as far away from him as possible. She should be damned wary of men in general, yet despite that, despite her puritanical upbringing, she had actually found the courage to slip into his room to make sure he was all right—whether he was dressed or not.

Alive, he remembered. She'd said she wanted to make sure he was *alive*. He'd honestly believed that that was an excuse at first—it had sounded that ludicrous to him. Now he understood that she might really have believed she had hurt him badly. She had probably never clobbered anyone before in her life.

Who *was* this woman? *Not your style, Jake. Leave her the hell alone.*

He touched a finger to the lump on the back of his head. One week, he told himself. Next week he would leave this place. He didn't really need to call Dallas. He'd actually taken three weeks off for the FBI seminars. He'd just told his brother he only had one left so as to leave an escape route open for himself.

He finally got out of the buggy and began unhitching the horse. The beast watched him knowingly. Jake wondered what it was thinking, then decided he didn't want to know.

"Okay, so where's the FBI on this?" he asked half an hour later, his mind starting to work. He was beginning to feel human again. He still felt tired, but it was the weariness of worked muscles, however brief his labor had been. It wasn't the kind of sleep-deprived exhaustion that had gripped him when he'd arrived here early this morning.

And he was eating. *This* was food. He shoveled braised beef and carrots and mashed potatoes onto his plate. If nothing else, he decided he liked these people for their no-nonsense approach to eating, cholesterol be damned.

"They cleared out yesterday," Adam answered, chewing. "The last agent to leave said he was going to work out of the field office in Philly."

"Not impossible," Jake allowed, "depending upon how much he got done while he was here."

"My guess would be not a lot," Adam said.

Jake tried to ignore the eyes of the women. The eyes of the one to his right, particularly. He could *feel* Katya watching him. As for the kids—all five of them, including Bo—they were all at the other end of the table, caught up in conversation and giggles of their own.

"That was Joshua Byler there today—the guy with the blond beard," Adam went on. "His Amalie was the second to disappear. She's been gone since November now."

"Any patterns you can discern so far?"

He asked Adam, but Mariah answered. "They were all just babies," she said quietly, sadly.

Jake shot a glance her way. She was sitting across the table from him. And out of the corner of his eye, he noticed Katya again. She wasn't eating, he noted. She was more or less pushing her food around on her plate. Her eyes were still on his face. As near as he could tell, she never even looked at her meal.

She was watching him just the way she had upstairs earlier, before he'd grabbed her arm. She'd been checking out his legs then, of all damned things. His ego told him that there'd been other more interesting things to inspect, but her gaze had been glued to his legs. And she'd been looking at him as though the sky had just started raining golden nuggets.

He felt something strange happen to the pit of his stomach. A sort of hollow flutter. He didn't much care for it.

"Anything else?" he barked suddenly. "Anything besides that?"

Mariah pushed her plate away and rested her chin in her hands. "Patterns," she repeated slowly. "Well, there have been an equal number of boys taken as girls—two each. The boys were taken at church suppers—you know, after services. No one noticed anything, but they wouldn't. There are so many people milling about then, children running, playing. The littlest ones just chase after the older ones." Her eyes turned pained. "One mother didn't even realize her baby was gone until it was time to go. They thought he'd wandered off into the woods. We searched for days."

"Find anything?" Jake asked sharply. "Anything at all? Maybe even something that didn't seem important?"

She shook her head. "No, nothing," she said quietly.

"What about animals?"

"Animals?"

He looked down the table at the children and dropped his voice. "Could an animal have gotten to him?"

She looked shocked. "Oh, no! We may *look* rural, but there

are cities and humanity all around us. We have badgers, of
course. And some deer. But that's it.''

Jake nodded. ''What about the other kids?''

''Amalie vanished at the little farmers' market in the village.
She was toddling along behind her mother...and then she
wasn't. Lizzie Stoltzfus disappeared from her own yard while
her mama was hanging clothes on the line. Oh, darn it,'' she
finished lamely, swiping at her eyes.

''I'll find them,'' Jake said hoarsely. ''I'll try.''

Katya felt a shiver dance down her spine. It was the way
he said it, she thought, fighting the urge to drop her fork and
hug herself. Oh, there was such danger in his voice now. There
was a very real threat there, a ferocious, determined anger. But
it was focused on whoever was doing this to them.

He wasn't...nice. But having him there made her feel safer
than she had in a very long time, even though she had been
hiding behind Adam's significant brawn for weeks.

Jake turned his head slightly and caught her gaze. She felt
heat wash through her. She meant to look away and couldn't.
His blue eyes were hard, questioning, measuring—then, bless-
edly, he looked away first. Katya breathed again.

''One other thing,'' Adam said suddenly. He looked at his
wife. ''You know, it only just now hit me. Correct me if I'm
wrong, but Lukas disappeared in October, Amalie in November, Michael in December—''

''And Lizzie the day after New Year's!'' Mariah cried. She
looked quickly at Jake. ''One a month! Is that what you mean?
Is that a pattern?''

Jake finished eating and pushed his plate away. ''Yeah, it
is. And it's a damned good one. It gives me something to work
with.''

The table went suddenly silent. He felt the prickle of too
many eyes. He glanced down at the other end of the table.
The children were all looking at him steadily. Even his own
nephew watched him as though he had just grown horns.

''What?'' Jake demanded. ''What are you staring at?''

''That's a bad word,'' Bo said. ''Tell him, Pa.''

"I did," Adam said. "I tried," he qualified. "Just ignore him."

Jake felt absurdly embarrassed, and that irritated the hell out of him. He stood abruptly and rubbed his temple, attempting to soothe a new headache growing there.

"I'll start by talking to the parents in the morning," he said shortly. "In the meantime, this is what—February eighteenth? Can you somehow get word around your...uh...?"

"Gemeide," Katya supplied in a whisper.

His eyes shot to her then he looked away again fast. "Yeah. Get word around the *gemeide* or whatever for people to handcuff themselves to their babies. To all of their kids, for that matter. If that pattern is deliberate for some reason, and no kids have disappeared yet this month, these people really need to be on their guard."

"I'll spread the word," Mariah said. "I'll send notes home with all the children at school tomorrow and tell the other teachers, as well. Unfortunately, this isn't Church Sunday, so we won't all be together to spread the word that way."

"Well, do the best you can." Jake rubbed his temple again.

"It hurts," Katya said suddenly. "Your head still hurts."

He moved his eyes to her again. And away. "Yeah. No. Not where you hit me."

"It's tension, then. I could—"

"I'm fine." Now that he was on his feet, he couldn't remember where it was that he'd meant to go. Away from here, he thought, to some other room where little kids didn't chastise him with their eyes for swearing. To some other room where this little wisp of a woman didn't watch him like she wanted to gobble him all up.

Get off of that thought. Now.

"What?" He realized she was still speaking. She was on her feet now, too, stepping closer to him.

"Sit down, sir. I'll—"

"For God's sake, will you stop calling me *sir?*" he roared.

Her hand flew to her mouth and she literally reeled away from him. Her elbow cracked hard into the wall behind her. Her eyes filled. Jake closed his own, cursing himself. He should have gone home when he had the chance, he thought. He should have gone home before his brother had had the opportunity to tell him about missing children.

But he hadn't. And that left him one option.

He reached for her and caught her wrist, pulling her hand away from her mouth gently. He told himself he did it because he had read somewhere that psychologically it was best to touch her right away, while she was shattered. It was a technique abusers used, though unwittingly, to keep a woman coming back for more, to keep her pliable. But it worked just as well the other way, to help a victim heal.

Touch her now, he thought, while she was vulnerable, before she could build up a brick wall against him. He'd prove that he wasn't an ogre, and get that notion right out of her mind. He had to show her that every time a man snapped at her, a blow wasn't going to follow.

But it wasn't just any man she was dealing with here. It was him. And suddenly, that felt dangerous. Suddenly, bridging any kind of gap between them seemed like a very bad idea. He felt his heart beating a little too hard.

"Come here," he said softly. He drew her toward him. She came, trembling, watching him with huge, wary eyes. He rubbed his thumb over the pulse slamming in her wrist.

"W-what?" she asked, her voice shaking.

"I'm sorry. I yell sometimes. It doesn't mean anything. Ask Adam. It's nothing personal. You're right. I'm just a little stressed out. Next time just yell right back at me."

"Of course." The words tumbled out of her on an expelled breath.

"You don't have to be afraid of me."

"Yes," she managed. "I mean, no."

"Good."

He was still holding her wrist. He finally loosened his fingers. And then his eyes fell from her own stricken gaze to her mouth, barely open, her breath soft.

The idea of kissing her blindsided him. Because when a woman stood close to him and looked at him in that way, he generally did just that. He almost—*almost*—started to lower his head before he even realized he was doing it. Because her mouth was pretty and enticing, and damn it, something about her drew him.

It was her eyes. It was the way she looked at him. Like he was something amazing and wonderful and good. He couldn't remember any woman ever looking at him that way before. Mostly they knew he was amazing, dangerous and bad.

He stepped back quickly. He became aware of the entire table staring at him. At them. "I need to find that pay phone," he said hoarsely. It was as good an excuse as any to get the hell out of this house while his head was still overruling his hormones.

Chapter 6

Jake roused the next morning to the smell of coffee. It smelled the same the world over, he thought, whether it was brewed in an electric coffeemaker or on top of a wood stove. It smelled good. He got up and ambled into the kitchen, following his nose.

"That couldn't have been comfortable," Adam said, inclining his head toward the sofa in the other room, where Jake had been sleeping.

Jake shrugged. "Somebody should be downstairs." He swigged from the mug Adam poured. "Just in case. Besides, there didn't seem to be anywhere else. I don't do corn husks," he added. That had been his other option—the floor mattress Adam had offered him.

But Adam shook his head. "Frank Essler is a coward. No way would he come here knowing two large men are under the same roof. He prefers to hit people who don't hit back," he said, his expression tightening.

"Let him try," Jake growled.

There was a sound of distress from behind them. They both turned sharply.

Katya stared at them, her eyes filling absurdly. She was touched—and astounded—that these men cared enough about her predicament to discuss it. And for one of the rare times in her life—although maybe not so rare lately, she realized sadly—she was angry and ashamed. Angry that Frank had put this on her. That there was even a *need* for these men to be discussing her. And she was ashamed that Jacob Wallace was looking at her so...pityingly. She hardened her jaw and stepped into the room. "I came to get breakfast for the children. Mariah is busy upstairs."

Both men moved away from the stove and the counter without a word, giving her room. She tried to ignore them, but it was hard not to be aware of them. She got cereal and poured it into bowls, as she took milk from the refrigerator that was powered by a hydraulic motor just outside.

She had four brothers, three brothers-in-law. Her family had gathered frequently until the *gemeide* had broken apart and her kin had stayed with the old one, mortified that one of their own was making such a fuss about the inequities of her life. Katya had often worked in a kitchen with all those men underfoot and others besides. And never had she noticed that the air changed with the overwhelming force of their maleness. These two men—especially Jacob—seemed to fill the kitchen with their very essence. She was exquisitely aware of him. She found it a little hard to breathe. When Jake spoke to her, she almost overpoured the milk.

"Who's handling your divorce?" he asked suddenly.

She looked at him, astounded.

He didn't seem to notice her expression. "You might want to get a restraining order," he went on. "That way, if he does bother you or the kids, they'll incarcerate him. That might dissuade him from trying it again and the kind of evidence that he's violent should help get you custody in a divorce. It doesn't always work—usually those things aren't worth the paper they're printed on, and I'll be the first to admit it. But it might work here, assuming he really doesn't want to get involved with the law of the...the outside world." He couldn't remember the term Adam had used. *Anner* something.

Katya was still staring at him.

"What's wrong?" He scowled. "I mean, why not just take a shot at it? If it doesn't work, you haven't lost anything but a few bucks for filing fees. It's worth a try." Maybe she didn't have a few bucks, he realized belatedly.

"I can't divorce him," she said quietly.

"What?"

"I said I...I'm not allowed to divorce him."

Her words sank in slowly. "You mean...what, because of your religion?"

"Yes. I—"

"So what are you supposed to do with the rest of your life?" he interrupted harshly.

"What I'm doing."

"You're not doing *anything!*" he said angrily, and she blanched.

He couldn't have said why he was so upset. Her religion was her own business. He'd always made it a point to argue neither God nor politics. But temper was hot behind his eyes. Burning, even. It made his blood move fast and hard.

"But I don't have to live with him!" she protested. "That's enough. Unless..."

"Unless what?" he asked sharply.

"Unless he comes back," she said faintly.

"That's what we were just discussing," Jake grated.

"No, no, I didn't mean...not 'come back' that way. I mean, if he goes to our new deacons and repents."

"Repents," Jake repeated.

"Says he's sorry."

"Easy enough. Just words. Then what?"

"Then I've got to go back to him."

"*What?*"

"I...would have to live with him again."

Jake wheeled on his brother. "This is bull—"

"Watch it," Adam warned quickly. "Anyway, he won't do it."

"You don't know that!"

"Yeah, I do. To repent, he'd have to admit that he hit her

in the first place. And he's still denying that. He's telling everyone in the old *gemeide* that Katya is crazy, that she ran off for no reason. I think we'd have some warning first. You know, he'd start saying, 'Well, *maybe* I pushed her around, but she deserved it.' We'd see it coming.''

''And then what?''

Katya realized he was glaring at her, not Adam. "I'd run," she blurted.

Her own blood started pumping hard. She had no idea where the words had come from. Her heart, she thought wildly. Yes, yes, the response had come straight from her heart. Because she had been thinking about it so much lately, wishing...

For a miracle.

It was a moot point, an impossibility. Where would she go? How could she survive? *Stupid, mousy, always making mistakes.* Frank's words echoed in her head. She felt tears burn at her eyes and she turned away to hide them.

Adam watched his brother's jaw working. "What else can she do but play the odds?" he asked quietly at last. "They're in her favor."

"For *what?*" he roared. "For being tied to a bastard who's not part of her life for the rest of her days?"

"Jake," Adam said carefully, "it's not your problem. You can't fix the whole world."

Jake turned sharply for the door. "I'm going to go see those parents," he said abruptly.

"How are you going to get there?" Adam asked.

"I'm—" Jake broke off, staring dumbly out the door. "Damn it."

"They all live in far corners of the *gemeide.* We just split from the old one a few weeks ago, so the homes of the two factions are sort of intermingled, like clasped fingers. There's no real delineation." Adam paused. "Besides, you're not even dressed," he noted reasonably.

Jake looked down at himself. Actually, he wore his jeans and the T-shirt he'd arrived in. He'd slept in his clothes for the sake of propriety...and to avoid a repeat of what had happened yesterday afternoon. But he was barefoot.

He looked at Katya. Her eyes were still shining. Her chin trembled. But it was up, thrust forward, bravely. It touched him more than he cared to admit. He wondered if he could be so strong, to accept as she did. And he hated her for accepting, though that made no sense at all.

He caught a whiff of something clean and springlike from her direction when she finally moved, stirring the air. How the hell could this woman get to him by just *being* there? And why was he so enraged by the fact that she was young and beautiful and trapped by a God who didn't care?

He slammed the door shut. Katya jumped, then deliberately caught and steadied herself. She gripped the edge of the counter. An odd quiet fell over the room.

When Jake finally spoke again, it had nothing to do with his clothes. His eyes stayed on Adam, and his voice seemed strangled. "It's just like Mom. That's all. That's why it gets to me." It was as good an excuse as any.

Adam could count on one hand the number of times his brother had specifically mentioned their mother.

"The Catholic church says divorce is a sin," he went on, "so she stayed and let him whale her and she drank and drank and drank until her liver gave out and she died. And I, for one, can't salute any religion that would demand that of a woman. How the hell can you condone it? Don't you even *see* it?"

Adam hesitated. He didn't believe—had never believed—that his mother should have stayed. He didn't believe Katya should ever go back to her husband. And that was at least one reason he was very cautious about joining Mariah's faith, no matter how much peace its ways had given him. Their union had so far only been blessed by a justice of the peace, and Mariah deserved—needed—more than that.

"I can't," he admitted finally, slowly. "I can't condone it."

Jake stared at him a moment longer, then he gave a quick, hard nod, satisfied by his brother's honesty. "I'm going to take a shower," he said at last. "And I need to borrow some clothes."

He cast one look back at Katya, still standing near the sink, her hands clasped together now. He opened his mouth as though to say something more, then he shut it again. He looked deliberately away from her and went upstairs.

The kids weren't done in the bathroom. He had the choice of waiting or showering with three boys and two girls underfoot. The boys wouldn't have bothered him, but the oldest girl looked to be about ten years old, so he waited in the boys' bedroom. And he stewed.

Family, he thought. Happy, cozy—no matter that they weren't even all related. Maybe that was the catch. Maybe familiarity bred contempt. He watched Bo in particular as the boys finally spilled into the room, his own blood.

The boy had recently broken his arm. "So what did you do this time?" Jake asked him.

"Tree," Bo explained, snatching trousers and a shirt off the hooks on the wall with his good hand. "I fell out. Pa says I did it before. It was a long time ago and I don't remember."

"Yeah. You did. Looking for a bird's nest."

"That's what he said. I thought I saw one this time, too."

"In February?"

Bo's face reddened. "Well, there was *something* up there. Something neat."

"I'll bet. What was it?"

His face reddened even more. "Never did find out."

"Maybe you were just trying to hide for a while," Jake guessed.

Bo turned blue Wallace eyes on him. Jake waited for him to trust again. He could be patient enough when he needed to be.

"Yeah," the boy said finally. "Maybe."

"So how's it going?" Jake asked. "Since you've been back here, I mean. Is it getting any easier?"

Bo hesitated. "I remember a little."

"That's good, huh?"

Bo didn't answer.

So the situation was still confusing to the kid, Jake thought. Small wonder. "He loves you."

"Guess he must, to stay here," Bo blurted. "'Course, he did that 'cause of Miz Fisher, too. I mean, uh…"

"I don't imagine anyone's going to expect you to call her Mom yet."

Bo shrugged uncomfortably. "Miz Wallace sounds funny to my ears, too."

No kidding. "Give it time, dude. Things have a way of working out when everybody's heart is in the right place."

"Yeah," Bo said just as two other boys came into the room.

Levi, Jake remembered, was Katya's oldest boy. He'd been introduced to them by name last night at dinner. Or supper, they called it. His hair was more yellow blond than his mother's—Katya's had that whitened, sun-bleached look, even in February. Levi was a stocky kid, with none of his mother's delicacy. Jake put him at maybe a year older than Bo's seven.

The baby, Sam, was dark-eyed and thin. He still had that blundering, sometimes stumbling way of walking. And he had the biggest, most serious eyes Jake had ever seen.

When Katya had walloped him with that rolling pin yesterday, Levi had been wide-eyed and amazed, and the littlest girl—Delilah, he remembered—had sobbed. Bo had seemed to think it was all pretty funny, and the oldest girl, Rachel, had looked terrified that Jake would pick himself up off the floor and charge all of them. But Sam had just watched everything with those wide, arresting dark eyes, sucking on his thumb to beat the band.

Levi nudged Bo in the shoulder as they dressed. "Guess you can't play hockey today, huh?"

"I gotta ask your mom," Bo said.

"Katya? Why?" Jake heard himself ask. He was startled. What could Katya have to do with Bo's broken arm?

Bo glanced at him. "Well, she fixed it. Guess she would know when it's healed enough so's I can't hurt it again, right?"

"Uh…right," Jake managed.

Mariah stuck her head in the door. "Bathroom's free, Jacob," she said quietly.

Everyone seemed so content, so cozy. Jake thought again. He stood from the bed, moving for the door. And he wondered, in spite of himself, if this was what life would have been like all those years ago if his own family had been normal.

Jake swore under his breath and pushed the thought out of his mind.

He showered and changed into Adam's clothing; the jeans were a little too short, but they would do. Then he went downstairs again. Everyone was gone. Everyone but Katya.

"What are you up to today?" he asked neutrally, still towel drying his hair as he stepped down off the stairs into the living room.

She moved past him into the kitchen, skirting around him carefully, not really looking at him. He thought again that she smelled of springtime. He stepped back quickly to allow her more room. And to clear the scent from his head.

"I've got to go see about Miz Miller's diabetes," she said softly. "It's under control—she saw a doctor—but she needs to maintain. Mariah took Sam. She'll drop him off to play at the Eitners' today so I'll be free."

The mention of diabetes reminded him of Bo's arm. Jake followed her into the kitchen without meaning to, dropping the towel over the newel post behind him as he went.

"You're a nurse?" he asked, even knowing it couldn't be. But maybe she had left the settlement and come back, the way Mariah had.

No, he realized immediately. That simply wasn't possible. Mariah had a serenity about her that came from experience, good and bad. Katya wore her heart on her sleeve and seemed to give that heart to everything she did. And always, right there at the surface, was her hesitation, her fear.

Now she looked back at him quickly. "Oh, no. We're not allowed to educate ourselves past the eighth grade."

He pulled his mind off it before their rules could anger him again. "So how do you know so much about medicine?" he asked instead.

"Medicine?" She gave him another quick, surprised glance. "I know nothing of medicine. But my grandmother was a folk healer. I know what she taught me, and that's good enough. It's enough for the little ailments. For more serious problems, people go into the clinic in the city. As I said, Miz Miller's diabetes is under control. We just need to keep it that way."

Jake nodded. Bemusedly.

She was busy snipping leaves off a plant on the windowsill. He watched her for a moment, looked at the plant more closely, then found his voice. "Arrowbruce?"

Katya stopped what she was doing to stare at him this time. She nodded slowly. "How did you know?" she asked finally, amazed.

He was vaguely embarrassed, though he had never been ashamed of his odd bits and pieces of knowledge before. "I read somewhere that it stimulates pancreatic health. That would work, right?"

"Yes," she breathed. "I make a tea with it. Blueberry leaf works well, too, but I only have access to that in the summer. And it's difficult to grow indoors." She put her attention deliberately back to the plant. "Adam left the wagon for us."

Honey, there isn't an us. Let's not get too cozy here. It jumped into his mind out of nowhere. He bit back on the words just in time. But the urgency was still there—growing even. He realized that the longer he knew her, the more he liked her. The more he hurt for her. And that scared the hell out of him.

"If you left here, you could go back to school," he said suddenly. "You could be a nurse. I've even read that there are those practicing holistic medicine now...." His voice trailed off at her expression. "What?"

"School?" she repeated.

His jaw tensed. "You said if Frank came back, you'd run. I was just pointing out an option in that eventuality."

"School?" she said again, focused and fascinated by that idea. Then she gave a little shake of her head, and her color heightened. "With no money and four children? Jacob, that's foolish. It's just...a dream."

And she wasn't allowed to have them, he thought bitterly.

"I'm finished here," she said quickly. "Let me just grab my coat and shawl. Oh, and Adam said you should use his same coat, the one you borrowed yesterday."

Jake looked around as she slipped from the room. He saw the coat on the back of one of the kitchen chairs. Perversely, he went upstairs to get his own sports jacket. He wasn't walking today. And...and he really didn't want to get too comfy here, borrowing a bunch of clothes, sharing wagons, settling in. There was still that obstinate feeling riding him.

They met back in the kitchen. This time he spotted a note on the table. He picked it up. Adam had left him directions to the farms of the four families who had lost babies. He stuck it in his pocket.

"Ready?" he asked and opened the door. And stopped again.

The horse was already hitched up to the wagon. Which was all fine and good, but he'd never played giddy-up before in his life. At least not this way, not in a buggy. He'd ridden before, long ago on that ranch, but as he had told Adam yesterday, that was *on* not *behind*.

Hell, how difficult could it be to drive a horse from a buggy? he reasoned. He was pretty sure the same rules applied. Pull this rein, the horse turned. Pull that one, he went the other way. "Okay," he muttered aloud.

Katya was already in the buggy, gathering up the reins. Jake went after her. He shut the door carefully behind him—there were actually no locks on it at all, he realized, amazed—and climbed up onto the seat beside her.

"Don't know why Adam couldn't have gotten one of those enclosed kinds," he muttered, already cold, pulling his jacket tighter. Wishing for Adam's coat after all. Stubbornness was another Wallace trait that he'd never considered particularly admirable, but that he succumbed to from time to time.

"They've ordered one from Abe, the buggy maker in the

village," Katya answered. "It should be ready in another week or so."

The horse trotted out onto the street at a steady pace. *CLOP-clop-CLOP-clop.* Jake shook his head as though to clear it. His heart chugged. *Oh, yeah, you're worrying me, bro.* Now Adam was buying a buggy? He was really settling in as though he planned to stay and keep up with this marriage.

Then again, he had said as much. Jake just preferred not to believe him. He shoved his hands into his pockets.

"I don't imagine your...uh, Mrs. Miller is any relation to the Miller family who lost Michael?" he asked finally.

She took her eyes off the road a moment. "No. Well, yes, but distantly. I believe they're second cousins. We're all descended from the same group of immigrants, you see, so in all the settlement there are only perhaps ten surnames. And most of our given names are either German or biblical. We're all related somehow, although fairly far removed in most cases."

"So there are a lot of Millers and Fishers and Lapps and Bylers," Jake said. But only one Wallace, he thought. That ought to have told Adam something.

"That's right. That's why we have so many nicknames. Like Sugar Joe, for instance. Because there are easily a dozen Joe Lapps, and we must differentiate between them."

His eyes narrowed as he looked at her. "So what's your nickname?" He could have sworn he didn't want to know, but the words were there.

She flushed a little. "I don't have one anymore."

"Then what did it used to be?"

She flushed deeper. "They used to call me Little Katie when I was a Yoder."

"Little Katie Yoder," he said with a smile in his voice. Then it faded. "But you're not Little Katie Essler."

"No."

"Why not?"

"Once I married Frank, I turned out to be the only Katya Essler. So there was no need for a nickname." Except, she thought, those that Frank had hung on her. She cringed inside, hearing them again. *Stupid. Mouse.* And, on those occasions when he had really been drunk, there were names she couldn't repeat, not even in her own mind.

Jake was watching her too closely. She forced a weak smile.

"This is it," she said a few moments later. She stopped the buggy in front of the Millers' farm. "This is where I need to go."

"How will you get home?"

"Seth will give me a ride when he breaks for dinner. Or one of his boys will. Miz Miller is Seth's mama. She lives in that *grossdawdy* house right there out back. She's a widow now."

Jake remembered that their "dinner" was the rest of the world's lunch, so she wouldn't be stuck here all day. No need to come back for her then, he thought. His relief was complicated, not quite as strong as he would have liked it to be.

She was out of the buggy now. He slid over and took the reins she'd left on the seat. Clumsily. He decided he'd wait until she got into that *grossdawdy* place before he actually tried to drive off.

"Jacob?"

At least she wasn't calling him sir anymore, though he vastly preferred just plain Jake. He looked down at her.

"If you like, I'll be finished here in just a few moments," she went on, nervously, he thought. "I don't have to stay and visit. I could go with you to see those families."

"Not necessary," he said too sharply.

"I could drive," she ventured.

"Hey, I'm cool."

"Oh! There's a blanket there under the bench. Jacob, you really should have worn Adam's coat," she chided. He stared at her. "Here," she added, reaching for it.

"Uh, no. Katya, no. I just meant...never mind."

She pulled her hand back but continued looking up at him earnestly. "Wait for me, Jacob. Just bundle up in the blanket, and I'll be right back."

She started to hurry away. His head was spinning.

"Katya." He clenched his teeth. "You don't need to drive

me. I can handle it. I've done it before.'' A small stretch of truth there, he thought, but his conscience could live with it. *Come on, Little Katie, go inside so I can breathe something besides innocence and springtime.*

She stepped back. "Well, then. Have a good day."

"Yeah, same to you."

She finally turned her back on him to go up the walk. He breathed and looked down at the reins in his hand. He'd watched her very carefully, had committed to memory every single move she'd made to make the horse go. He jiggled the reins as she had done. The gelding began stepping along. Good enough.

He was a quarter mile down the road before he looked back. She was still watching him. Just standing there outside the *grossdawdy* door, her shawl gathered tightly against the cold, watching him.

Something in his stomach rolled over again. What *really* scared him was that he was getting used to the sensation.

Chapter 7

Katya was home, mending some of the children's clothing, when she heard the approach of a horse and buggy. She was curled on the sofa, stitching and thinking, that burning, helpless feeling lingering in her chest again as she remembered her conversation with Adam and Jacob that morning. A restraining order! she thought wildly. Not even *God's* rules had kept Frank in line. And school...

It all sounded so wonderful, she thought wistfully. A piece of paper, a *written* rule that said Frank could not hurt her. And learning things. What an amazing world it was out there. A world she was too dumb and frightened to fit into.

Still, she'd dreamed about it until she heard the clatter of hoofbeats—too fast—and wagon wheels—too loud and too close. Then her thoughts shattered. She threw Sam's little trousers aside and leaped to her feet before rushing to the front window. She saw nothing there, but the commotion grew even louder. The wagon was passing too close to the side of the house.

She ran to the kitchen, looking out the door there, then she gasped. It was Adam and Mariah's wagon, and Goliath, their horse. The reins trailed loosely, cutting snaking swaths through the snow.

Jacob was nowhere to be seen.

Panic seized her. She cried aloud and rushed outside, then she hovered there, uncertain what to do next. The horse appeared to be fine. He wasn't able to get into the barn because the wagon still attached behind him was too wide. But he was complacent, unperturbed, nibbling bark off a tree.

Where was Jacob?

She whirled back into the house. She went inside just long enough to grab her coat and shawl off a hook inside the rear door. Then she raced to the wagon and clambered up onto the seat, gathering the reins.

"Come, Goliath. Where did you leave him?" She closed her eyes briefly. What a dumb question. *Stupid mouse.* A horse was not even as bright as a dog. Goliath would never be able to lead her to Jake.

The Lapps, then. She would find Sugar Joe. He was their closest neighbor, and he would know what to do.

She set the wagon to rolling, biting her lip. She cracked the reins a little, urging the horse faster. "Please," she said on a whisper, not sure whom she was pleading with.

She careened into the Lapps' driveway a few moments later. She jumped down and looked about. She did not see either Sugar Joe or Nathaniel, their oldest son, who still lived and worked at home. She turned for the house and ran that way.

No one answered her knock.

She could feel her heart start booming against her chest. She wondered if Jake was lying unconscious in the snow somewhere. And if he was, she thought of things like pneumonia, bronchitis, all the nasty infirmities that would befall him from lying wet and injured in the bitter cold.

She should never have let him drive off in that buggy. She groaned aloud and banged her fist on the door again. Why *had* she? She had guessed that he couldn't drive the conveyance. Something about the way he had gathered the reins...

Shame blasted through her, hot and almost unbearable. She had let him drive off because she was afraid to mention right out that no matter what he said, he didn't appear to be able to. Because although she was far from worldly, she had learned one painful truth over the years; the male ego was a frightening thing. It was delicate, vulnerable, unpredictable. She had not insisted that Jake couldn't drive the buggy because she had been terrified of his temper. She had been purely afraid that he would lash out at her if she embarrassed him.

Silly, stupid mouse. She chided herself, near tears, and waited for Sarah Lapp to answer the door. If something had happened to him, she would never forgive herself for her cowardice.

"Sarah, *please!*" she all but shouted, then, beside herself, needing to do something right if only this once, she barged in without waiting any longer.

The entry was silent. Sounds of weeping came from the kitchen. Katya raced into it and found Sarah at the table. She was more alarmed than ever now.

"Sarah!" she cried. "What is it?"

The woman came to her feet so quickly the chair toppled behind her. She looked embarrassed and horrified. "Katya! What are you doing here?"

"I knocked. I..." She didn't finish. She understood a woman's tears better than she understood anything else in life. She moved instinctively to the other woman, holding her arms out. "What is it?" she asked again, enfolding her.

"Nothing."

"Is it Bo still?" Sarah and Sugar Joe had raised and loved little Bo for four years before Adam had found him. Katya knew the loss of the boy to his true father—no matter how right that was—still had to leave a painful hole in the fabric of Sarah's life. The whole situation was made even sadder by the fact that Sarah couldn't have any more children of her own. An *anner Satt Leit* doctor had told her that if she tried, she would probably die.

But Sarah shook her head. "It's not Bo." She pulled away, shoving a hanky into the pocket of her apron. "I didn't hear you knock." Her voice had become stronger. "I should be asking you. What's wrong?"

Katya had been momentarily distracted—*distracted*, while Jake was out there, perhaps really dying this time. "It's Adam's brother!" she gasped. "He took the buggy out to see the parents of the missing children, but Goliath came back without him."

Sarah's own panic lasted no longer than a commendable heartbeat. "I'll get Joe and Nathaniel," she decided. "And Adam is straight across the woods at the Stoltzfus place today. That's where they're building the last new school to replace the ones we lost when we left the new *gemeide*. Why don't you go find him?"

"Yes, yes…I'll do that." She knew where Adam was today. Why hadn't *she* thought of that?

Because she fell apart in times of trouble.

Katya raced out the back door. She gathered her shawl more tightly about her shoulders and ran for the creek, then for the long tree line behind it. It truly wasn't so far. The spreads beyond the woods were invisible because Shaker Hill rose right on the other side. The treetops were deceiving, giving the impression that the woods rose straight up without a break, but there were actually two more spreads tucked in there.

She made it through the woods and onto the fringes of the Stoltzfus place. As soon as she waved for Adam, she saw Jacob. He was coming up from the road. Walking. *Not lying unconscious somewhere.* But he was limping. She cried out and ran for him.

Jake saw Katya approaching and it took everything he had not to turn around and disappear the other way. Her skirt whipped around her legs, outlining them clearly. Her hair was coming undone again. This time the bonnet was in place, but shimmering white blond strands slid down her back and forward over her shoulders, bouncing as she moved. Behind her neck, what little remained of her tidy bun slid lower and looser with each step.

He jerked his eyes away from her. "I'm fine," he snapped as soon as she got close enough to hear him and before she could even ask. "This was the last place I had to go today, so I just decided to walk." Even he realized how inane that sounded. God, how he hated that horse.

Katya's steps faltered as she reached him. "You're not fine," she said. "Jacob, you're bleeding."

"The hell I am." Blood dripped from the gash on his forehead squarely onto his nose. He scrubbed it away with the heel of his hand, angry. And embarrassed. He looked up and saw people streaming toward them through the trees. "What did you do?" he demanded. "Call the whole damned county out for this?"

"No, I..." she began, then stopped. Her chin came up in a show of courage. "Yes," she breathed. "Yes, that's exactly what I did. I got help." Then she braced herself as though, despite everything he had said, she was sure he would hit her or yell.

Well, he thought, she had good reason to expect the yelling part.

"Damn it," he groaned, then before she could react, he hooked one shaky arm around her shoulders and pulled her closer. He smelled the flowers, the springtime. It was just that she was so urgent, so damned sweet. "I'm all right," he said, and he thought his voice sounded odd. "You didn't need to worry."

"But the horse came back—"

"Too bad. I was hoping he'd play in traffic."

Her eyes widened. "What happened?"

"He started bucking like a fool and took off." At which point, Jake had somersaulted right into the back of the wagon and out again onto the road. He was really taking his lumps on this trip and was only grateful there hadn't been anyone around to see the spectacle.

"What did you do to him?" Adam demanded from behind him.

Jake turned to glare at his brother. "Maybe you ought to go ask that cantankerous beast what he did to me!"

"Cantankerous?" Sugar Joe Lapp asked, catching up with them from the other side of the property. "*Goliath?* He used to be Abe Miller's horse, the one he loaned out with buggies

to novices. That gelding doesn't have a cantankerous bone in
his body.''

"He does now," Jake snapped.

He had met Sugar Joe Lapp on his last trip. He liked the
man. Now, as usual, there was a lingering humor in Joe's eyes.
He was as tall as Jake was, as big as Adam, and his face was
tanned and rugged, even in the winter.

Suddenly, Jake heard himself laugh—actually *laugh*. Adam
cracked a smile.

"Where is he?" Adam asked again. "He's the only horse
I've got.''

"Beats the hell out of me," Jake muttered.

"He's in Joe's barnyard," Katya offered. "I drove him
here. The wagon is fine, also."

Jake glared at her. "Thanks a lot."

Her jaw dropped. "For what?"

"You might have lied and said it was battered all to hell.
You could at least make this whole thing look good, earn me
some pity.''

"But that's simply not true!" she protested.

She was absolutely guileless, he realized as she blinked at
him in clear consternation.

"Come on inside," the other man said, the one Jake didn't
know. He had arrived with Adam. "Katya can neaten up that
mess on your forehead."

"I'm fine," he grumbled.

"No," the man said, "you're not. You're bleeding."

Jake thought about it. "You're Simon Stoltzfus?"

"That's right."

"You were next on my list anyway. To talk to."

"About what?"

"Your daughter, Lizzie."

The pain that flashed across the man's face was so real, so
deep, Katya felt it herself. She tugged on Simon's arm to get
his attention. "Jacob is here to help. And I just know he'll
find them, all the children. He's very smart. You just need to
talk to him."

And just like that, Jake was angry at the same thing that

had touched him a moment before. At her innocence. Her urgency.

She was tying him in knots. He wanted to grab her and shake her. He wanted to tell her that she had no way of knowing that he could find those kids. Damn it, he wasn't a god. He was just a man, and not an altogether good one at that.

She looked at him with an appreciative smile that grew even as he watched, and he felt the air leave him. *Damn it, don't look at me like that.* But he heard himself say, "I'll try. It's all I can do, but I'll try."

Simon studied his face a moment. "I'd be obliged. But let Katya fix you up first. Don't reckon you'll be much good to anybody 'til then."

Jake looked down and realized that the whole front of Adam's borrowed shirt was marked with ample red droplets. He just managed to refrain from swearing again.

They all trooped into Simon's farmhouse. Into another kitchen nearly identical to Adam's. The unrelenting sameness of this place would make him crazy, Jake thought, if he were already crazy enough to stay here longer than a week. There were the same hardwood floors, he noted, the same white walls. The same miles of counters, the hum of a hydraulic motor just outside, a flame flickering in the lamp hung over the table. There were green things growing, and he felt something inside himself die a little.

This was the way other people lived.

He sat at the table. Katya busied herself at the counter, then she descended upon him. He couldn't quite see what she had in her hand, but it smelled like a submarine sandwich. He reared back. "What are you doing?"

She stopped just short of him. "Stopping the bleeding," she explained nervously.

"With what? What is that?"

She looked at the towel in her hand. "Minced onion. A poultice."

"Onion," he repeated.

"It will clean the wound out nicely, and it helps the blood clot."

"It's going to sting."

She blinked. "Well, yes."

"Take it away."

She started to step back, then she stopped and frowned, unsure if he was serious or not. "But—"

"Let me drip, Katya. I promise to wipe up anything I get on the floor."

"I can't do that!"

"Why not?"

"You're *bleeding!*"

"We've established that. It's my blood. I can put it anywhere I like. I'm not going to let you sting me."

He *was* serious, she realized. "Why, you're nothing but a big baby!"

His eyes narrowed. "Watch yourself there, woman."

"You're going to bleed rather than succumb to a little bitty sting?"

"How little bitty is it?"

"Very. And I'll do it quickly."

Jake shook his head. "No. You won't do it at all."

He was more than a little aware of her faint blush. In fact, he *was* playing with her, enjoying her. He had a pretty high pain threshold, though he never went out of his way to inflict any upon himself. He tried to remind himself again that there were easily a million reasons he had to leave this woman alone. She thought he was a good man. She thought he was worthwhile. She thought he was wonderful.

She couldn't be more wrong.

"Give me that," he snapped suddenly, snatching the poultice out of her hand. As he had known she would, she jumped. He took no gratification from it, though he'd been hoping he would. He looked at Simon Stoltzfus and deliberately, with great effort, shut her out. "Go ahead and tell me what happened to your daughter while I sit here reeking," he went on, slapping the onion-y towel to his head. "Please," he added, biting the word out carefully.

The man stared at him uncertainly. "You need a pen or something to write all this down?"

"No, he'll remember it," Adam muttered.

Katya smiled whimsically, almost proudly. Jake caught the expression out of the corner of his eye and swallowed another growl. "Here's the thing," he said, pulling his attention off her again. Then he couldn't for the life of him remember what he had been about to say next. She'd returned to the counter, but now she was coming at him again with a handful of something white and powdery. His eyes narrowed. "*Now* what?"

"Alum."

He relented because he knew it would help the situation. God knew he didn't want the fuss of stitches or an unsightly scar on his forehead.

He turned his attention back to Simon and let her work on him. "Something changed during the days immediately preceding your daughter's disappearance," he declared. "Something had to have happened. Someone was here in this settlement, someone who wasn't supposed to be here, either with the intention of taking Lizzie, or looking for the first available baby to take. Can you think of anything?"

His eyes cut to Katya again, then away. He was having a damned hard time concentrating. Her fingers brushed his cut, touched as gently as a whisper. Then—God help him—she blew softly on the wound.

Her breasts were inches from his nose. He thought of clasping his hands around her waist, of putting her bodily away from him, but that would involve touching her. So he simply sat. And he felt her instead.

She combed his hair back from his forehead with her fingers, keeping it clear of the cut. And when she did, she leaned into his shoulder. Soft. She was soft. As tiny as she was—and she was definitely too thin—her body gave, yielding to the solidity of his shoulder. He felt his own body reacting. Impossible. He had never before in his life gotten...well, turned on by a woman just leaning into his shoulder.

He shifted uncomfortably in the hard chair. Katya was looking into his face now as though whatever came to his lips next was going to be a nugget of wisdom far beyond comparison to all nuggets that had ever come and gone before. He cleared his throat.

"Uh, Lizzie is our best bet for getting to the bottom of this because her mother was right there with her when it happened, right? In Lizzie's case, we know exactly when and where this abduction occurred. The others were…uh, in crowds." He dragged his gaze to Simon again. "I'll need to talk to your wife. I'll need her to show me exactly where this happened. I want to cover that ground tomorrow. Damn it," he snapped suddenly at Katya. "Will you stop touching me?"

Katya jumped back, clear of him.

"She's quilting with her sisters today," Simon answered. "But she should be home shortly to make supper."

Jake looked at his watch and decided he was too hungry, too tired—and too sore—to wait. "Could you ask her to hang around here in the morning? I'll come over around eight o'clock and she can show me to the site."

"How?" Katya asked. She sat primly in the chair beside him now, clasping her hands in her lap.

Jake scowled. "What do you mean, how?"

"How will you get here?"

"In the buggy, I guess. Or I'll walk."

He watched her actually seem to brace herself. She drew herself up. Squared her shoulders. No good that, he thought, because it made her breasts thrust toward him a little, and he was angry not only that he noticed but also that he knew he would have been worried about himself if he hadn't.

It was her fault that he had had this mishap today, Katya thought. She'd known earlier as well as she knew right now that Jake was not able to drive that buggy. She had let him go off on his own because she was afraid of confronting him over it. As she was afraid now. He would certainly be angry with her for embarrassing him in front of all these people, but she wouldn't be able to live with herself if he tried again and was hurt even worse.

She stood and leaned into him again. "I'll take you," she whispered in the direction of his ear.

He scowled up at her, tilting his head back. "What?"

"I said I'll take you," she whispered again fiercely. "I'll drive."

Distance. He couldn't be amused by this. And he sure as hell wasn't going to start spending his days with her.

"No," he said shortly.

"But—"

"I said *no!*"

She jumped back. He saw immediately that her blush had become one of anger. It was fascinating. He stared.

Just yell back. He'd told her that. Katya gathered herself for it and thrust her chin out. "You're as stubborn as a mule!" she cried.

"And it's gotten me this far through life in one piece," he remarked.

"Because God protects drunkards and children and *idiots!*"

He continued to stare at her. "Are you calling me an idiot?"

She began trembling. "If you insist upon driving that conveyance by yourself, then yes, sir, I am."

"Don't call me sir!"

"Don't shout at me!"

Somehow he had ended up on his feet, glaring down at her. She had taken a step toward him. She had to crane her neck back to look into his face. She barely came to his collarbone.

The room was quiet. All eyes were on them.

Jake snapped his head around to find his brother. "We need to rent a car, bro. That would be easiest."

"It's not possible."

"What do you mean it's not possible?" Jake demanded.

"Just what I said. I mean, get it in your own name if you want, but it's not something I can comfortably do right now. I don't want to bring any more censure down upon Mariah's head than our civil marriage already has."

"There hasn't been censure," Sugar Joe said. "We're just waiting for you to come around, is all."

Jake understood and he didn't like it one bit. "So what the hell am I supposed to do?"

"Actually, this is about the place where the FBI hit a roadblock," Simon volunteered. "Our customs. The way things are around here. Their agents couldn't accommodate the *ord-nung,* our religious guidelines. Jacob, I'd like to suggest that if you start driving up to doors the way they did, you're not going to get anything out of our women. You'll scare them off. You'll frighten them."

"I got information out of them before, the last time I was here," Jake argued, getting irritated.

"You talked to the *men* before," Sugar Joe corrected him. "Myself included. But it's the women who know the most about *this* situation. It's the women who go into the farmers' market in Divinity for this or that, who take care of the children, who would know if a stranger had been hanging about."

Silence fell again.

"You should stop acting like a foolish, pigheaded man and let me drive you." Katya's soft voice broke into the quiet. "I have nothing to do with my days anyway." She looked pleadingly at Adam. "Let me help with this."

Adam remembered something Mariah had told him, that Katya was uncomfortable and distressed because she couldn't contribute anything to their household. Here was something she could do. Except, he thought, he felt like he was throwing a lamb to the slaughter, a sacrificial virgin into the mouth of a volcano. He didn't particularly want to send her off in the wagon with his notorious, three-date-limit brother.

"It could work," Jake said reluctantly, aloud.

Adam glanced at him and saw, too late, the look in his brother's eyes. Jake was thinking about Frank Essler again.

"It's probably not safe for her to hang around in that house all day by herself anyway," Jake went on.

Katya looked away. "Frank won't come for me. He blusters, but...I think he's probably just as glad to be rid of me, except he has to wash his own socks." Her skin flamed with the admission.

Sugar Joe made a sound in his throat. Simon Stoltzfus uttered a word that was as close to swearing as any Amishman ever came. The word did not speak highly of Frank Essler.

Adam felt himself sinking into a situation he had created

when he had brought his brother here, a situation that seemed to be spiraling rapidly out of his control.

"You know," Sugar Joe said finally, "it's an arrangement that really does cover a lot of bases. Not that I think Frank would really do anything, either, but you never know."

"It's not up for democratic vote," Jake said. "We'll do it."

Katya beamed. She felt her pulse scurry. For the first time in days, weeks, *years,* she had something to look forward to tomorrow. She would be doing something *useful.*

And that, of course, was the only reason her heart was acting so frantically, the only reason at all.

Chapter 8

Katya was awake before the sun rose the next day. She watched it lighten the sky on the other side of the window, feeling shivery and expectant and wonderful. But she held herself very still.

In truth, a little part of her was afraid that if she rushed downstairs, *when* she rushed downstairs, she would find out that she had dreamed it all. That Jacob wasn't going to take her with him. That he didn't need her. *Need her*—what a delightful phrase that was. She was afraid she would go downstairs and find out that none of this had happened at all, that she wasn't going to ride along with him today and do *something*, however small, toward finding those babies.

She waited until the sky turned yellow-gray, then gradually blue, then she couldn't stand it anymore. She sat up and dropped her legs over the side of the bed. As always, the room was frigid. There was no stove in here, and the fire in the hearth had died many hours ago. Goose bumps trekked immediately over her skin when she slid free of the blankets. She stepped over her daughters and around the crib before creeping into the hall.

Jacob was just coming out of the bathroom.

"Oh," she said, startled, stepping back a little. He looked at her, then away, in that funny way she had started noticing.

Her skin flamed. She knew why he did it. She was unpleasant to look at. Tiny, plain, pale. He was just too polite to stare. At least he hadn't told her that he had changed his mind about today. She waited, bracing herself, but he only slung a towel around his neck and stood there.

"I...uh, thought I'd beat the crowd this morning," he said awkwardly.

"Me, too," she managed, drawing his attention back to her face.

"Well, it's all yours." He stepped away from the bathroom door and waved a gallant hand in its direction.

"Thank you."

But she didn't move. She watched him head off toward the stairs. He did not wear a shirt. She had just scrubbed the goose bumps from the cold off her arms and now they came back.

His naked shoulders moved with an almost lazy grace as he went down the steps. He didn't even seem to feel the cold. He was amazing. She saw him hesitate and she darted into the bathroom, afraid he would look up and find her staring at him.

She was just finishing in the shower when her girls burst in. Delilah had had her bath last night and she just washed up in the sink. Rachel scrambled into the shower as Katya stepped out. Then there was a knock on the door and Adam's voice drifted in.

"How much longer in there?" he asked.

Katya flinched. "Uh...five minutes." She turned quickly back to the shower to hurry her daughter along.

"Where's Sam?" she asked Rachel. If the baby woke and started crying before she could easily get to him, if someone else had to pick him up and soothe him, she would die a little more at the way she always seemed to put these people out.

"He's still sleeping, Mama," Rachel assured her.

Oh, they needed their own place, Katya thought desperately. A little of her earlier euphoria slid away. It was so unfair to put Adam and Mariah out like this.

She found herself glancing down the stairs again as she hustled the girls back to their room, even standing on tiptoe a little to be able to see more. But Jacob was no longer in the living room. She found him in the kitchen when she finally made it downstairs, a sleepy Sam in her arms. Jake was drinking a cup of coffee, leaning back against the counter, dressed in more of Adam's clothing. She could tell because both the sleeves and the jeans seemed just a little too short, and she didn't think he had brought a suitcase with him.

"Ready?" he asked. "I told Simon I'd be back over there by eight."

"Yes, I remember. I'll be just a minute." *He hadn't changed his mind.*

Mariah came into the kitchen. "No, Katya, go. I'll gather the children up and take them to school with me. Jake says they mustn't walk alone anyway."

"If you're sure," she said uncertainly.

"Of course I'm sure. We're all going to the same place, aren't we?"

Katya kissed each one of her children in turn as they spilled into the kitchen. She gave Rachel a squeeze. "Don't spend your day worrying," she chided. "Keep your mind on your studies. As for you..." She looked at Delilah worriedly, smoothing her dark hair off her forehead. "You're so pretty today. If that boy teases you, just punch him in the nose. Promise me you won't cry about it."

"Thank you," Mariah said dryly, but she was smiling. "Violence and mayhem in the classroom. Not to mention what resisting in such a fashion does to the *ordnung.*"

Katya looked abashed. "Oh, I hadn't thought of that."

Mariah's smile held. She shrugged. "Our little one here isn't yet bound by the *ordnung,* and it seems an effective solution to me."

"Levi, no hockey today unless a grown-up goes with you," Katya went on.

"That means you, too, Bo," Adam contributed.

"Miz Essler says I can't play yet with my arm anyway," Bo grumbled.

"Geese," Sam said, looking crestfallen. "Geese, Mama."

She gave him a little squeeze. "We'll go later, after we finish with Mr. Wallace." She looked at Jake apologetically. "I promised to take Sam to the pond today, to see if some geese have returned there. They usually flock there in the afternoons. I'm sorry. I'll have to take him with me today, and if you wouldn't mind just stopping a moment on your way home..." She trailed off. "It won't take very long, I promise."

"Uh...sure."

They went outside. Adam went to the door to watch after them, then he looked back at his wife. "You practically shooed them out of here! You couldn't get them on the road fast enough," he said darkly.

Mariah blinked. "What's wrong with that?"

"I just don't think she should spend any more time with my brother other than what's necessary with them under the same roof this week."

She stared at him, then laughed and tucked her arm into his. "You're too young to be her father," she chided.

"Yeah, well, her own father turned his back on her."

Mariah flinched. Hers had, too, when she'd been shunned, and the comment brought painful reminders. Then her expression calmed again. "Jacob has been with us for two days now," she remarked. "I don't think he's as bad as you said, Adam."

"There's not much trouble for him to get into here."

"Well, there you have it."

Adam opened his mouth, then closed it again. "Damn it," he muttered. "I hate it when you win an argument."

She put her finger to his lips, then followed the finger with her own mouth. "Watch your language, Adam. And don't worry so. Katya is much tougher and smarter than she looks." And one of these days, Mariah thought, Katya herself was even going to realize it.

For the life of him, Jake couldn't get those images of Katya—and her kids—out of his mind. She'd had something to say to each one of them, he thought, something special. He didn't want to dwell on it. He thought about it anyway.

"You're a good mother," he said finally, swinging up into the wagon beside her and Sam. The baby was bundled into a blanket so that only his face peered out.

Katya experienced a feeling of surprise, then a rush of pleasure. She gave a quick little shake of her head, and just like that her neatly bound hair was loose again. She gathered up the reins. It was the first compliment she'd received in so very long. She shook its echo deliberately out of her head because it was too tempting to wallow in it.

She remembered what he had said about his own mother yesterday morning when they had been arguing the topic of divorce. "It's probably not that I'm so good," she observed, "as it is that you've known only bad."

It had been the wrong thing to say. She felt the anger come off him suddenly, in almost physical waves. "There was nothing wrong with my mother," he snapped. "She just wasn't there."

"Oh."

"I mean, physically she was, just not...emotionally. She was kind enough, when she was sober." But he couldn't recollect one single time when she had paid him specific attention, he realized. Emma had needed all her emotion for herself. She'd sure as hell never promised to take him to a pond to see if some geese had returned.

"Do you...?" she began, then left her question unfinished as she guided Goliath and the buggy out onto the street.

"Do I what?"

"Do you not have children? I wondered what *their* mother might be like."

His face hardened even more. "No. I don't like kids." Though, in all honestly, it wasn't really a matter of *liking,* he reflected. It was more a matter of not trusting his own Wallace genes—his father's genes, possibly determining his own behavior. Adam was a good father, but it was entirely possibly that the little buggers had skipped a sibling and were lying in wait inside him. He would never find out. He didn't dare.

Katya thought he was lying. She'd watched him with Bo last night, with her own children. He was so gentle with Delilah. He'd seemed so attuned to little Sam. He had a marvelous way with children, she thought, a way of getting down to their level. He didn't worry too much about rules and authority. She didn't think he cared much about rules of any kind.

Jake decided he wanted to get off this subject fast. "How did you do that?" he demanded, glancing over at her.

"What?"

"Whatever you just did with the reins to make this beast go."

"Oh. I jiggled them."

"That's what I did yesterday." He'd watched her yesterday. He'd seen her do it and he had done it himself. At which point he'd landed in the snow. "So how come he doesn't kick and bolt for you?"

Katya thought about it. "You must have let the reins touch his back."

He decided it was entirely possible. The damned things had been all over the place, hard to control. "Well, now that I know that, you really don't have to tag along. You could go back. I don't need you."

The look she sent him hurt. Her eyes were suddenly wide, stricken. He could feel her plea almost as though she had spoken aloud.

Well, he reasoned uncomfortably, there was still the little matter of her husband. It really was best to keep her close and protected. In which case Frank Essler only had to wait out the week until he was gone and he couldn't protect her any longer. Jake shook that possibility right out of his head. Adam would be here. Adam had already taken Katya under his wing. He was a little lax about precautions to Jake's way of thinking, but that could be remedied. Jake figured he would just give his brother a good talking-to on the subject before he left.

"Never mind," he said finally. He shook his head. "Come on, make this pony pick up the pace a little. We're going to be late."

She smiled at him beatifically. Jake had to look away.

When they reached the Stoltzfus farmhouse, the children were just spilling outside, then piling into a waiting buggy. Simon was giving them a ride to school. Jake was gratified to see that people were taking his warnings to heart.

A heavyset woman stood just outside the door, watching him warily. She looked older than Jake might have expected. It was probably just the care and the heartache that were etched into her face.

He leaned over in the seat, across Sam, closer to Katya. "Could you introduce me, smooth the way here?" he asked her.

"Yes, of course. I'd planned to." She scrambled down from the seat.

He watched as she collected the baby and went up the walk. He followed at a distance.

"Deborah, this is Jacob Wallace, Adam's brother. He's come to find the babies."

He should have known she'd put it that way. "I've come to try," he corrected.

The woman clasped his hand in a surprisingly hard, desperate grip. "Please come in. I have coffee and sweet rolls."

"That's not—" he began, then broke off as Katya kicked him smartly in the calf.

He looked down at her, frowning. She gave a shake of her head as the woman went ahead of them into the house.

"What?" he asked in an undertone.

"If you don't let her serve you something, you'll take her dignity, Jacob."

"Her *dignity?* I'm just trying to find her kid."

"There's no 'just' about it. Let her do something for you, as well. We're a proud people, accustomed to paying our way."

Jake stared at her a moment longer. "Good thinking," he said finally, then he moved to catch up with Deborah Stoltzfus.

He didn't see the look of wonder that came over Katya's face.

Good thinking. Her chest swelled until it almost hurt. Of course, he didn't mean it. It was just...just something to say.

But she hugged the memory of his words just as she hugged Sam as she followed him.

Deborah had laid out plates and coffee mugs. She bustled around the table, bringing the rolls, pouring coffee. Katya slid into a chair, bouncing Sam on her lap. He immediately stuck his chubby fingers into a roll. Jake reached over and tore it apart for him seemingly without thinking, then took a bite himself.

"This is great," he said, swallowing, biting again.

Deborah gave her first strained smile. "Thank you. It's my grandma's recipe."

"Don't lose it."

"No! Oh, no. It's in my head. I could never lose it. I even taught Carola and Birgitte, so it will be passed on." Her smile faded.

"Her daughters," Katya supplied softly. "Lizzie's big sisters."

Deborah nodded vaguely. Jake washed down the roll with some coffee, and that was great, too—strong and black, just the way he liked it. "Can you tell me what happened that day, Mrs. Stoltzfus? Everything you remember, even if it doesn't seem important."

She sat in the chair at the end of the table. Her eyes glistened. "It was my fault," she said, so quietly they almost didn't hear her.

"No," Jake said sharply. "It was the fault of whoever has taken her."

"But—"

"No buts about it, Mrs. Stoltzfus. You've got to get that guilt out of your mind right now if you're going to help me. Come on. Get hold of yourself. *Think.* Castigating yourself isn't going to bring your daughter back."

Katya stared at him. He was being awful! His voice had taken on a bite, and—and then she saw Deborah straightened in her chair. The woman's eyes took on a glaze of purpose. Oh my, she thought. Jacob had done that deliberately.

Katya held Sam a little more tightly. At last Deborah nodded.

"Start at the very beginning," Jake said.

"Yes," Deborah agreed. "But…there's not much to tell. I was hanging laundry, putting clothes on the line. I didn't want to leave her inside by herself so she was right there playing with her dolly while I finished." Her voice cracked.

"Where?" Jake demanded.

Deborah began to rise to her feet.

"No," he said quickly. "Show me later. For now, just give me an idea of how many feet she was away from you."

Deborah scowled. "Ten? Fifteen?"

Close enough that she should have seen something, heard something, Jake thought. Why hadn't she? "Go on."

"Well, I reached down for one of my husband's shirts. Into the basket, you know. I clipped it up and looked around the clothes again, and she was gone."

Around the clothes. Jake bit back a curse. "Sheets?" he asked. "Big stuff? Were you putting up large items?"

"Yes, of course."

The kidnapper must have loved that, he thought. Whoever it was had still taken a hell of a chance, but Deborah had helped him—or her—out. "This clothesline was between you and your daughter," he said, and it wasn't a question.

Deborah nodded. She had begun to cry with remorse and anguish and a guilt so terrible Katya couldn't even imagine it. She reached instinctively for the other woman's hand.

"Can you show us where it happened now, Deborah? Exactly where you last saw her?" she asked softly.

Jake glanced at her and shot a brow up. "Getting into this, are you?" he asked wryly.

Katya blushed. "I just…I want to help."

He hesitated, then nodded. "She's right, Mrs. Stoltzfus. Can you show us where the clothesline is now?"

Deborah nodded. "But my husband and the others went all over the place. They looked and looked and found nothing. And it's snowed eighteen inches since then."

"Actually, that's good," Jake told her. And bad, he thought, but there was no need to get into the downside at this point.

"It is?"

"It is?" Katya echoed, surprised.

"Yeah. The snow might have sealed in evidence. There's less chance that the wind, animals, kids, whatever, could have disturbed it." He wasn't wild about the idea of all those men having trooped around through there, though. He stood. "We need to borrow a couple of rakes, too, if you have them."

We. Katya stared at him, amazed and delighted. *We need rakes.*

"Will pitchforks do?" Deborah asked. "We've got those."

"That'll be fine," Jake answered.

The woman went to the back door and called out. A few moments later, an older boy came in with the pitchforks. He nodded at them solemnly and then went right back out.

They all bundled up again and went out through the front. They made their way to the side of the house. Katya wielded one pitchfork, Sam in her other arm, straddled over her hip. Jake carried the other, though he'd offered to take both. She'd refused. He thought she marched along like a determined soldier.

The snow crunched under their feet. Jake kept his eyes down, watching for anything the cows and horses might have left behind. It had nothing at all to do with the fact that the sight of her urgency touched him.

"Here," Deborah said after a moment. Her voice grew thick with tears again. "Right here."

Jake looked around.

The clothesline was between two trees, roughly twenty yards from the house. There was a tree line maybe thirty yards on the other side of it. He wasn't sure why—maybe it was just instinct—but it all led him to believe that Lizzie had been handpicked ahead of time. She hadn't been left alone in a crowd. She had ostensibly been protected and under her mother's eye. He thought her kidnapper must have been watching her, watching this house, this family, waiting for an opportunity to take her.

It chilled him.

Beyond the clothesline were barns and various outbuildings. And beyond those were fields, fallow and hidden deep in snow. Most likely they would have been snow-covered then, too, he thought. If he had his bearings right, and Jake was pretty sure he did, then those fields eventually came up against one of the few paved settlement roads. Other than the woods and the outbuildings, there was really nowhere to hide and wait.

"Where was your husband when this happened?" he asked suddenly.

"He and Jamie—my four-year-old—were working the farm."

The kidnapper probably hadn't hidden in the outbuildings, then, Jake decided. Too risky. Simon could have entered any one of them at any time.

"Did the FBI agents go into the woods?" he asked.

Deborah frowned. "I don't...they must have, wouldn't you say? I don't rightly remember."

They might not have, Jake thought, thinking of his continuing education courses with the federal government. It was entirely possible that they had measured off a precise circumference to search. If they *had* gone in there, they wouldn't have gone far.

"Did you notice any footprints in the snow?" he asked.

"No," Deborah said wretchedly. "There wasn't much on this side. The sun hits this side, and it melts quicker. And anyway, Lizzie had trampled all through it."

Okay, Jake thought, scrap that. "And you never heard *anything?* No voices? She didn't cry out?"

"Oh, I couldn't bear it if she did!" Deborah cried irrationally.

She was sobbing again, beyond speaking. Katya took her hand in her free one, resting the pitchfork against her other hip. They had all hashed this over a thousand times, she thought. She knew the answers as well as Deborah did.

"Deborah peeked over the line, but Lizzie just wasn't there," she explained. "There was no car or buggy on the road."

The woods, Jake reasoned. Had to be the woods, then. "Good. That's exactly the sort of thing I need to know."

Katya's heart swelled again. She thought frantically for other information she might give him. His approval was sweet. She wanted to clutch it close, to hold it. She wanted more. She blushed at her own silliness.

"Okay, Sherlock, let's go. You can go back inside, Deborah. We can take it from here. I'll stop in again before we go."

"Yes." The woman backed off more quickly than Jake might have expected, almost stumbling in her haste. "I hate coming out here," she explained. "I haven't even hung clothes since...since..." Her voice cracked again.

"Go," Katya urged. "We'll talk to you later."

"No, wait," Jake said suddenly. "Why don't you take Sam? Free up Katya's hands so she can help me."

Deborah stared at him. Katya felt her heart thump. Her first reaction was protest. *No, not now. Babies are being stolen. I need to keep him right by me.* Then she understood, and her heart thumped harder.

Deborah blamed herself. There was precious little she could do for her, but she could trust her, and maybe in trusting her, she would help to ease some of that terrible guilt.

Jacob had thought of that. Her heart moved with something softer as she looked at him, then back at Deborah. "Yes," she said softly. "That's a wonderful idea. Sam, would you like to play here for a little while?"

"Pay," he said. "Pay, pay."

Deborah took him with a tremulous smile and turned toward the house. Jake watched her go, Sam's big brown eyes peering over her shoulder.

Keep him safe, Deborah. Though he tried never to get too involved, never to let himself care too deeply about the kids, the parents, any victim, Jake felt a piece of his heart crack a little.

He shook his head. It was plainly stupid to allow that. Still, he realized that he wanted to find little Lizzie Stoltzfus as badly as he had ever wanted anything before in his life. He was getting a real bad feeling about this. Something stank here. Something maybe more evil and wrong than even he could bear to think about.

Chapter 9

Jake started toward the trees, his mind working, then he realized that Katya wasn't with him. He looked back at her.

"Who's Sherlock?" she asked. "Why did you call me that?"

Jake stared at her. "Holmes?" he prompted after a moment.

"I don't know him."

"Are you kidding me?"

He saw her stiffen. Her eyes slid away. "No," she said in a small voice, then she marched into the trees with her pitchfork.

"He's a fictional character," Jake called after her, unaccountably disturbed. "A detective in a book."

She didn't look back. He went after her and just barely heard her response.

"We never read make-believe books in school. There were just lessons." Then she brightened, smiling slowly, her eyes coming back to him. "You were calling me a *detective?*"

"I was kidding." He was bemused. His head felt foggy.

"Oh." The light went out of her eyes again.

"I was—never mind." How was he supposed to deal with

a woman who wore her heart and everything in it on her sleeve this way? A woman who didn't even know who Sherlock Holmes was?

"This Sherlock man," she went on after a moment, "is he very entertaining?" She thought how wonderful it would be to sit down after the children were in bed and read a book. She had so few chores now. Adam and Mariah did not have a farm. There just wasn't as much work for her to do as there once had been when she was living with Frank, even though she looked for things to keep her busy.

As for Frank, he would have hit her for sitting down and indulging herself in a book about a fictional detective. But oh, it sounded delicious.

"Well, it's a good read in an old-fashioned sort of way," Jake explained, and thought that might suit her. "It was written a long time ago. I tend to go for more modern stuff myself. True-crime things."

She nodded thoughtfully. "What must I do to be like him?"

He almost laughed. "You mean to help out here now?"

"Yes, please."

He gave into it. A bark of laughter escaped him. He couldn't help it. He rubbed his forehead, feeling that bemused sensation coming on again.

"Well, I'll show you," he said finally. "It's not an optimum technique, but given the weather and what we've got to work with, it'll have to do." He started walking again.

She followed him eagerly. He felt rather than saw her shiver.

"Cold?" he asked, frowning, wondering if she would hold up through this chore.

She shook her head. He saw a strand of white blond hair come loose and curl under her chin. "I'm excited."

He made a sound in his throat. "Don't be. Odds are that we're going to spend all day out here freezing our butts off and not find a damned thing."

"But it must be done, right?" she asked hopefully. Her heart was beginning to pound with anticipation. This was more

than she had counted on. She'd thought all she'd be able to
do was drive the buggy.

He watched her face change. She was too innocent, he
thought again. Too sweet. Too willing. "Yeah," he agreed
finally.

"I just...rake?"

"Uh, no."

She was already standing close enough to him that he didn't
have to close any distance between them. He put his hands on
her shoulders. Carefully. He turned her around until her back
was against his chest. He felt her shiver again. Then he realized his hands were lingering and he snatched them back.

And he could still feel her shiver.

"Now what?" she asked.

"Uh, like this." He put his arms around her. Carefully
again. He closed his hands over hers on the pitchfork and
dragged it toward them through the snow.

"Just keep doing that?"

"What?"

"Just keep moving the fork like that?"

He shook his head as though to clear it. "No. Stop between
each swipe. Look and see if you've turned up anything. Then
move the tines, say...half an inch to the right. Do the same
thing there, in neat lines, until you've covered all the ground
in whatever given area you've set for yourself." He paused.
"See anything?"

"Where?"

"In the lines the tines made."

She leaned forward to peer down. Her bottom nestled comfortably and warmly into his groin. Jake stepped back fast.

She looked over her shoulder at him. "What?"

"What?"

"Is something wrong, Jacob?"

*Innocent. Sweet. Somebody's mother. Somebody's wife.
Worse, a lot of somebodies' mother.*

There were so many reasons for not getting turned on by
this woman. Big mistake. Wrong avenue. Too many compli-
cations. Tentacles. Ensnarements. Problems. She wasn't for

him. No way. Not at all. Black tights, a longish dress and sensible shoes, he thought desperately.

He tried hard, damned hard, to remember those little red bandannas on the waitresses' hips at Clyde and Bob's just a few short days ago. And he kept seeing the way her hair was spilling out from that knot at her nape. One long, thick strand had come free.

His hand came up again and he found himself touching it. It was gossamer. It was silk. It was cool and thick to the touch, and it slid through his fingers like water.

"What are you doing?" she whispered, her eyes growing.

Damned if I know. He jerked his hand back and turned away from her. "Just…rake. Look into the furrows and see if there's anything in there that shouldn't be," he repeated hoarsely. "Anything that doesn't belong in a forest. Gum wrappers. Cigarette butts. That sort of thing. If there's nothing, do it all over again and dig the tines deeper, until you get to the ground. Got it?"

"Yes."

"We don't have to go too far into the trees. He almost had to have waited right near here, so he could see Lizzie, so he would know when to strike."

"Yes," she said again.

"I'll work this side," he finished.

He began wielding the other pitchfork with a vengeance. He looked back once to see her brow furrowed in concentration. She was doing fine. He looked at his watch. Barely nine-thirty. It was going to be a very long day, he realized.

They worked for a good hour before she called out to him. He propped his fork against a tree and went to look down at the place she pointed to. There was a candy-bar wrapper at the bottom of her most recent furrow. She'd had the good sense not to pick it up herself. He took a plastic bag out of the pocket of Adam's coat that he'd had the foresight to bring from Mariah's kitchen. He nudged the scrap of paper inside.

"What does it mean?" she asked, wide-eyed.

"Either that our kidnapper likes Snickers candy bars, or that one of the kids has a sweet tooth."

"Oh, no." She shook her head. "Not for this sort of thing. Deborah would *never* buy sweets when she could just as easily make them at home."

Which meant, Jake thought, that the Amishmen who had trooped through here probably hadn't been munching on chocolate, either. "So what are the odds that Lizzie—or any of the kids—sneaked some for themselves?" he asked.

"How? Where would they get it?"

And why would any of them come into the woods to munch on it? he asked himself. To hide such a travesty from their mothers? "That's what I'm asking," he said. "A store in the village?"

Katya shook her head. "Jacob, for heaven's sake, Lizzie was—is—barely *two*."

"Maybe one of the older kids bought it for her."

"No, they wouldn't go into Divinity alone. And what would they buy it with?"

"Allowance money?" Or they shoplifted it, Jake thought, trying to convince himself that kids were the same everywhere. Not really believing it, not from what he'd seen of Katya's children and Bo.

"What's that?" she asked, frowning.

"What's what?"

"Allowance money."

He stared at her, dumbfounded. "It's sort of a little salary kids get at the end of the week for doing their chores."

"Your children get *paid* for it?"

"Mine don't," he snapped, unaccountably irritated. "I've always been real careful not to acquire any for myself. I told you that."

She blushed. "I meant *anner Satt Leit* children in general."

Of course she did. He rubbed a frown off his forehead. What was she doing to him? "Then, yeah. They get paid. In most instances. In good homes anyway." Not that he had had a lot of experience with one of those, but as a kid he'd had a few lucky friends who'd enjoyed perks like spending money.

Let *them* populate the earth, he thought.

Katya shook her head as if deep in thought. She tucked the

strand of hair behind her ear again. He caught the reflex. He felt a vague itch in his fingers, as though they wanted to do it for her. Jake shoved his gloved hands deep into his pockets.

"That's amazing," she murmured finally. "And strange."

"Why strange?"

"That a child would need such incentive to make his family's farm thrive."

"Well, for God's sake, most other kids don't live on farms!" He didn't know why he was so angry about this. "I don't know," he went on more levelly. "Maybe those who live on farms *do* work just to make their land prosper. But the majority of *anner Satt Leit* kids live in towns and cities."

"Yes, of course," she said softly.

He went back to his pitchfork. "Get to work. We've got a lot to do here in a short period of time," he said stiffly. Then he added, "That was real good, finding the wrapper."

He tried belatedly to remember how far down in the drift it had been without going back over to the spot, without standing close beside her again to look. Six inches, maybe. Could have been there since the abduction. Lizzie had been the last child taken, right after New Year's. Deborah had said eighteen inches of new snow had fallen since then, but that much wouldn't have accumulated here in the woods. It would have been filtered somewhat by the limbs above, naked though they were at this time of year.

So the kidnapper might well like Snickers, he thought. Which told him not a damned thing, although he would send the wrapper to Dallas anyway and have it checked for possible prints. Still, paper was one of the worst surfaces for holding fingerprints. Slick, shiny paper was even worse. And in this weather, whoever had tossed it had almost certainly been wearing gloves.

They worked for another two hours without finding anything other than the usual detritus of reasonably thick woods. He finally leaned the fork against a tree and pushed his shoulders back, stretching the kinks out of his spine. There were distinct knots of discomfort between his shoulder blades and at the small of his back. He turned and looked at Katya.

She raked on eagerly. If she was stiff, it didn't show. Well, hell, he thought, disgruntled. He was a lot taller than she was. He'd had to bend over to do the job right. She didn't. Still, it was time for a break, for a little comic relief here.

Without thinking, he scooped up a handful of snow. He compacted it just enough, bouncing it from one palm to another to give her ample time to look back and see what he was up to. She didn't.

"Well, honey, you've got this coming, then," he murmured under his breath, grinning. He let the snowball fly.

It struck her squarely between the shoulders. She jerked so violently the pitchfork flew from her hands. Then she whirled, her hands up, ready to ward off another blow. Too late, he realized how cruel he'd been.

"I'm sorry, baby. Oh, God." He moved for her quickly, but she was still shaken and she backed up instinctively. He stopped in his tracks, holding his hands up. "Hey, hey," he said quietly, "I was just playing around. It was only a snowball."

She stared at him. "A snowball?"

"Yeah. Guess you guys don't have fights with them, either."

She blinked. "Of course we do. Or, the children do." She looked around vacantly as though expecting to see some. "The adults don't have time."

"Well, then."

"I just—you startled me."

"Sorry," he said again, feeling small, feeling like hell. She wasn't going to let him get much closer, and it was just as well. He turned his back on her abruptly and went back to his pitchfork. He'd apologized. What else could he do?

Comic relief. What the hell had he been thinking? Not a good way to keep his distance from her, he realized belatedly. He'd just been growing a little stiff and bored with the sameness of the job. She was easy to relax with. He'd lost his head for a minute—

Thwap!

As far as snowballs went, it wasn't a good one. Too loose.

Not packed enough. Still, it got the job done. It hit the back of his head and rained nice, cold snow down inside his collar.

Jake turned slowly. "You know that means war."

She was standing with both mittened hands clapped to her mouth as though she couldn't believe what she had done. But her eyes were alive. Something moved inside him. Oh, yeah, he thought. This was war.

She saw him reach to scoop up another handful of snow. Katya backed up fast. Oh, it was going to be cold. She started to twist, to take it on her back again where it would be the most tolerable, but she only got halfway around before the missile came sailing. It caught her in the neck and she shrieked and dived for snow of her own before he could get more. She never had time to make a ball of it. He was advancing toward her. She simply flung the handful and ran.

He had such long legs. He would catch her. But that didn't matter. No, she realized, it didn't matter at all. When was the last time she had actually *run?* She felt her shawl coming loose and managed to snag one end of it, but the rest of it trailed behind her. And the wind was icy and biting, even in the trees, but it felt so *good*, she thought, tingling all over her exposed skin. She tipped her face up to take it on her cheeks and laughed in sheer joy.

Jake heard her and stopped cold.

He had never heard her laugh before. He wondered if anyone had, or if she had been caught up in her own private hell for so long that the reflex had died in her heart. The sound drifted back to him, sweet, high, special. It hit him like a blow to the chest. He'd made her laugh. Worth the delay in their work, he decided. Definitely worth it.

He wondered if she'd laugh with a good handful of snow shoved right inside the neckline of her plain wool jacket. The snowball she'd landed above his collar still chilled his skin with its cold wetness. He started jogging again, knowing if he went after her at an all-out run he'd only frighten her. And he'd catch up with her too soon. He wanted to prolong this a little. He saw her look back over her shoulder for him, her cheeks cherry red now. Laughing, she was still laughing. Then she ducked behind a tree.

What was she doing? Jake laughed too, when he saw. She was hiding back there, out of his aim, building a whole damned arsenal. She was too busy to keep an eye on him. He crept around to her left, soundlessly, deeper into the woods. He came up behind her, snow in hand.

She finally heard the crunch of his footsteps and her head snapped up, her heart hurtling instinctively. She pushed the fear away because she hated it. For once, just this one time, she wouldn't be a slave to it. She grabbed as many finished snowballs as she could and shot to her feet again.

Too late. One of his came flying.

She shrieked again and ducked. It missed her. She tried to back up as he lunged for her, another handful of snow at the ready, but she only collided with the tree she'd been trying to hide behind. He lifted her right off her feet and dropped her in the snow—like a calf about to be tied, she thought indignantly. But he was laughing and she wasn't afraid.

She rolled—or tried to. Oh, that stupid tree! She came up against it again face first and felt him pull the collar of her jacket wide in the back. She knew what was coming and she gasped, half-laughing, before she felt it. Crunchy, hard snow spilled down against her skin.

She squealed and tried to get away from him, but he straddled her quickly, trapping the snow in her dress with his hand, then forcing her onto her back to hold it in there. Gasping, she tried to roll again anyway, so he dropped his full weight upon her to hold her.

"Oh, no, you don't. Hold up the white flag. Honey, you've been bested by a master."

She managed to work one arm to the side, her fingers still searching for the snowballs she had dropped. He caught her hand as quickly as he had once before, when she had crept into his room. So fast she didn't know what had happened. One moment her fingers were fumbling, spidering across the snow. Then her arm was over her head, and somehow so was her other one, and he was pinning them there, both her wrists in one strong hand.

But this time, instead of keeping her immobile with his thigh, his whole body pressed her into the snow. Something ticklish moved deep inside her. She couldn't get her breath.

"Give up your ammo," he growled.

"Y-yes."

And that was when it stopped being funny.

He stared down at her. He realized what he had done. What he was *doing*. He'd moved without meaning to, didn't even realize he'd done it until he had. He'd used his knee to push her leg out, to give himself room to settle between her legs, more fully against her.

He tried to swear and couldn't find his voice. The scent of her, springtime fresh, hit him again, filled his nostrils, seeming incongruous as they lay there in snow. And it was good. It was right, warm, intimate, and he felt himself respond more or less as he had yesterday when she had combed his hair off his forehead, but the wanting this time was suddenly a lot more than before. He tried to remember all the reasons he'd had for not getting involved with her, and at the moment he couldn't even recall the first one.

He looked down into her face. His mouth was maybe three inches from hers, and that was only because he was still angling his upper body away from her to be able to hold her wrists. Slowly, carefully, he moved his gaze from her mouth to her eyes, needing to know what he would find there.

Her eyes were huge. Not wary. Amazed, not scared. She was breathing a little too hard, but it wasn't from the exertion.

"What have we gotten ourselves into here, Little Katie Yoder?" he murmured.

Jake knew he was playing with fire. He did it anyway. He had to. He lowered his mouth to hers and tasted her.

Katya's blood was tripping through her veins now, scurrying fast and without reason. She felt sure she was trembling, but she didn't seem to be; all the tremors were inside. Her heart was moving fast and erratically, suspended somewhere between her chest and her throat. His weight was delicious and special, and her nipples tightened and something wonderful happened low inside her. It was as though her muscles were gathering, tightening, readying.

He told himself he'd make it quick. Keep it playful, although most of the giddiness had gone out of this whole business moments ago. He could get it back if he wanted to. He'd keep it light.

He slanted his head, going from a brush of his lips over hers to something fuller, deeper, better. She tasted the way she smelled. Clean, new, like spring on the verge of bursting into the full ripeness of summer.

He wasn't sure when he let go of her wrists, when he settled his upper body upon her, too. He wasn't sure how his hands got into her hair, holding her face, one on either side, keeping her still, suddenly afraid, very much afraid, that she was going to stop him. One moment he was in control, then he wasn't. One moment he knew exactly what he was doing, as he always did; one moment it was a game, as it always was. Then he was sweeping his tongue through her mouth, hungry, wanting. Needing her. He never needed. He never allowed himself to need. But he couldn't have dragged himself away from her now if his life had depended on it.

When she first felt his tongue, Katya was startled, repulsed. Everything inside her cringed back, away from rude, ugly memories of Frank. Ah, but it hadn't been this way with Frank. Jacob didn't pummel her. He didn't grunt and paw. He was so gentle, his touches featherlight as he finally moved his hands a little, trailing a finger down her neck. His tongue swept; it didn't just probe and invade.

When he freed her hands, Katya knew one moment of awkwardness, wondering what exactly she should do with them now. It lasted only as long as it took her heart to boom one more time against her chest. Then she drove her fingers into his hair.

He was so incredible, so strong and smart and...yes, he was a little wild. Dangerous. Certainly no other man of her acquaintance would have dared to kiss her without even asking first—and certainly not now, not when she belonged to Frank.

And he was so handsome. She couldn't believe, could scarcely accept, that he was kissing *her*.

Everything erupted inside her. A certain desperation came to her that he might never do this again—he probably *wouldn't* do it again, that just seemed too incredible—so she wanted to feel, to taste everything she could right now. His hair was just as soft and damp as it had been when she had hit him with the rolling pin. It slid through her fingers and that made her shiver, and when she shivered, she felt something changed within him, as well.

She moved her hands, too, wanting to find out if his shoulders were indeed as hard as they had looked that day when she had crept in on him sleeping. She wished she could get her hands underneath his coat, his shirt, so she could feel how smooth his skin really was. She made a humming sound in her throat, a sound of pure pleasure.

She didn't hear the cracking sound at first, but she felt the ground give beneath her a little. She felt it because, for a brief moment, she thought she was actually floating. The second crack was louder, longer, turning into a shredding sound.

She lost his mouth as he pulled away. She made a sound of distress even as Jake swore.

"What the hell—" he began.

And then it happened. The ground literally gave way beneath them.

She screamed as they fell, but his arms came around her, and somehow he rolled with her, using his own body to absorb most of their fall. But more uncomfortable than the impact of landing was what they landed *on*. Jagged branches and twigs, dried and brittle and dead. And wet and cold with the snow.

"What the hell?" Jake demanded again.

Katya tried to push away from him, tried to sit up, but there was little room. They'd crashed through the top of a deadfall.

"They're all through the woods," she gasped. "There was a tornado many years ago—it ripped right through here and crashed everything over. A lot has grown back, but the dead stuff is still here, and—"

He took her face in his hands. "What are you talking about?" he asked with great patience. He was still shaken.

"Deadfalls," she whispered, losing her voice a little because he was touching her again. "All the...deadfalls. That's what happened. I believe we were on top of one. It gave out."

His body was still alive and he still wanted her, but painful reality was settling in. His conscience wasn't howling yet, but he knew that, given enough time, it would start screaming at him. He couldn't deal with that. More immediate was the problem of how he was going to get them out of here.

It struck him now—belatedly—that he'd had to go *up* an incline to get to the spot where she'd been crouched behind the tree. A small incline. An incline only in that specific location. Not a hill. It was only a few yards wide.

A deadfall. Hidden beneath smooth, pretty, deceptive snow.

He looked up. The hole they had fallen through was all ragged edges. It wouldn't be sturdy. He probably couldn't pull himself out, but she could. She certainly could, being as small as she was.

"Okay, here's what we're going to do." He got to his knees, gingerly, not sure how much farther down they could fall if the bottom gave out again. "Kneel here in front of me."

She knelt. He caught her waist then slowly, carefully, he stood with her, lifting her toward the hole above their heads. Katya was amazed by the strength that would require.

He found himself nose first to an area just beneath her waist. *Don't think about it.* He wanted her still. That shook him. Shook him badly. Despite their circumstances, the need was still there, and he was a man who could turn off like a light switch when he chose to. Not now. Now the need stuttered at first, then it grew, pounding for his attention.

"Jacob!" she squealed.

"What?" he asked hoarsely.

"You're hurting me."

Carefully, deliberately, he loosened his fingers where they bit into her waist. "Can you reach anything up there to hold on to, to pull yourself out with?" he asked. "Is there anything sturdy up there?"

"Yes." One of the tree roots was exposed. The tree had been partially uprooted by the twister. She reached for it. "But what about you?"

"Just go."

"But—"

"*Go*, Katya. Just pull yourself out and I can take care of myself."

He felt the burden of her lessen in his grip. Whatever it was she had found was taking most of her weight now. She finally got one knee on the brittle edge and scrambled out the rest of the way.

The hole wasn't all that deep. If it had been made of anything but the dead limbs of trees, getting out would have been a cinch. But he doubted if any of the debris around him could bear his weight. He was contemplating the problem, sifting through his memory, wondering if he had ever read of anyone in a similar situation, when she screamed.

Fire shot through his blood, galvanizing him. Someone out there was going to hurt her. Her husband? The kidnapper? A million possibilities raced through his mind.

He looked up. She was staring down into the hole, at a point past his shoulder, her eyes wide and stricken, a hand clapped to her mouth.

"What?' he demanded. "You scared the hell out of me, woman. What the—"

"We…we…we…" she interrupted. Or tried to. She didn't quite seem to be able to get the words out.

"*What?*" he asked again, frustrated. He finally inched his way around to see for himself what she was staring at. Then, in disbelief, he mentally finished her sentence for her.

We had company. We weren't alone.

A hand stuck up out of the broken branches he was standing on. It was inclined at a strange, unnatural angle. A single hand. A woman's hand. He knew it was a woman because it wore a ring, something delicate and feminine that glittered even in the scant sunlight that made it through the forest canopy and down into the hole. Otherwise he wouldn't have known. There was no way to tell. The hand was skeletal, only bone.

He heard a strangled, mewling sound from above him. He looked up again just in time to catch Katya as she fell, in a dead faint, right back into the hole.

Chapter 10

Katya swam back to consciousness to find herself on Mariah's sofa. She was peripherally aware that many, many people were present. A tragedy always brought friends with helping hands extended. The hum of various conversations was buzzing around her. But the only person she cared about was the man leaning over her, his dark brows knit together in concern.

"Damn!" she burst out. It felt so good, so gratifying to say it. She didn't care who heard her. Tears burned at her eyes. She refused to let them fall.

Jake reared back from her in shock. "Huh?" He straightened and looked worriedly for Adam. "She's not right, bro."

Adam hurried over to look down at her, too. Katya sat up shakily. She realized that most of the people present were women. Mariah and the older children were still at the school. Only a few men had been able to get away from their farms.

Thank goodness. She couldn't bear for any more people than necessary to see her like this.

She looked down again, ashamed. "I've never been very good in times of trouble," she said quietly, speaking to her clasped hands.

So that was what was bothering her, Jake realized. "That's not true," he said quietly. "You brought the whole county out to find me when Goliath dumped me on my backside."

She didn't answer. He stared at her, at the top of her head, her bonnet long gone now. Her blond hair shimmered in the lamplight. More snow was falling outside. The day had darkened as though in silent mourning for the woman they had found.

"Hey," he said finally, sitting beside her. He put his arms around her and drew her toward him.

Letting himself touch her was easier now, after what had happened in the woods. That was both good and very bad. But at the moment, she needed comforting. Hell, for that matter, so did he.

"Do you know," he began quietly, "how very many times I've encountered someone dead or dying?" So many times, he thought. Life was ugly and people were unconscionably cruel to each other. "So many times," he said aloud. "And I'll let you in on a secret. What just happened to us was one of the worst."

She pulled back to look at him. "You're lying, Jacob," she said softly. "You're lying to make me feel better."

"No." And it was true. "No, there was something...spooky about that one. Something weird." He thought about it, trying to put his finger on the difference, for his own sake as much as hers. "When I'm working and I get a call that there's trouble, I know what I'm going to find. When I'm looking for a kid—with ChildSearch—I'm always aware that I might not like what I'm going to find when I get to the place where the clues lead. But that—what we came across today—hit us out of the blue. It thrust its way into a really nice moment."

Nice. Something shimmered inside her, almost glowing. He thought kissing her was nice? She'd already convinced herself that he regretted it. He'd been so irritable afterward, even before they'd found the body.

"Neither one of us had any reason to expect what we found," he went on. "If I hadn't had to catch you when you fell back into the hole, I probably would have fainted myself."

"Now I know you're lying," she said tremulously, but he did make her want to smile. "You'd never faint. You're too…brave."

"I did once," he said awkwardly.

Katya shook her head. "I don't believe it."

He decided to let it go. Actually, he'd been sixteen and he'd been knocked unconscious by his father's fist when he'd tried to save his little sister from bouncing off her bedroom wall one more time.

"Oh," Katya breathed, suddenly grabbing his hand.

"What?"

"What's happened to you? You're hurt."

He looked down at his scratched and gouged palms. This trip was really killing him. "The deadfall happened," he answered wryly. "With you unconscious, I pretty much had to take it apart limb by limb to get us out of there."

She flinched.

"Damn it." He caught her chin, made her look at him. "Don't make me keep saying it, Katie. Your response was normal."

She didn't looked convinced. He leaned close to her, so that their mouths were only a breath apart.

"Then try this," he murmured. "I never kiss tough old Amazons who can take a skeleton without reacting."

That got to her. Her mouth opened on a silent "Oh." God, he thought, her responses were delightful.

Then she paled yet again.

"Was it…was that…oh, Jacob, please tell me that we didn't find Lizzie," she whispered.

He jolted. "No. God, no, it wasn't Lizzie. You can put that idea out of your mind. It was a woman." And he was pretty sure he knew what woman it was.

The sheriff had already come and gone, as well as the county coroner—a fumbling, overweight man who had set Jake's teeth on edge. No matter what he'd been told, no matter what he'd learned here, Jake had been startled when the crowd of Amish that had gathered to see what the excitement was about had simply…well, disappeared at that point.

As soon as they'd found the skeleton, as soon as he'd worked them both out of the hole, he'd collected Deborah and Sam and brought Katya back here in the buggy. He'd taken Adam to the deadfall to show him what they'd found. Deborah had ostensibly been staying with Katya, but somehow the woman had managed to spread the word. Five minutes after Jake and Adam had returned to the deadfall in the woods, a good fifty people had joined them there.

It had been a nightmare, trying to keep them away from what remained of the hole, trying to keep from destroying evidence. Until the *anner Satt Leit* authorities had arrived. Until the outsiders' ''law'' had trooped into the woods. Then the Amish people had quietly vanished back to their homes. And here, to Adam's house.

The coroner had taken the skeleton away with him. Jake had been moderately gratified to hear that the man would call in a special forensics team from the University of Pennsylvania as there was very little left of this woman for him to autopsy.

Adam had already gone out to one of the pay phones and placed a call to Dallas. His ex-wife's dental records would be sent up by overnight delivery. They were almost a moot point. Adam had already identified the ring on the woman's hand. It was one he had given Jannel several years ago.

This really put a new spin on things. Jake's gut clenched. He continued to hold Katya, but now he did it absently. His brain was buzzing.

When Jannel had hidden Bo here in the settlement four years ago, she had dropped the little boy off at Sugar Joe and Sarah Lapp's door. She had told them that she'd heard the Amish were not likely to go to the police, to get involved with the *anner Satt Leit* authorities—and she certainly had that right. She had begged Joe to keep her child safe for a little while and told him she would be back for Bo shortly. She had told Joe neither Bo's name nor his birth date, indicating that they wouldn't need to know because he wouldn't be there that long. She really *had* intended to return.

But she had never come back. Adam—actually Child-

Search—had finally found Bo four long years later through a picture on a milk carton that Mariah had identified.

Jannel had been a con artist. She and her partner—one Devon Mills—had set Adam up. Adam had been a visible man in those days, very much in the public eye, playing baseball with the Houston Astros in a year when the Astros had made a respectable grab for the pennant. The deal had been that she would marry Adam, relieve him of a few million of his dollars, then she and Devon would take off and live on easy street.

Conceiving Bo had never been part of the plan, but in the end she had cared enough about her child to try to protect him. Jannel had burned her partner, disappearing with all the money rather than give Mills his share, but she had had the foresight to guess that Mills might go after Bo for revenge. Mills had been briefly in custody last month while Jake and his friends had grilled him to learn what had happened with Jannel. But they hadn't charged him with anything. Bo had been present and accounted for by then. As for Jannel, she was an adult, and Mills's story about her double-crossing him had seemed logical.

They all presumed she had disappeared of her own volition, that she was sunning on a beach in Tahiti by now. That skeleton proved otherwise. Neither a coroner nor a special forensics team needed to tell Jake that the back of the woman's skull had been shattered. That much he'd seen with his own eyes when they'd started pulling the dead wood away from her.

"I've got to find Mills again," Jake muttered to himself. Was there a connection between that whole mess and the missing kids? Things like kidnapping and murder did not often happen in this peaceful settlement—in fact, to his knowledge, they had *never* happened before. That both should occur in a relatively short period of time seemed indicative of some sort of tie-in to Jake's way of thinking.

Katya was looking at him. He realized she'd heard him speak.

"Who is Mills?" she asked.

He shook his head and let go of her, needing to stand again.

She caught his hand and stopped him. "You're angry at me."

He looked down at her and scowled. "No, I'm not."

"I wanted so badly to be…valuable to you," she said in a whisper. "I wanted to do something. I wanted it desperately. Instead I messed everything up."

Something shifted inside him. What was he supposed to do with this woman? He didn't want to take on responsibility for her feelings.

"You didn't mess anything up," he heard himself say. "What did you mess up?"

"Well, I did fall on the evidence."

"Honey, *we* fell on the evidence. We messed up anything that was there long before you took a dive back in."

She looked at him hopefully. "Really?"

Don't look at me that way. "Really." He pulled her to her feet. "Let's go."

She came too willingly, too trustingly, too eagerly. "Where?"

"Lancaster."

"The *city?*" she asked breathlessly.

"Yeah." He stopped short. "Are you allowed to, or is that verboten?"

"Of course I'm allowed. It's just…" She had never been back there, she thought, never once in all these years, not since she had seen that Santa Claus. Suddenly her heart was thrumming as wildly as it had that day. "My children…"

"I'll keep Sam," came a voice out of nowhere. Katya looked to see Deborah Stoltzfus coming out of the crowd. "Please," the woman went on. "It was nice this morning…distracting…to have a little one around."

As before, she found it hard to deny the woman the pleasure, the vote of confidence. And oh, she wanted so badly to go with Jacob.

"I could keep him until Mariah brings your other children home from school," Deborah said earnestly. "Then I'll have one of my older boys bring him home. Simon could do it. Please."

"Of course," Katya whispered, her heart hurtling now. She was going to go.

"Have Simon do it," Jake said. "With everything going on...that would be safer."

"Of course." Deborah nodded hard.

He went outside. Katya rushed after him.

"I've got some clothes waiting for me at the post office," he explained. "At least, I hope I do. And something tells me I ought to go pick them up today." Something told him that this whole missing-kid thing was going to blow up in his face at any time, and he wouldn't get another opportunity to go into Lancaster.

A skeleton, for God's sake. They'd fallen down smack-dab on top of what remained of Jannel's body. It had been very hidden. It should never have been found. It was a miracle—a convoluted set of never-again circumstances—that had allowed them to stumble upon it.

He didn't particularly want to think about those circumstances. They made his stomach fill with nerves. Why the hell couldn't she have been stiff, awkward, prudish, as he'd half expected? He could still hear the way she had hummed deep in her throat with pleasure when he had kissed her.

Why the hell was he taking her with him? Because he wanted to, he realized. Plain and simple. Because he wanted her company. Because maybe she would smile again. Maybe she would even laugh.

"Adam!" he barked. His brother had gone outside. He was standing at the front fence, talking to some of the local cops. Jake had already spoken to them about Jannel. He suspected Adam was just shooting the breeze. At least he hoped so. Jannel's body had been deposited beneath that tree before the tornado three years ago that had created the deadfall, at a time when Adam probably had never even heard of this Amish settlement. But it still might occur to the authorities here to question him.

Jake was amazed at the sheer number of people who were still gathered outside, as well. The women had brought cakes and casseroles. Some of them hadn't even made it inside yet.

Jake hadn't a clue what they thought the food would accomplish. They'd brought huge thermoses of coffee and home-canned jars of vegetables, too. They waited for God only knew what, but they kept their distance from the fence and the cops.

Jake didn't understand it and he didn't like the ache it gave him inside, a sense of need for things he would never have, couldn't have, because of who and what he was.

Suddenly, an old memory flashed in his mind, of a pet store in Dallas, one he had visited regularly as a kid. He'd been seven, maybe eight years old. He'd passed by it every day after school. And there'd been a beagle in the window for a while—actually a whole litter of them—but one of the pups had been just about the ugliest dog he'd ever seen. And every day, that ugly pup had pressed his nose up to the glass to greet him. Every day, Jake had wanted him. But the sign in the window said he cost fifty-two dollars.

The litter had dwindled as people had bought the pups. One day there had been only two puppies left—the ugly one and a little female. On that day he'd watched a boy arrive with his father, and the father had bought him that little female puppy. Jake had watched them leave, get back into their car with the boy's prize...and he had ached just as he did now.

The next day the pet shop owner had offered him the ugly pup. For free. He was getting too old to be cute, the man said, and even as a kid of eight, Jake had realized that that was a pretty kind way of putting it. The truth was that that pup had never been cute to begin with. The owner said the odds of actually selling the dog were long and that he just wanted the little thing to have a good home.

Jake had had his hands outstretched to take him, his heart pumping with wonder, when the man's words had stopped him cold. *A good home.* He didn't have that. He couldn't give the pup a good home. His father would kick the daylights out of the beagle sooner or later, maybe even kill him if he got mad enough. Sooner or later, Edward would get drunk, and if no one else was around, Jake knew his father would take it out on the dog.

Jake had left without him. He'd never gone back to the pet

store. From that day on, he'd taken a detour to get home after school. He couldn't bear to look in the window anymore. It wasn't the first time he'd felt like he was on the outside looking in, into a world where fathers bought boys puppies, a world that would never be his own. It wasn't the last time it had happened. But it was one that stuck in his mind loud and clear.

"Jacob, what's wrong?" Katya asked, her voice filled with concern.

"Hey, come back," Adam said, waving a hand in front of his brother's eyes.

Jake shook his head to clear it. "Uh, yeah. Got any cash on you?" he asked. "I need to call a cab. I need to get into the city, get my clothes, make a few phone calls. I need to start putting a few things together here."

Adam pulled thirty-odd dollars out of his pocket and handed it to him, then he scowled at Katya. "You're going, too?"

She nodded eagerly.

Jake started for the street.

"Katya—" Adam began.

She never gave him a chance to finish. She ran after Jake, her feet flying.

Adam let out his breath on a ragged, worried sigh.

The cab came right to the pay phone to pick them up. It was a good thing because snow had begun falling steadily. They were covered with it. Jake looked so rugged with it crusted on his hair, with the wind chapping his cheeks. She watched him, mesmerized.

Their first stop in the city was a bank.

"Stay here," Jake said, opening the car door on his side. "I'll be right back."

She followed just as soon as she made sure that the driver wouldn't leave if she got out, as well. She scrambled from the automobile and raced up the stone walkway to the bank building. Or she started to race. Halfway there she had to turn around to look behind her, then she walked more slowly, backward, taking it all in.

Everything was so *alive!* No doubt the street would be even busier if the weather wasn't so bad, she thought, if the low, gunmetal gray sky hadn't kept spitting small, hard flakes. Still, humanity spilled from the buildings and the stores. Many of the women wore short skirts and thin nylons. She thought their legs must be freezing. A lot of the men wore suits with no topcoats. But she saw jeans and heavy jackets, and longer skirts, as well—knee-length and vibrant with color. There were a million kinds of hairstyles on both the men and the women. There were exhaust fumes—the air was unpleasantly thick with them—but she loved it. There was noise—horns and the hum of traffic and the rush of tires through the sloppy wetness of the street.

And there were so many different kinds of automobiles. Some were big, some shiny, some old with dull paint. An especially fascinating model passed her, a flash of bright blue, low-slung, with an engine that rumbled.

"Oh, my." She stared, taking small steps in reverse, until her back came up squarely against the glass of the bank's entrance. Jake's hand snaked out and caught her arm, then he dragged her inside.

"Get in here before you kill yourself," he said absently. He was staring down at a little piece of paper in his hand.

"What's that?" she asked, leaning close.

"It's some computerized wizard telling me a lie."

Her eyes went huge. "What?"

"They're trying to tell me I have ninety dollars less in my checking account than I thought I did."

"How do they know? Do you keep your money here?"

He shook his head, his mind still elsewhere. "No. My bank is in Dallas."

"Then these people are probably wrong," she insisted. "How would they know what someone is doing in Dallas?"

"It's an automated teller machine." He was getting impatient until he looked at her.

Her color was high. Her eyes were alive with excitement. And she had taken her hair down. She was beautiful.

"Why did you do that?" he growled.

"Do what?" She backed up a bit.

"Your hair."

She touched it self-consciously. She opened her mouth, then closed it again. She couldn't tell him. How could she tell him what it was like to be stared at, to be scorned and pitied and judged, to feel the weight of so many eyes as happened whenever tourists drove through the settlement? A man like him, so physically perfect, would never understand.

Now, for just this one afternoon, she couldn't bear it. For one little space in time, she didn't want to have to. She could not do anything about her plain clothing. She could not do anything with her straight hair to make it pretty, to make herself look like those other women on the street. But she had inadvertently left her bonnet either at Adam and Mariah's house, or possibly in the deadfall. She didn't have to accentuate how pale and plain she was by scraping her hair back off her face.

She brought her chin up defiantly. Jake stared at her. "Want to buy a pair of jeans?" he heard himself ask.

She stared at him. "I beg your pardon?"

"Jeans. Blue jeans."

"How?" she breathed.

"We'll just go into that store across the street there and buy them. You can change in the dressing room."

"Why?" she gasped.

"I don't know. Just because." Something squirmed inside him. Because she wanted to, he thought. He could see it in her eyes. It would be a wonderful adventure for her. And he wanted to give her that.

"Because is no reason, Jacob," she managed.

"Honey, it's every reason in the world."

She continued to stare at him. He was crazy. But she wanted to. She wanted to do this so badly. She yearned. But then reality hit her. "I have no money, Jacob. Certainly none that I'd spend on myself."

Watching her eyes slide away, that whole thing with the puppy came back to him all over again. There was no help for him, for the little boy he had been, but damn it to hell, this woman was going to have her blue jeans.

"I have money." He'd taken a hundred and fifty dollars from his account. And he might even have a buck or two to spare on his credit card.

"How…how much do they cost?" she ventured.

"Hell, I don't know." He'd never bought a pair of women's jeans before in his life. "Fifty dollars? Shouldn't be more than that."

Her eyes went huge. "So *much?*" It was a fortune! It was more than a week's worth of groceries! Frank had only given her thirty dollars every Friday to buy in Divinity those things that the farm didn't provide.

Jake read the horror in her face. "Probably less," he corrected himself. "As long as we don't pay for somebody's fancy name on your seat."

She hadn't a clue what he was talking about. "Why would I want to do that?"

He didn't answer. He left the enclosure and started down the walk toward the street. She watched him slap his hand on the hood of the taxi. He thrust a bill at the driver when the man looked up.

"Take off," he told him.

"But she said—"

"She was wrong. Bye." He looked back at her. She was still standing frozen inside the little enclosure. She inched outside to stare at him.

"Jacob, I can't let you do this!"

"Why not?"

"Because…" She thought frantically for another reason. "Because it really is so very wasteful. How can we spend money on something I'll never wear again?"

"Then wear them again."

Her eyes widened in horror once more. "I can't *do* that!"

Jake swore under his breath, then he came back to her. He took her chin in his hand. "Then stick them in a drawer," he said softly, "and every once in a while, open that drawer and touch them and pretend. Or remember. Katya, there's no going rate on dreams.''

Her eyes filled. *He understood.*

"Will you stop that?" he demanded.

"What?" she asked tremulously.

"Getting all misty-eyed like that."

"No one ever did anything like this for me before." She was shaking, she wanted this so badly. "Can I pay you back?"

He thought of what Adam had said about her needing to find a way to support herself. And her four kids. She wasn't going to come up with the cash any time soon. "Sure."

"O-kay, then."

"Yeah?" He realized he was delighted. And surprised. He'd fully expected her to back off. He knew that Adam's Mariah had clung to the ways of her faith during her *meidung,* her shunning, even though she didn't have to. Because they weren't restrictions to her. The *ordnung* rules provided walls and foundations to her world. She'd still dressed in her plain clothing, had still eschewed a telephone and electricity, because she believed in the sanctity that sameness and simplicity brought to Amish families.

This woman was different. He was beginning to understand that she was so different, in so very many ways.

"Yeah," he said again, and grinned, then he felt a shot of good, old-fashioned anticipation. "Okay, stay with me here. Something tells me you don't have a lot of experience at dodging traffic."

He caught her hand and pulled her across the intersection against the light. Horns blared. She cried out, but she was laughing. She was laughing because her feet never even touched the pavement and because he was holding her hand.

Her heart boomed with a new, wonderful, giddy kind of fear. She was floating on air.

Chapter 11

Katya was in the dressing room for nearly twenty minutes, until Jake began to worry that something had gone wrong in there. Normally, it wouldn't even occur to him. What could happen to anyone in a store dressing room? But Katya's wide-eyed simplicity made anything possible.

When she finally came out, his breath left him in a burst of relief. Then his heart staggered. She stood there, her eyes darting. He was standing by the cash register, and that was the one direction her gaze *didn't* go. He had a few heartbeats in which to watch her unaware.

He tried to decide if she looked as though she thought a lightning bolt was going to spear through the ceiling and strike her—or if she thought everyone in the place was staring at her. Everyone wasn't. From Jake's vantage point, it seemed to be only the men.

"Uh, I think she'll take them," he said to the salesclerk. He dropped money on the counter without taking his eyes from Katya and began to move toward her.

The jeans hugged her legs, her backside, her hips. They weren't a fancy designer brand, but they had been created for her body, for her precise curves. He'd thought she was too thin. He'd thought she wouldn't *have* many curves—though admittedly it had been hard to tell beneath that shapeless dress. Now, clearly, they were all right there, plain as day, just where they ought to be.

His heart moved harder.

He worked his gaze upward from her legs with an effort. She'd chosen a boxy lavender sweater to go with the jeans. It only reached to her waist, and as she turned this way and that, looking for him, tantalizing glimpses of skin peeked out. She must have felt the air, or his eyes, because she tugged at the hem of it, then she gave a gusty sigh and let her hands fall.

Her hair was still wild, free, almost waist-length except for those strands that always found a way to curl just underneath her jaw. In that moment he could almost forget that she had a staggering number of children. That she had a strong faith in a God who had abandoned him. He could almost forget that she was good and pure and she seemed to think he was wonderful for some unknown reason. He could forget that he needed to stay clear of her, for her sake as much as his own.

Her gaze finally found him. "Oh, Jacob! Thank goodness! I'd thought you left!" She hurried toward him. She had her dress and apron clutched in one hand, her coat and shawl in the other. "I feel foolish," she said when she reached him. Her mouth trembled.

"You look..." Jake struggled to remember when, and if, he had ever been at such a loss for words before.

Katya couldn't meet his eyes. *You look...* Of course he wouldn't finish. During all the short time she had known him, he had never been cruel or unkind.

What was he supposed to say? *You look ridiculous. You don't belong here. Go home and cover yourself with plain cotton. Keep your eyes down.* She began trembling harder.

Why, oh, why had she allowed him to talk her into this? It wasn't even just a waste of money! It was pure naiveté, absolute stupidity, to think that she could ever look anything like those women she'd seen on the street! She was about to bolt back to the dressing room, had even taken a single step in that direction, when he spoke again.

"Uh, incredible," Jake finished.

She finally met his eyes. Her own went wide and wondering. "Incredible?" she repeated as though tasting the word.

He did the only thing he could think of to prove it. He caught her elbow and spun her suddenly into his arms. He leaned down and captured her mouth quickly while it was still widened in a little "Oh!" of surprise.

"Incredible," he repeated.

He'd change the rules, he decided suddenly. It was the only option now, really. The old ones weren't working. He couldn't avoid her, couldn't stay clear of her. Not that he had tried incredibly hard, but she just wouldn't let him. She was there, warm and inviting, all the time. She was there every time he turned around. So he'd have to try a new avenue. He pulled back and looked into her eyes.

"What?" she whispered, still dazed by his action. She could still feel his mouth on hers.

He'd give her pleasure, he determined. For the short time he was here, he would make her world glow as best he could. He'd take that darting fear from her eyes. That uncertainty. That lack of faith in herself, so unwarranted. He'd give her touches that made her feel good. He'd give back anything he took from her, tenfold.

Good enough, he thought. As rules went, these felt far more comfortable.

"Jacob!" she protested against his mouth as he abruptly kissed her again. This time it was hard, fast, decisive. Then he backed off after touching his forehead to hers. "We're in a *store*," she gasped. "There are *people!*"

He looked up, around, then grinned. "I guess you knocked the sense right out of my head, Katie."

Katie. Oh, my Lord, she thought. He had called her that before, too. And just like then, it made her feel as she had a lifetime ago before she had married Frank. It made her feel young and strong and good—maybe even pretty—with a million vistas open to her, unlimited possibilities for her life.

Jake caught her hand. He took the bag the salesclerk had left on the counter and pushed the dress and the apron inside. "You'll need your coat, but let's lose this shawl thing," he decided. He shoved that in, too. "Let's go."

Katya let him drag her out of the store. She threw one frantic, apologetic look at the woman at the cash register. And what she saw on that woman's face made her stumble. *She envies me.* It was in her eyes, in the set of her jaw. *Me!*

Jake was nearly pulling her arm out of its socket. She hurried to keep up with him. She was sure, absolutely sure, that everyone in the entire store was staring at her bottom. She could *feel* their gazes as surely as if she were stark naked. She almost might as well be, she thought wildly. The jeans certainly didn't hide the shape of her.

She lost her breath for a moment as she made up her mind that she just wasn't going to allow herself to care. *Just today, just right now.* No one would ever know.

For all her years of hell, she decided that this one afternoon was *hers.* It would be her own special secret, her own wicked delight, to hold close to her heart for all the long, lonely rest of her life.

They went to the post office first. While Jake collected a duffel bag from General Delivery and posted the package with the candy wrapper to Dallas, Katya hung back, watching him. Butterflies danced not only in her tummy, but in her limbs. They made her whole body feel light, ticklish, airy. She was torn between disbelief that this was happening to her and a dizzying happiness. Jake glanced back once to see if she was okay, and he smiled. Her heart did a funny flip-flop.

She finally pulled her eyes off him for sanity's sake. She studied every detail of the post office while she waited. The electric fluorescent lights over her head hurt her eyes, made them tear, when she looked straight up. The shiny floor even *looked* cold. Big, thick, plastic ropes hung from short metal posts. They seemed to tell people where to walk.

And the people themselves! There was a woman in jeans much like hers, but she wore them tucked into black boots with very high heels. She wore a black leather jacket with a wonderful furry collar. There was a man in jeans with a bulky red plaid coat and a baseball cap. His teeth were yellow. There was a plump woman in stretchy pants even tighter than her jeans, struggling with two unruly children. Compared to her, Katya felt infinitely more modest.

There were rows of pictures on the wall. The men in them looked evil.

She jumped and gasped as Jake's mouth grazed her neck. She hadn't realized he'd finished. "Ready?" he murmured.

"For what?" *Yes, yes, I'm ready for anything. Just tell me what to do.*

"We'll grab a bite to eat before we go back."

Katya wasn't the least bit hungry, but he'd made the alternative clear. *Before we go back.* Not yet, she thought. Oh, please, not yet. "Yes," she murmured. "Let's eat."

Eating in a restaurant was against the *ordnug,* too. But she was already standing here in blue jeans that showed the world nearly everything she had been born with, and a sweater that let the cool air tickle her tummy once in a while. If the deacons ever caught wind of all this, she'd be shunned so completely she would never find her way back, not if she repented for years. Then again, if the deacons were in a restaurant in Lancaster to see her, then she thought they might have a few sins of their own to worry about. That was all the justification she needed.

Jake was quiet as they went outside. There was a whole handful of other things he should do while he was here in civilization, he realized. He should call New Jersey and track down his buddy, the guy who had picked up Devon Mills the first time, last month. He should ask him to go have another talk with the dude. He should call someone he knew in Washington and get them to run what they knew of the settlement kidnapper through the VICAP computer. He knew the FBI would already have done that, but it did *him* no good. He needed to know himself if there were any similarities between this one and cases elsewhere in the country, and as a general rule, the Feds didn't share.

He should be doing all those things while he was here, and all he wanted was to touch her, taste her, hear her laugh again. It was suddenly an overriding urgency.

"I noticed a place down on the corner," he said. "That way." He thrust his thumb in that direction. "Do you mind walking?"

"Of course not."

"It might have been three blocks," he allowed.

"That's fine."

"Four?"

"I believe you're the one who's out of shape, Jacob."

"*Me?*" He almost stopped walking.

"You couldn't keep up with the raking this morning," she observed mildly.

"I didn't...I wasn't..." He let his words trail off, dumb-founded.

She had, he thought. She had kept up easily. The muscles beneath those new jeans would not be just fluid, but strong. He forgot what he'd been about to say as he actually contemplated finding out.

He glanced over at her. She was catching snowflakes on her tongue as she walked, and he had one of those near-paralyzing moments of bemusement again. He did not think he had ever walked the street with a woman who caught snowflakes on her tongue. He did not think he had ever known a woman so guileless, so innocent and vulnerable, in his life.

She felt him looking at her and laughed self-consciously. "It's something we used to do when we were girls. My sisters and I."

"Growing up is no fun," he muttered absently.

She smiled a little sadly. "Yes, I do think things go down-hill after seventeen or so."

Or ten, or twelve, he thought. Sometimes even seven or eight.

"Jacob?"

"Huh?" He stopped in his tracks.

"Is this the place you meant?"

"Stay here. Let me check."

Her brows went up. "You can't remember from the out-side?"

What he wasn't sure of was whether or not the establishment would suit her. It *looked* cute, with a green-and-white canopy over the corner-facing door, but he didn't know the neighborhood. He stuck his head inside. It was perfect.

"Come on," he said, glancing back, holding a hand out to her. She scooted to him. As they stepped inside, he thought she was holding her breath.

Katya was. In that moment, she felt seventeen again, waiting with her eyes closed, ready to pop them open and see a wonderful surprise. And that was what she got. She had never been inside a restaurant before in her life. She had not read about them in novels, so she had no clue what to expect.

It was very dark. The golden light glowing from wall sconces was low, murky, intimate. It looked like candlelight, and she was comfortable with it.

"Oh," she breathed.

There was music, slow and sultry. It seemed to be coming from a large box not far from where they stood. In contrast to the room, the object was alive with light—red, pink and green tubes of it, blinking off and on, off and on.

It was only one room, a big one, she realized as her eyes adjusted. There were round tables scattered all over one side. There was a counter with high stools on the other. As she stood there, rooted, taking it all in, someone bumped into her from the side.

"Oh, excuse me!" She skittered out of the way to let a man and a woman pass to the door. The woman wore the shortest skirt she had ever seen in her life. Like the woman in the stretchy pants at the post office, this one made Katya feel almost decently dressed. "Oh," she whispered again.

Jake laughed.

It was a warm, rich sound that lifted her skin into goose-flesh. She looked at him quickly to see if he was mocking her. He didn't seem to be. He was leaning back against the lighted box, one arm resting atop it, watching her. He looked happy.

"Like it?" he asked.

"Oh, yes. What do we do first?"

Jake pushed himself off the jukebox. "We go over to one of those tables."

She began moving toward the tables without him. He hurried to catch up, swinging her into his arms. Her heart started hammering at the simple closeness. "You said go to a table."

"Don't you want to know what we'll do after we get there?"

She nodded seriously.

"We'll lean close to each other." He put his mouth to her ear. She was stunned when she felt his tongue there, dipping so briefly inside. Then her breath caught and her skin pulled even tighter.

"Okay," she managed breathlessly.

He laughed. "You're easy, Katie."

She scowled. "Is that bad?"

He thought about it. "To some frames of mind." His had never been one of them. "And not in your case. I just meant...there's no deception with you."

"Lying is a sin."

"Well, yeah, I guess it is." He felt briefly uncomfortable, then he laughed again, a low rumble. "After we lean close to each other, I'll whisper sweet nothings in your ear."

"That's not possible."

"What?"

"Jacob, you can't whisper and say nothing at the same time. Or, at least, what would be the point?"

That foggy feeling came back, just behind his eyes. "Wait and see."

She smiled slowly, mesmerized. She was really starting to believe he could do anything at all.

He led her the rest of the way to the table. He pulled a chair out for her with a flourish. She laughed again, a light, nervous sound. Then she sat and shrugged out of her coat. And she waited.

When the waitress came, both she and Jake looked at Katya expectantly. "What?" she asked uncertainly.

"Something to drink?" the woman suggested.

She was tongue-tied. She didn't know what to ask for.

"Two coffees," Jake said. Then it occurred to him that she probably drank coffee every morning of her life. "No. Wait. How about...I don't know. Some kind of ice-cream float?" Something special, he thought. Something different.

The waitress blinked. "In February?"

"We're living dangerously." And he was, he realized, though danger had heretofore meant a few extra shots of bourbon.

When the waitress brought the concoctions, Katya sipped tentatively, her eyes on Jake's face. Such strong lines, she thought. And that mouth, always that mouth. It had touched her. She felt a little thrill scoot through her all over again.

"Well?" he asked.

"Well what?" She blinked, not sure what he expected of her.

"The float."

She scowled. "You haven't had any."

"I'm filling up on the sight of you."

She cocked her head to one side. "That's silly."

"It's one of my best lines." It wasn't, actually, but he thought it was one of the few he could use on her without shocking her.

"Perhaps you should work on more," she suggested honestly.

He stared at her, then he laughed. It came up from deep in his chest. It was sudden, unstoppable. She was the most naive woman he'd ever met in his life, and damned if she hadn't put him in his place.

"I like you, Katie Yoder," he managed finally.

She had never heard sweeter words in her life.

He touched his tall, foaming glass to hers and couldn't believe he was sitting in a café, drinking an ice-cream float, feeling mesmerized. "Here's to new experiences," he said, his voice low this time, seductive, "in the most astonishing of places."

She wasn't sure she understood what he meant, but then, she understood only a portion of the things he said anyway and she hated asking for clarification all the time. So she pretended, smiled tentatively and drank a little, finally scooping out the ice cream with the long spoon the waitress had brought.

It was sinfully delicious. She laughed in delight.

Jake leaned forward again abruptly. "I think this would be a good place for those sweet nothings I mentioned."

Her eyes widened. "Okay."

He shook his head slowly. His eyes were on her face, roving, as though to find some secret there. He touched a finger along her cheekbone, then leaned over and caught her mouth.

He didn't know what to do with her. He didn't know how to be with her. Yes, all the old rules had vanished; he'd decided they no longer applied. But he wasn't sure what he was left with here. He couldn't laugh things off with a woman who wouldn't play games. He couldn't pry off the fingers of a woman who didn't cling, who asked for nothing. This was, he realized, getting a little too close to the core of him, easy and comfortable and right.

Alarm kicked in. Panic threatened again. But he couldn't heed it, at least not at the moment, because the lure of her was stronger.

He slanted his mouth over hers. She shuddered again and moaned something that sounded like "Oh my." No, he didn't know what to do with her.

If this was sweet nothing, Katya decided, then she wanted all of it she could hold. She had gone beyond being totally shocked that he seemed to want her. She had gone beyond her fear. Both had been impossible to hold on to in the face of his frequent touches. That was his way, she'd come to learn, always using his hands. Each graze of his palm, each capture of her hand in his own, every time his mouth brushed over hers, he was saying that he wanted her, he really did, no matter how preposterous that seemed to her. And if she had stiffened, had yanked back in fear each time, she would be exhausted by now.

So she accepted. And in a part of her heart, she also accepted that sooner or later it would all end. But she was reasonably convinced that for some reason she couldn't fathom, an angel had come to sit on her shoulder for a little while. A sweet angel, a kind angel, who said that for each attack of Frank's battering fists, she should also have one touch to cherish.

Jake's mouth left hers. His tongue skimmed her lower lip.

"Was that nothing?" she whispered.

"What do you think?" His voice seemed to her as dark and smoky as the room. "I'm through handing out lines for a while."

She thought about it. "It was everything."

He kissed her again. The overriding feeling she got from him was *time,* Katya decided. He would stretch this out forever. He would nibble and murmur. There was no plundering, no cruel and hurtful rushing through to his own pleasure.

She groaned a little against his mouth.

He felt her trust like a palpable thing, like something she held in her hands and extended to him. And he felt the weight of it, the responsibility. Something he'd always avoided. That brought him back to his senses a little. He sat back again, away from her.

"Would you...?" she ventured.

"Would I what?"

"Do that again?" The words were hard to get out.

He was doomed. "We're in a café, Katya." He tried for sanity.

"I thought that was okay. You said it was a place for sweet nothings."

Damned by his own lines, he berated himself helplessly, then he found her mouth again.

He smelled like something spicy and rich. It filled her head. Slow, everything was so slow. Then suddenly, his kiss changed to something deeper, almost needy.

"I don't want to hurt you," he heard himself say, and that shook him, too, because he hadn't even realized he was thinking of the possibility.

"How could you? How could you possibly?"

Don't trust me. Don't you get it? You'll need me and I won't be there. But the words wouldn't come, and that made him angry.

Then her head tilted back a little so that he lost her mouth. A sigh left her.

"No, baby, no." His voice was raw. "You can't do that here."

"What?" She came back to reality and looked at him dazedly.

He hooked an arm around her neck, pulled her closer, but into a kind of hug this time. *You can't throw your head back like I was making love to you and we were the only two people in the world.* He realized he was shaking.

"Jacob."

"Yeah."

"Why did you stop?"

Because maybe, he realized, just maybe there was some small shred of decency left inside him after all.

Chapter 12

"Jacob?" she said a few minutes later.

"What?" He surreptitiously shifted his chair a couple inches from hers.

"You're not talking anymore."

He'd ordered hamburgers, and the waitress came and set them in front of them, giving him a moment to think of a response. He stared down at the burger fiercely. His appetite was gone.

Talk, he told himself. Okay, she wanted talk. He'd focus it on her. "How come you were so willing to break out today?"

She looked at him, her eyes wide. "Break out?"

He waved a hand. "The jeans. Your hair."

She smiled a little. "That's exactly what it's like," she answered wistfully. "*Breaking out*. Being free. I never knew…it's so glorious."

He considered Adam's wife. Made himself consider her. "Mariah cherishes every restriction of her life," he returned.

She pondered that. "Almost everyone does. It's why my people left the church in Europe all those centuries ago, why we came here to Pennsylvania. It happened over an issue of baptism. The old church performed the rite much as many of your faiths do. Shortly after birth. But we felt that people should have the choice. That their faith would be stronger if it was something they chose of their own free will. We don't feel people should be baptized into it until they're old enough to know what they're getting into, until they're old enough to make a responsible, conscious choice.''

She thought he relaxed a little as she spoke. For a while, he'd seemed very tense. She'd wondered if it was something she'd done or said. But now he seemed to be focusing hard on her words.

"You were baptized," he said hoarsely.

"Yes."

"So you made a conscious choice." Even he realized there was something too rough about his voice. He couldn't have said why this seemed so damned important.

She shrugged one shoulder and nibbled on a French fry. "The Amish church, the deacons, won't marry a couple if both partners aren't baptized."

"A little coercion there, he snapped. "So much for free choice."

"But most people are baptized years before that. Very few embrace the church *just* so they can get married."

"Why'd you do it then? *Why?*" She wasn't happy. He *knew* she wasn't happy. She was trapped and she was miserable.

Katya felt a burning sensation come up in her throat. "Because I had to."

"To get married?"

"No. I was sixteen. I married at seventeen."

"Then *why?*" he persisted, almost shouting. He found he badly needed to know, to understand. Suddenly, knowing was the most important thing he'd ever needed.

"There was nothing else I *could* do!" she burst out.

"You don't believe in all this...this *ordnung* stuff, then?" It was her life, he reminded himself. It had nothing to do with him. But it felt like it did. The whole thing bothered him tremendously.

"Of course I believe," she answered.

He felt like a horse had kicked him in the chest.

"You see, it wasn't terrible at first." She struggled to explain. "I got baptized because I couldn't imagine doing anything else. I was raised in the settlement, Jacob. This is only my second time in the city. I was fine with the decision until I started seeing things that were just...that were just *wrong*. I believe in almost all the *ordnung,* Jacob. But some parts are just...senseless." She dropped her voice, unable to speak the blasphemy above a whisper. "Some parts just hurt people."

Jake felt each of his muscles tighten, one by one.

"Now I'm in and they've closed all the doors," she went on. And oh, it felt so good to *say* it. She wondered if she would ever have been able to say it to anyone but him. "They won't let me out, Jacob. That's better than being expected to allow Frank to hit me day after day after day. At least the new *gemeide* threw the *meidung* on him and allowed me to separate, but this is all there's ever going to be. Ever. Just me and my children. And sometimes I just...sometimes I just want to *dream* again. Like you said. There's nothing specific I want to do and am prohibited from, not right now, but all my dreams, all my possibilities are gone."

The way she said it hurt him. "So leave," he said, his voice raw. "Live like the rest of us. Get a divorce. For God's sake, Katya, there has to be a way out!"

"There isn't." She looked at him as though he were crazy. "Oh, Jacob, I could never survive out here."

That made him angry. Frustrated. Something hurt behind his eyes. "Why not?"

"I've just told you. I'm not...smart enough. I'm not educated. I have four babies! And this...the people in the settlement are all I've ever known. I need them, Jacob. If I lost them, it would be like walking down the road naked."

He knew better than to let that image get stuck in his mind.

"Thank you," she said suddenly, fervently.

"For what?" he growled.

"For opening this one little door. For bringing me here today. I'll remember this forever."

She looked at him with her heart in her eyes. Everything

inside him stiffened. It was what he had wanted to do for her, to give her, and now, somehow, it hurt.

"Eat," he snapped. "Just eat your hamburger."

She took another dutiful bite. Actually, she found, her own cooking was much better. Jacob wolfed down his burger, and she didn't see how he could taste it. Maybe, she thought, that was the point.

"Ready?" he said abruptly, wiping his mouth with the napkin, tossing it down.

It was over.

She nodded. She'd felt it coming, of course. She looked down sadly at the paper bag sitting beside his chair. "I'll need to change," she said quietly. "I guess we should go back to that store."

But Jake shook his head. "You can do it here in the rest room."

He threw some money on the table and went to a pay phone against the wall. By the time she came back from changing, he'd hung up. "I called a cab. You stay in here and keep warm. I'll go out to the curb and keep an eye out for it." And just like that, he was gone.

She went after him despite what he had said. He didn't notice her right away, didn't hear the swishing sound of the door. For a moment, she could watch him without him knowing it.

The expression on his face took her breath away. Inexplicably, tears sprang to her eyes. His face *hurt*. It was miserable. Hard. She didn't understand.

She must have made a sound of distress because he looked her way suddenly and sharply. "Hey," he said neutrally, "what are you doing? I told you to keep warm."

"I didn't like it in there without you."

His face went even harder. "Don't say things like that."

"But—"

"Just don't. Damn it, Katie, *don't.*"

She stayed silent. This time she listened to him.

The cab pulled up. Jake held the door for her. She scrambled inside and went to the far window. It was over, she thought again.

Almost.

She watched the lights of the city flash past. She leaned forward, nearly pressing herself against the glass, not wanting to miss one last glimpse of this place. But before she knew it, they were back at the phone booth. She took the bag with her treasured jeans from the floor wordlessly. While he paid the driver, she waited on the road. A tear fell down and plopped wetly on her shawl. It was big enough that she could see it even in the darkness. She dashed her hands over her cheeks angrily. If there was one thing she knew, one thing she had learned long ago, it was to cherish the brief moments of good in her life, then just…release them. Let them go. Mourning them, the loss of them, would only make the bad parts of her life feel worse.

But oh, this time it was so very hard. This time had been almost more good than she could hold.

Jake didn't want to look at her and he couldn't quite figure out a way not to. He saw her chin tremble in the moonlight. *Damn it.* He felt angry. He had never promised her anything. He'd never offered her anything but this one damned afternoon. Why did she have to look at him like that, like he was taking everything good in her world and stomping on it just by bringing her home?

He decided he'd walk her back to the house, then he'd just get the hell out of Dodge. Or paradise, as the case might be, with all its sweet, simplistic values. With this woman who smiled so tremulously, and the others who carted food into a neighbor's house because a skeleton had been found. He'd go back to the city if he had to walk. He'd spend the night there, burn it off.

He took her elbow a little too roughly. "Come on."

They trudged through the night. Even the moon went away, ducking behind a cloud. They rounded the first curve in the road, and then they saw it. They both began jogging at the same time. The bag Katya held with her precious jeans and sweater fell from her nerveless fingers. She knew. Somehow she knew.

Adam and Mariah's house was alive with lights. Lanterns were lit in every room. There were horses and buggies all over the place, lining the street. *Something was wrong.* Katya began making a keening sound in her throat. Their jogging footsteps turned into a flat-out run.

Jake scarcely heard her. Their shoulders bumped hard together as they tried to get in the front door at the same time. Katya almost fell and she had to grab the porch rail to steady herself. Jake raced inside first, like a madman. She wheeled away from the rail and went in after him, almost in one motion.

"What is it?" he demanded of the people—all women again—crowded into the living room.

"What?" Katya cried as soon as she spotted Mariah. "What's happened?"

Mariah's face was as pale as the moon. "Sam," she whispered. "It's Sam. Bo says they went to the pond to look for the geese after all when you didn't come back. And now he's gone. I'm so sorry. I thought they were playing out back, but they slipped away when I wasn't looking."

Katya's heart stopped. Her blood seem to drain down to her feet and out through her heels. She swayed. *No, no, no.* But she had known. From the moment she'd seen all the lights, she had known. She looked around wildly for Jacob. He was still standing in the doorway, and his face was parchment white. "Help me," she said, her voice strangled. "Jacob."

She didn't know why she turned to him so instinctively. Maybe it was as simple as the fact that he had come here in the first place to find the babies. Maybe because he knew that her babies were all she had. Maybe because he was strong, he was fierce, he was smart, and he was the only person she could imagine saving her from this nightmare.

She couldn't catch his eyes. When he swore, it was with words she had never heard, not even from Frank's mouth. "*Jacob,*" she pleaded. And his gaze finally came to her.

He heard his own voice as though from miles away. He

recognized neither the tone nor the words—especially not the words. He was filled with something hot, then cold, as he took her in his arms. "I will. I'll get him back. I promise."

Jake had no recollection of getting to the pond. *It's happening again.* The words were thunder in his head, a litany. He wasn't thinking about the babies who were disappearing. He was thinking about his own rotten, mistake-riddled life. He'd broken all her rules and his own, and now a child would pay for it. Katya's child.

He forced the guilt away, the panic. He needed to think like a cop. He began yelling, roaring at the top of his lungs. There were easily a hundred men milling around, their feet obliterating everything, and he'd had so precious little to go on so far.

"Don't move! *Don't anybody move!*"

Everyone froze. Then Adam's fist came out of the darkness and landed squarely on Jake's jaw. Jake went sprawling backward in the snow.

"What the hell did you do that for?" Jake snarled.

"Where were you? Where the hell have you been?" Adam growled right back.

Jake wiped the blood from his mouth. He got to his feet very carefully. "The city. You know where we were."

"For *five and a half hours?* What did you do there? If you laid a hand on her, so help me God, Jake, I'll kill you."

Jake's voice became deadly, too calm. "Stay out of it," he warned.

"The hell I will."

Jake ignored that. "All I want to hear from you are facts. Where. When. How. What you know so far."

Adam watched him a moment, his eyes narrowing. Then, finally, he nodded. "When Katya didn't come back, Bo and Levi took it upon themselves to take Sam to the pond," he said.

"What did they see?" Jake snapped. "Were they all here when it happened?"

"Yeah," Adam answered. "We've got something this time.

A beat-up, gold Cadillac, maybe a Lincoln, pulled up on the road there. A man got out and grabbed Sam, then burned rubber getting away again. Bo spent just enough time in Texas earlier in the month to be able to describe the model. Levi hadn't a clue.''

Jake's eyes became feral. He nodded and turned away.

"One other thing," Adam said. "The guy had a beard and he was wearing Amish clothing.''

Jake snapped around to look back at him. Too much light suddenly filled his head. *Yeah, yeah, of course!* He should have realized it before. The guy had been dressed like an Amishman. It was the only way he could have gotten unnoticed into those church socials. It was the only way he could have gotten close to an Amish woman and her child in a farmers' market without raising undue suspicion.

"I've got you, you bastard. You screwed up this time," he muttered under his breath.

"Jake," Adam said, "I don't think he's Amish. No Amishman I can imagine would have reason to steal someone else's kid, not even Frank Essler. They all have kids enough of their own, and kidnapping is so much of a sin *I* can't even imagine it.''

Jake looked at him briefly. "No. He's not Amish. But he's been here and he knows how to act the part.''

Now he had something to go on. He turned away from his brother again, hungry and desperate to do something, anything to set things right.

He had promised. Sweet God, he had promised. He had promised his sister, and he hadn't been able to save her. He had promised his mother, and he had done nothing to save her, either. But he wasn't going to let this bastard hurt Sam. And he sure as hell wasn't going to let him hurt Katya.

Chapter 13

It was like a nightmare, Katya thought, and she had no hope of waking up any time soon.

The women waited in Mariah's living room with her, attempting to console her, holding her hand. Katya didn't want them. She felt claustrophobic. The feeling in her chest was unlike anything she had ever experienced before in her life. It was intolerable, unbearable. It was a breath-robbing pain that kept her eyes wet, that wouldn't let her get air.

Her baby. Someone had taken her baby.

She wanted to scream it out. Instead, she stood up from the sofa. Someone reached out to touch her shoulder. Katya recoiled and fled into the kitchen. After a moment, Mariah followed her.

"Katya, tell me what to do," she said softly. "Tell me anything I can do to make it stop hurting just a little."

Katya pressed her knuckles against her mouth and went to look out the window into the dark night. *Her baby was out there, scared and alone.* "There's nothing," she murmured. Then she thought about it. "Talk about something else," she decided faintly. "I need to try to keep my mind off it all while Jacob looks. If I think about it too much…"

Mariah understood. And she heard the almost reverent way her friend said Adam's brother's name. She took in a shaky breath. "Okay, then," she said finally. "There *is* something I want to say. Katya, I fear for you."

Katya turned away from the window. "*Me?* Why?"

"Don't love him!" Mariah burst out. "Please, don't fall in love with Jacob. I know it would be easy. He's charming and he's handsome. And I think, no matter what Adam says, he's a very good man. But Adam is right, too, and I see it. I sense it. Jacob never lets himself get too involved in anything he enjoys too much. If he wants something too badly, he turns away from it. That's just the way he is. You'll get hurt," she finished. "One way or another, he'll leave here."

Katya felt the strangest thing happen. For one brief heartbeat, her grief shrank. It didn't vanish—that would never happen until she held her baby in her arms again. But it got smaller because there was only so much her heart could hold. And at this moment, her heart was full of rage.

"Do you think I'm that silly?" she cried, then her voice took on a singsong quality. "*Poor little Katya, we must protect her.* I am not that stupid! I see my life. I see what it is. I am under no illusions. There's nothing here for me, Mariah! There is *never* going to be anything here, and there's nothing I can do about that. But Jacob makes me feel happy for a little while.

"I know he'll go," she finished more quietly. "Of course he'll go. He's not meant for this country, and what would he ever want with a woman like me? He's only shown me attention because he's here, and there's no one else. Everyone else is married. *Really* married. I've known that from the start. But I won't deny myself these memories, these days, just because they won't last. If I did that, I would *really* be dumb."

"I never thought you were dumb!" Mariah protested, stricken.

Katya scarcely heard her. "I'll tell you something else," she went on fiercely. "I'm beginning to hate it here. I'm beginning to hate our church and our ways, and I'm not even sure how I feel about God right now! Because He takes everything away, all the pleasure, everything good. And He doesn't give anything back! *All I had was my children!*'' She was sobbing now and she hated that, too. She scrubbed her hands over her cheeks hard and fast. ''All I had was my babies, and He couldn't even protect them! Our mighty *ordnung,* all the sacrifices—what's it for, Mariah? What *good* is it if it won't even protect the little I have?''

She didn't wait for an answer. She fled into the living room and up the stairs.

Jake shoved change into the pay phone and punched out a number he knew by heart. Not that he had called it often, but his mind just stored that sort of thing.

''Lawrence Spina,'' he snapped when an operator at FBI headquarters answered. His voice shook a little with the strain of control. He could have called the local cops and let them drag the Feds back here. But he'd made a promise so he would go straight to the top himself.

''He's not in,'' the bland voice replied. It might have been a recording except for the slight throat clearing that accompanied it.

''Then patch me through to his home. I need to talk to him about the fifth kidnapping in a small, protected area in five months,'' Jake snarled. ''Your guys were here briefly, then they backed out when they didn't get anywhere. Now another kid has been taken. I need some cooperation. I need information.''

The voice said nothing, but he heard a series of clicks and hums as the call was transferred.

''Jake Wallace,'' Jake said as soon as the man answered. ''Dallas P.D. I met you in Quantico a couple of years back. You tried to hire me. I need your help.'' He outlined the problem.

''Well, if our guys have left—'' Spina began.

''I need you to get them back here,'' Jake interrupted harshly. ''Tonight. Within the hour. Your guys have equipment that I don't have access to." And a promise left little room for pride when it came to admitting he needed help. "I need to cast some footprints." By some blessed miracle, the men hadn't trampled over some he'd found right near the road. They hadn't been plain, flat, like Amish boots. "In snow," he added.

"Cover them," Spina said immediately.

"I have. It's possible, right? To cast them?" He seemed to remember it was, though he hadn't had much opportunity to tangle with snowy evidence in Dallas.

"It's difficult, but possible," Spina agreed. "We've got some stuff called Snow Print Wax. We lay it into the tracks before we fill them with the liquid dental stone. Then if the stone is cool enough and the snow is frozen hard enough—"

"It's down to eleven degrees right now."

"Good. Then we shouldn't melt any of the evidence. I'll send a team out from Philly by helicopter. Should take no more than an hour."

"Thanks," Jake said tersely, then he made another call. This one was to Toms River, New Jersey. "Ernie," he said when the man answered, "it's Jake Wallace." Ernie O'Brien had helped him out with Devon Mills earlier in the month. Ernie was a senior detective with the New Jersey State Police. He'd pulled Mills in for questioning when Jake had ID'ed the man through the settlement's description of him and Child-Search's Web site on the Internet. Ernie donated time to ChildSearch cases, as well. "I'm back here in Pennsylvania," he told him, "in the Amish settlement."

"Again?" Ernie asked. "I thought you had that business settled with your brother and his ex-wife and the kid."

"So did I," Jake answered grimly. He paused to clear the words that wanted to get stuck in his throat. "Another kid has been snatched, Ernie. The fifth." He filled him in. "I'm thinking there's got to be a connection here," he added. "It just seems like a bit too much to me, all this bad stuff happening to these pious folks all at once, after centuries of being stoic and trying to worship in peace and quiet." He grimaced a little at that, his gut tightening again. "It smells."

"Yeah," Ernie agreed. "So what do you want me to do?"

"Pull Mills in again."

"Hey, buddy, I need some grounds. We all but wore out that kidnapping thing last month."

"I found Jannel Wallace's body this afternoon."

Ernie whistled. "That would do it. You think he killed her?"

"Yeah. We know now she didn't run off to Tahiti. I'm thinking Mills caught up with her here after all and offed her. I'm thinking *Mills* got Adam's money, and I'm thinking he figured out a way to get more."

"The guy ain't living large," Ernie replied thoughtfully. "If you're right, my guess would be that he blew his first booty on drugs or drink. And maybe that gaudy Cadillac."

Jake's heart stalled, then exploded. "Cadillac," he repeated.

"Gold. Silver trim and hubcaps. Pretty damned ugly, if you ask me. I got a good look at it when I picked him up the last time."

"Bingo," Jake said quietly. He'd gotten him. He really had him. "Do me a favor. Put out a pick-up-and-hold on the vehicle in case he's headed back that way. One of the boys with the kidnap victim saw a big gold car. Something tells me you're not going to be able to find him at home tonight. And get me the license plate. I'll turn it over to the FBI. They can put a multistate APB out, as well."

"You think Mills is acquiring more funds by kidnapping these kids? Have there been ransom demands?"

"No." And that was the heinous part. That was what was giving Jake nightmares, and he wasn't an easy man to scare. "These folks don't have much in the way of money. A ransom demand would have to be for a horse and a couple of cows. I think he's selling them, Ernie."

"Oh, hell," Ernie said tensely. His voice had taken on a kind of hum Jake recognized. Ernie was in on the hunt.

"No older kids have been taken," Jake explained tightly. "A seven- and eight-year-old were right there with the victim tonight. This guy ignored them in favor of a not-quite-two-year-old. Because nobody wants to adopt older kids. The younger the better. But it's tough as nails to get a baby anymore. There are just too few of them, and too long a waiting list. If you go through legal channels anyway.''

"The last legal thing Mills probably did was be born," Ernie said flatly.

Jake winced. "Exactly."

"And there's a big demand for healthy white infants," Ernie went on.

"Yeah. And the Amish provide some of the healthiest around. There are no drugs here, Ernie. They're damned near disease-free. The worst-case scenario is maybe they have a few quirks from inbreeding."

Ernie let out a sound of disgust.

"Worse, they have this rule about not protesting God's will. So if Mills picked up on that while he was here looking for Jannel, then he'd have realized that he could grab a baby whenever he wanted and get away with it. The Amish wouldn't run howling to the law."

"But they did."

"No, not right away. Four kids vanished before they did that. It was a monumental decision on their part, Ernie. My brother's new wife pushed them into it with the help of a guy named Joe Lapp." Jake paused. "Mills is selling these poor kids. I'd bet my last dollar he came here chasing Jannel, took a look around and said, 'Wow.' There was never any sign of a real struggle because he dressed like they do. That's why they're sort of popping off into thin air like this. That's why nobody noticed a stranger. That was bugging me, too. I kept thinking they should have seen a car or an *anner Satt Leit* coming too close. But he just blended right in. You know, they've got kin coming and going through here from other *gemeides* all the time. People would probably expect this guy was just someone else's cousin. Then, ten to one, he lured the little ones with candy." He told Ernie about the Snickers wrapper. "Katya says the mothers just don't buy their kids that kind of stuff," he finished.

"Who's Katya?" Ernie asked, startled.

Jake's heart spasmed. "Never mind."

"I'll alert our highway patrols," he said finally. "Listen, what's the status on the skeleton you found today?"

"I don't know much yet. Why?"

"How sure are you that it was Jannel?" Ernie asked.

"Ninety-nine percent. My brother ID'ed her ring."

"Good enough. Based on that, I can probably get a court order to toss this dude's house. We probably won't find anything to tie him to the murder after all this time, but maybe we'll find something that'll lead you to where he's placed these kids."

This, Jake thought suddenly, was where God waited. In the hearts of guys like this, guys he knew all over America, guys who would bend a few rules and step into a few gray areas for the sake of a child.

His throat tightened. "Thanks, Ernie."

Jake hung up. He felt the slow, sick ebb of adrenaline. Temporarily, his hands were tied. There wasn't much else he could do. So he'd do everything over a second time, he decided. One more time. Damned if he was going to sit idle.

He had promised.

"Katya?" Mariah knocked tentatively on the bedroom door. More than an hour had passed since her friend had fled upstairs.

Katya hugged herself and went to the door. She felt like a fool, like she was pouting in her room. But the truth was that after her outburst, the ungodly pain had come back, pressing in on her chest. She couldn't bear to be around anyone.

She opened the door anyway, Rachel and Delilah crowding up behind her. "What is it?" she asked. "Have they found anything?" *Please, God, tell me they found something.* But God didn't answer her anymore. Had He ever, even once, since she had married Frank?

"I don't think so," Mariah answered. "But Adam is here. He wants to talk to us. I imagine he's here to give us an update." They both knew that if Sam had been found, Adam would have said so immediately.

Katya nodded and stepped around her, pulling Delilah by

the hand, shepherding Rachel ahead of her. She had an irrational fear now of leaving them alone, even in Mariah's home. Levi's necessary absence was gnawing a hole in her stomach. He was still at the pond with the men.

They went downstairs. The women were still there, seated in every available chair in the living room. They spilled over, filling in all the little spaces between the furniture. They pressed against the walls, and a couple were crowded in the kitchen doorway. They were all watching Adam. He stood by the door, looking pale and haggard.

Mariah, Katya and the girls stopped on the stairs. They couldn't go any farther. Women blocked their path.

"What's happened?" Katya asked Adam. "What do you know?"

Adam's eyes seemed to skim over her without settling. She thought he seemed uncomfortable looking at her.

"Jake sent me back here," he said finally. "He's busy, but he thought you'd want to be filled in. First of all, the guy left some evidence this time."

There was a collective gasping sound as the women drew in their breaths. Katya felt herself sway a little. She knew her first hope in hours. It was like the sputtering flame on a candle, just lighting. If there was evidence this time, Jacob would do something with it. Surely he would.

"What?" she demanded.

"Footprints. And Bo and Levi saw him. Bo recognized the kind of car the kidnapper drove—at least to some extent. Jake's working on it."

She gripped the banister for support. Her knees almost gave out. There was not a single doubt in her mind that Jacob would find this man, this vile man who was stealing their children, if he had this much to go on.

"Anyway, he thinks it might be prudent to get the other children out of the settlement as soon as possible, until this whole thing is settled. Our precautions haven't worked. Kids will be kids. They'll slip away by themselves as Bo and Levi and Sam have proved. So they need to go somewhere else until this guy is caught. We need to make absolutely sure this can't happen again. I just came from the pay phone. I've made arrangements to lease a bus.''

"No!" Katya cried instinctively. The word was torn from her heart. Delilah and Rachel and Levi were all she had left.

She shook her head frantically. Her hair tickled her neck, her cheek. No wonder everyone was still looking at her as though she had gone heathen, she realized. She was standing here with her hair spilling to her waist, when God intended that only a woman's husband should see such a thing.

"No," she said again, more quietly. "Please don't ask me to do that."

"Look," Adam said carefully. "Jake's been in touch with the sheriff. He's learned that there have been no kidnappings of *anner Satt Leit* children in this county in over three years. And if it was happening in other settlements, in other counties, we would have heard."

Katya nodded halfheartedly. Everyone had kin in other settlements, she thought. Yes, they would have heard.

"This is only happening here," Adam finished. "So we've got to get the kids away from here."

Slowly, carefully, Katya let her breath out. He was right.

"But *where?*" someone else asked.

"Sugar Joe Lapp has friends in Berks County," Mariah said suddenly. She looked for Sarah Lapp in the crowd. The woman's face was inordinately pale. She seemed to be taking this worse than anyone, for some reason Mariah could not fathom. Or maybe something else was bothering her. With Jake descending into their lives, Mariah hadn't had much of a chance to talk to her friend lately.

Sarah finally nodded. "Yes," she said faintly.

Adam nodded. "I think he's still at the pond. I'll go talk to him." He looked at the women again. "Why don't you all go home and get your families together, then bring the kids back here? The bus will be here in an hour."

Katya turned back for the stairs. She knew all she needed to know now. Sam hadn't been found yet, and Jake was working on it. She would have to send Rachel and Delilah and Levi away.

When everyone was gone, Mariah went to her husband. He hadn't moved as the women began swarming past him out the door, collecting coats and shawls as they went.

"How's Katya holding up?" he asked, his voice raspy. It got that way when he was very emotional.

Mariah thought about it. "She's very shaky, of course," she said quietly. "And there's nothing I can do for her. Only Jacob can restore her faith, I think, by finding the baby." One of the other things Adam had said about his brother was that he had one of the most impressive, deductive minds he had ever encountered. She prayed that in this instance, Adam was right.

His face twisted. "Did he—" He broke off. "Do you think he—they—you know. Did he touch her?"

Mariah's brows popped up. "It's none of our business."

That, he thought, was pretty much what Jake had said.

Adam left because there was no sense in arguing with her. He knew how futile it was when his wife got that expression on her face. Nothing he could say or do would sway her. When she looked at him like that, he always found himself going along with her blindly and without question.

But he was upset. And he was worried. Not just about Sam Essler, but about Jake. Each time he'd encountered his brother in the past hour, it seemed to him that the man was literally vibrating with tension. Something was boiling in there. Something was going to explode.

He'd thought the settlement would save his brother. He'd been shortsighted. Now he was very much afraid that his brother might rock the settlement off its foundations. And that Katya Essler was going to blow sky-high with the rest of the debris Jake left behind.

Most of the men had left the pond by the time Jake returned from the phone booth. He had hit upon the idea of sending the kids away as much to get the fathers out of here as to protect the little ones. Then he noticed that Bo and Levi were still sitting on a fallen log near the edge of the frozen water.

"Uncle Jake?" Bo said.

Jake groaned aloud. They had been told to stay there and be still, and they were doing just that. But in all the commotion, the men had forgotten about Sam's accomplices. Jake went to kneel in the snow in front of them. "Hey, boys. You about ready to clear out, too?" He looked at Bo. "Your dad got a bus."

"Yeah," Bo answered sullenly. "He said."

Jake looked at Levi. The boy's chin trembled in the moonlight. Jake's head swam all over again. He wasn't equipped to deal with this kind of trauma. He didn't *want* to deal with it. He wanted to go on doing what he did best—looking for the bad guy. Unfortunately, he had done all he could do for the time being, and here was Levi, needing something, someone, to hold on to.

"My ma's going to tan my hide for this, ain't she?" the boy finally asked in a small voice.

Jake thought about it. He thought about it hard.

"Has she ever done that?" he asked finally. Frankly, he couldn't imagine Katya ever raising her hand to any of her kids. No, he thought, there was always that sweet, steady gentleness about her. She would never hit her kids.

Levi shook his head, just as Jake had expected. "But I never did something this bad before, either," he admitted.

Jake let out his breath. "Well, this was pretty bad. Or, at least, it was foolish."

"Glad my dad didn't come to help look," Levi muttered, rubbing his toe in the snow. "My dad would have pounded me one for sure."

Jake flinched.

"We thought we could watch out for each other," Bo said suddenly, his chin jutting. There it was again, Jake thought— that stubborn Wallace gene.

"Yeah? Against some man?" Jake countered. "You thought the three of you were a match for him, with Sam not even two years old yet?"

"We coulda got him," Bo insisted. "Levi and me. If we'd been there, you know, close enough to Sam."

"Sure, that was your first mistake. You should have stayed

together. Then..." In one motion, he came to his feet again. He caught Bo—he was lighter—in the crook of his left arm, lifting him clear off the log. He tossed him over his shoulder before Levi could react. He used his right hand to shove Levi backward. The kid fell flat in the snow on the other side of the log with a startled little grunt. Jake stepped over it fast and straddled the boy, pinning him with his thighs, while Bo wriggled on his shoulder. He gave Bo a quick, light smack on his bottom. "Quit that before I drop you headfirst on the log," he warned.

Bo went still.

"So is this how you were going to bring this guy down?"

"Guess not," came Bo's voice from over his shoulder.

"You just surprised me," Levi complained. "If I wasn't surprised—"

"Point is, you were," Jake interrupted. He stood and let the boy up. He set Bo back on his feet.

Off in the distance, a helicopter was landing.

"Tell you what," Jake said. "Why don't you two wait until you're sixteen or so before you try something like this again?"

They were looking up at him with expressions he didn't like at all. Levi's reminded him a little of Katya. It was almost...adoring. In fact, in that moment, the boy looked a great deal like his mother all the way around.

"Come on," he said uncomfortably. "You guys have a bus to catch. Let's step on it. I'll race you back."

He let them get a good head start and jogged behind them, never quite catching up. He figured their pride had taken it in the teeth enough for one night.

Adam's bus wasn't at the house yet, but the whole settlement seemed to be. Jake stopped well short of the place. Bo went on without him, but Levi hesitated and turned back.

"What?" Jake scowled down at him.

The boy hugged him hard, fast, around the waist. *Ah, hell.*

"Go inside," he managed hoarsely. "I've got to go and meet that helicopter."

"Who's in it?"

"The FBI."

"Wow. I used to pretend I could be a spy if I could go to school," Levi said wistfully.

Jake's eyes narrowed. "How do you know about spies?"

"Matt Lapp's pa is from Berks. He's got kin over there. They go to big schools. *Real* schools. He told me 'bout spies. 'Course, you got to go to high school to be one. Probably even college, too. So I can't never be one."

"Can't ever," Jake corrected absently. The kid's words hit him hard.

Don't get sucked in here, he thought. *Don't do it.* But it was too late, and he knew it might have been for a while. Out of the blue, he heard Katya's voice again. *Now I'm in and they've closed all the doors. Sometimes I just want to dream.* A throbbing sensation began to develop at the back of his head. Free choice like hell, he thought. You could give people all the choices in the world, but if they were only familiar with one avenue, they would take that safe route time and again.

He wanted to save her. He wanted to save Levi and give him his dreams. And he was a man who had failed too miserably before to believe he could do so.

Jake abruptly turned away from Levi and went to the helicopter.

Katya watched from the upstairs window as Jacob brought the boys back. He stopped well short of the property, out on the road. She swallowed carefully against a lump in her throat. After everything else tonight, this was small, inconsequential. It shouldn't have bothered her, but it did.

He wasn't going to come inside. He was avoiding her.

She closed her eyes and hugged herself, leaning shakily against the glass. She'd intended to accept it with good grace, just as she had told Mariah. But it wasn't happening for the right reasons. She could have accepted it if Jacob had just moved on, but she thought he was probably steering clear of her now because of guilt, and that wasn't right at all.

He thought this was his fault, she realized, because he had taken her to Lancaster, had kept her from accompanying Sam to the pond. She knew it as certainly as if he had spoken it aloud. And, unless she badly missed her guess, Adam thought it was Jacob's fault, too. That was what she'd seen in his eyes downstairs, what she hadn't initially been able to identify.

She straightened abruptly. She had to talk to him, to both of them. Since Jacob was here, and Adam wasn't, she would tackle him first. But when she looked down at the road again, Levi was racing into the house and Jacob was gone. He had disappeared into the night like an animal of the darkness who couldn't bear the light.

"Looks like about a size ten Nike," Agent Ted Rizzel said, straightening away from the molded shoe print. "There's the brand right there, stamped into the sole. I guess you couldn't see it clearly before we molded it."

Jake let out a breath of relief. Not one of the fathers' prints, then. There had been the lingering, worrisome possibility that he might have made a mistake about that.

An Amishman in Nike shoes. He imagined they were black, so as not to stand out too incongruously. He guessed the kidnapper had chosen to wear them rather than real Amish boots, in case anything went wrong and he needed to run.

Jake eased to his feet, as well. He let out a ragged breath as he looked around. As far as physical evidence was concerned, the Feds had sewn things up here. They'd covered the entire area—or at least the one within their prescribed perimeter—and hadn't found anything else. And this time Jake considered that their perimeter included everything that needed to be included.

Snow began falling again. Soft, wet flakes this time. Big ones. They'd stay. Didn't matter, he thought. They'd gotten the prints and the evidence up.

He was all out of things to do. He shoved his hands in his pockets. It was time to go back to Adam's house. He started walking like a man going to meet his Maker.

Chapter 14

He had every intention of going straight to the sofa and staying there. He'd catch a little sleep. It was well past midnight, and he wanted to be back at the pay phone by no later than five.

He didn't want to see Katya. Couldn't bear to. He'd let her down. He couldn't bring her baby to her, and he couldn't approach her without him. And yet, somehow, he found himself standing at the foot of the stairs.

He looked up into the thick darkness on the second floor. The house was dead quiet. There was a stillness to the night, a waiting. But more than that, there was an absence of life, as though everyone had gone.

The children had left. Bo, with his stubborn Wallace chin, and Levi, with the weight of the world on his little shoulders. Delilah, who was scared of her own shadow, and Rachel, who'd lived much more than she should have in...what, ten years?

And baby Sam was still gone.

Katya would be up there alone. He knew better than to believe she was sleeping. He took the stairs one at a time, pausing on every step. There was nothing up here he wanted to get involved in, but he found himself at her door.

"Katie." He didn't knock, though that sound would have been no more intrusive in the quiet than his voice. He flinched at its echo in the upstairs hall.

She didn't answer.

Maybe she was sleeping after all. It was what he wanted for her, a brief respite from all this fear and helplessness and waiting. But he still didn't believe she'd be able to do it. He put his hand on the knob and eased the door open.

She was standing by the window, a quilt wrapped around her shoulders. It took him a moment to find her in the relative darkness. Something about her posture told him that she had been there for a very long time.

She heard the door open and spoke without turning around. "The children have left."

Jake cleared his throat. "Yeah. I figured that."

"I miss them already. I need them now, so badly."

I'm sorry. But that would be a stupid thing to say. Of course he was sorry. What comfort was that?

He needed desperately to be able to do something for her, and the one thing she had asked of him—the only thing she had ever asked of him and the thing he had promised to do— remained just out of his grasp.

"They're safer this way," he said finally. As far as comfort went, that was lame, too, but he didn't know what else to say.

Katya turned to look at him. "It was very kind of Adam to pay for the bus."

She wasn't going to ask him, he realized. He felt like a coward for the incredible relief that swept through him. She wasn't going to ask him about Sam. No doubt she knew that if there was anything, anything at all, he would have told her right away.

"I didn't want to come back until I could bring him with me," he heard himself say. The words came all the way up from his soul and they tumbled out of him fast. No one was more surprised by them than he was. "I kept doing the same things over and over, until there was nothing left to do. I kept doing busy work so I wouldn't have to come back here without him. So I wouldn't have to tell you that I hadn't found him yet. I would have done anything to have brought him home with me, Katie.''

"I know," she said simply.

There was a fire banked low in the hearth. The last glow from its embers was just enough to make her face shine. She'd been crying, he realized. He felt a hot fist clench around his heart and tear it right out of his chest.

"God, you should *hate* me!" he burst out suddenly.

Her eyes cleared into genuine surprise. "For what? For not bringing him back yet? You'll find him. We've just got to be patient. We must give it some time."

"Don't *do* that!" he shouted. He stepped quickly into the room, closing the door behind him for privacy. "For God's sake, Katie! You don't *know* that! Odds are, if things run true to form, I *won't* find him. No matter what I've figured out so far, something will go wrong, something will get screwed up, and he'll slide right through my fingers like sand!"

"I don't believe that."

"Well, you damned well better believe it so you can brace yourself for it!"

She only watched him, steadily and without censure. He felt himself grinding his teeth together, something he hadn't done since he was a kid.

There wasn't anything more he could say. He turned for the door.

"Do you think that if you hadn't taken me to the city, none of this would have happened?" she asked. "Jacob, that's purely ridiculous."

He stopped and turned to stare at her.

"If you hadn't taken me to the city, then I would have taken Sam to the pond," she agreed. "And then what do you suppose would have happened? Look at me, Jacob. *Look* at me. Do you think for even one moment that I could have stopped that man from snatching my child?"

Jake had trouble finding his voice. "I know that." That issue haunted him, tore him up inside with conflicting emotions. If she had been there, *maybe* Mills would have hesitated. He had waited until Deborah Stoltzfus was behind her line of sheets after all. Maybe Sam would still be here, because Katya's attention would have had been focused on him. In all likelihood, she would have been holding him.

But then, maybe, Mills would have hurt *her*.

"So now what?" she asked.

He brought his thoughts back to her. "I was going to catch an hour or two of sleep."

"There's nothing that can possibly be done in the meantime?"

He winced. "God, Katie, I wish there were. Believe me, I'd be out there doing it. But there's not. I know who's doing this now. The highway patrols in five or six states are looking for the car. I've gotten the guy's license plate number. The FBI has an interstate APB out on him. His home is covered. Assuming he ever goes back there, my buddy in New Jersey will grab him. So, no, there's nothing to do now but wait for someone to lay their hands on him."

But so much could go wrong, he thought again. Mills could abandon the Cadillac. The post offices were full of pictures of men who were wanted, who'd managed to elude the law for years and years. All Jake could do was pray that Mills wasn't smart enough to pull it off. And praying had never held him in particularly good stead before.

Katya was wearing that awed expression again. "How in the world did you ever manage all that?" she whispered.

He realized that she didn't know half of what had occurred tonight. Guilt tore at him all over again. There *were* things he could tell her. He had been so wrapped up in himself, he just hadn't thought.

He tried to tell himself he never shared all his cards, not even with the ChildSearch parents. It generally tangled up an investigation, having them overly involved. He always warned them to back off and let him do his job. He rarely shared, period. Why then, did he feel ashamed that he hadn't now?

Because in this instance, not telling Katie had been a decision based wholly upon not wanting to come back here sooner. Instead, he had sent Adam with vague messages about evidence that didn't tell the whole story. Because he was a coward. Because he hadn't known how to face her.

And that was just another way of letting her down.

"It's a long story," he said at last, carefully. "The skeleton helped. The candy wrapper fed into it. It just started to make sense that the same guy who killed Jannel has been snapping up your babies. And he lives in Jersey, and I've got a buddy over there who works with ChildSearch. He gave me the plate number. Police work is like that," he went on. "Sometimes I've gone round and round on a case for years, turning up nothing. Then one weird little *something* happens, and everything else starts falling into place. I call it the domino effect. It just takes one thing, one little push, to start the blocks toppling over. In this case, it was the body we fell on. A million-to-one long shot, but it happened, we found her, and then everything else started clicking together." Too late, he thought. Too damned late to save Sam. "Plus he got lazy this time," he added. "He left clues and witnesses at the pond."

"Ah," Katya said, clasping her hands together in front of her. "So Sam is…in New Jersey? Is that what you think?"

Jake's stomach rolled. It was always so easy for her to simplify things. "Not yet." And he could have been. It was only a three- maybe four-hour drive. "But Mills will have to turn up there sooner or later." He would *probably* turn up there sooner or later.

"Can we go there and wait?"

"For God's sake, Katie, we don't know how long it's going to take!"

"Oh. Well, then, I suppose I must wait here."

Suddenly he was angry again. "How the hell can you be so calm?" he demanded.

"I'm not. I'm simply functioning."

No, he thought, that wasn't entirely true. Oh, he didn't doubt that her heart was tortured. A piece of it was gone, missing, out there somewhere with Sam. But she was doing better than functioning. He'd come up here to give her what pathetically little he could, to make it *different* this time. And from the moment he'd set foot in her room, she'd been calming him, soothing him, instead.

"Ah, Katie," he said finally. "You make me feel so small."

"Small?"

And strong, he thought. Invincible. Worthwhile. Just because she seemed to believe in him.

He cleared his throat. "I should let you get some sleep."

"Please don't."

He scowled at her.

"I won't. I won't sleep. I can't." She thought of what she had told Mariah earlier about distracting her. And it had worked. There was only one way she was going to get through this. One way she could bear this intolerable waiting. "Could you do something for me?"

"Anything." Then he thought about it. "I can try," he amended. He'd made one too many promises tonight already.

Katya's heart pounded. "Could you make me forget for a little while?"

His heart stalled. His eyes narrowed. "What are you asking?"

"Could you make the next few hours pass in a...well, in a blur? Until something happens. Until you can go back out there and do something. Until I have something more to hold on to, some kind of *hope*."

His heart started beating again, slowly, cautiously. Hell, he probably wouldn't sleep, either. What was the sense of trying? "What did you have in mind?"

He wasn't making this easy. Her fingers twined together into a knot. "Would you touch me again?"

Jake felt the floor shift under his feet. "Touch you?" he repeated.

"The way you did this afternoon."

"Adam would come charging in here like a white knight, trying to save your honor," he said hoarsely. It was the first protest that came to his mind.

"How would he know?"

Because ten to one, he already knows I'm in here, Jake

responded silently. But damn him, he's not my keeper. Or hers.

Katya's face flamed. He didn't want to. He'd already changed his mind about her. She turned away, back to the window. "Never mind," she whispered. "Of course, you need your sleep. You—"

She broke off, her breath catching, as she felt him lift her hair from her nape and touch his mouth there. She hadn't even heard him cross the room. She turned back to him fast and chided herself helplessly as soon as she did, because her hair fell back into place and the moment was over.

"Jacob?"

"Katie, I've wanted you since I woke up with half a concussion and saw your face swimming above me," he said quietly. "You're selling yourself short again."

"I just—"

"You've got to stop that." If he didn't leave her with anything else, he had to fix that. "I know what you thought. You thought that when I touched you before it was a case of temporary insanity or something. That now I've come back to my senses. What did Frank tell you?" he demanded, his voice suddenly harsh. "No, don't bother. I think I know. He told you that no other man would want you."

Pain sliced through her.

"Do you know why Frank said that?" he went on. "To keep you under his thumb. To keep you *his*. Because if you believed in yourself, you might find it within yourself to fight him. Because if you thought somebody else might want you, you might find a way out, a way to leave him."

Her eyes widened. "But the *ordnung*—"

"*He* never believed in it, Katie!" he interrupted. "If he had, he could never have hurt you! Why should he believe it would stop *you* when he didn't respect it himself? Why would he have thought it would stop you from leaving him?"

"I...I don't know," she whispered, realizing it.

"Well, I do." Men like Frank Essler were the same world over, he thought. "You're beautiful, Katie. You're a beautiful woman. You're beautiful when you're wearing those plain dresses. And when your hair is pulled back, even though it never stays there. And in jeans, with your hair loose, you're a knockout." If he could give her nothing else, he resolved, he would give her this. "Don't believe him anymore, Katie. Don't do it. He was lying."

She began to tremble. "Pride is a sin."

"No," he said fiercely. "*No.*" He would never believe that. If that was what Frank Essler and her God had taught her, then they had effectively destroyed her. "Pride is nothing more than believing in yourself," he went on, "and *every* human being has the right to do that."

"You don't have to say these things."

He swore, frustrated. "I'm saying it because I'm scared to death to *show* you."

Her mouth opened in a little sound of surprise. Then she shook her head. "You're never scared, Jacob," she said, as she had once before.

But this time his answer was different. *I'm always scared.* And he had never fully admitted it, even to himself, until he met her and understood the true meaning of fear. In that moment, he knew why he had so desperately needed to steer clear of her from the start. He had worked long and hard to accept his own inadequacies. He had blamed himself and hated himself for letting down those he loved. And so he had fixed himself—or he thought he had. He had turned away from that puppy, knowing that to love it would mean destroying it. He had stopped making promises because there had been too many promises he had been unable to keep.

Katya wouldn't let him be that way. She wouldn't leave him alone. He had known from the start that she could reach past the barriers. Because she was beautiful, and he wanted her, but she wouldn't accept what he was trying to tell her about himself, wouldn't let him be the way he knew he had to be.

"I'm scared now," he managed to say.

"Why?" she whispered, stepping closer, searching his face.

"Because I'm not good enough for you. Because you deserve so much more than me, and you don't believe it."

She shook her head slowly, thoughtfully. "No. But I won't argue with you because I think you believe it."

She amazed him. Somehow, she just kept amazing him.

"It doesn't matter anyway," she went on.

Something jolted in the area of his chest. "Why not?"

"Because you're here, at least for now. And no one else, no other man, good or bad or otherwise, ever will be. I've accepted that."

"You don't know that," he said harshly, feeling the panic set in again.

Katya realized that she was utterly calm now. Her heart had stopped clamoring. That amazed her, but it made sense, too. So few things were within her ability to change. But she might be able to change his mind right now, about this.

She was tired of waiting for God to bestow favors and kindnesses. Too often, He was too busy to remember her and hear her pleas. She had realized tonight that she was more or less on her own. And maybe, just a little bit, she wanted to defy Him. She wanted to defy the upbringing that had brought her to this place in her life.

"No other *anner Satt Leit* man is going to come into my world, Jacob," she went on in a rush. "Someone like you arrives here so rarely. And no Amishman will ever touch me because in their eyes I will always be married. I want this *now*, Jacob. With you. While I have the chance. Please don't turn away from me and leave me with nothing forever."

He realized almost distantly that his hands weren't steady. There was a thrumming sensation in his chest. How the hell was he supposed to turn away from that?

He couldn't.

He went back to the door. Her heart plunged. Katya felt it virtually hit her heels. It hurt. It hurt so much more than she had thought it would. He must have been lying when he said she was beautiful. Otherwise, how—why—would he turn away?

But he only pushed the lock on the door.

He leaned back against it, watching her a moment. This was

wrong. He knew—God help him, he knew—that if he did as she asked, he'd only end up hurting her when he left.

He couldn't live with that.

But...the solution he had hit upon earlier in the department store came back to him. The criteria that would maybe make it all right. He could give her something. Maybe something as simple as what she had asked for—a short time of respite, time passing in a blur. Or maybe he could give her something bigger, like a belief in her own beauty and strength.

If he gave her that, he thought he might possibly be able to live with himself afterward. Or maybe, maybe, she would end up finally and fully destroying all the things he had ever believed about himself...if he let her come any closer, if he let her in.

Fear, he thought. It was there again, howling through his blood. It demanded that he leave *now.* Right now. Before everything could change. Before both of them were left with none of the things they needed. She needed her God, and he needed his own rigid rules of behavior, those tried-and-true guidelines that had grown out of his own years of hell.

"Jacob?" she whispered.

He crossed the room toward her. He didn't trust words or his voice. He placed his hands carefully on either side of her face and he kissed her.

For the longest time, for whole booming heartbeats, Katya had felt as though she were extending a handful of grain to a wild deer. She had felt his yearning—and that in itself was astounding, that he should yearn for *her.* She had felt his fear. She didn't understand it, and then she didn't need to. His lips were on hers and she could let herself breathe again.

She caught his wrists with her hands as his tongue swept her mouth. The quilt slid from her shoulders.

There was a certain desperation to his kiss this time, as though he thought he would be damned for every move he made now and couldn't help but make them. She shivered. Then he stopped and bent to retrieve the quilt that had fallen from her shoulders to the floor.

"You're cold."

"No," she whispered. "Leave it."

"But—"

"You must leave it. Pull it aside, Jacob. *Please*."

He stood, letting it dangle from his fingers, and looked at her oddly. Then he looked at the quilt. It was pale ivory, with large blue rings interwoven all over it.

He felt his throat tightening. He was confused by her urgency, and he hungered for her. Too much. Too easily. Because it was easier than arguing, he threw the quilt onto the bed.

She came into his arms hard and fast then, with a small cry, as though that was all she had been waiting for. So he kissed her again, because doing anything else seemed impossible.

Katya felt his fingers tense, tighten in her hair. His mouth was hard, almost bruising. Kissing him was delicious, heady, but he kept space between them, just a few inches. She slid her hands up his arms to his shoulders with the thought of drawing him closer.

She felt no fear. None at all. And she knew that that had less to do with trusting him than trusting herself to give him something. She wasn't sure what it was, but she sensed it within herself. So rarely was she able to give anything to anyone. *That* made her heart pound.

He still wore Adam's coat. She tried to push it off his shoulders. He finally dropped his hands from her face and shrugged out of it without taking his mouth from hers. He flung it away blindly. It landed on the floor near the door.

He was vaguely aware of that, as though it were blocking him from his sole avenue of escape. Then she nestled closer to him in the few seconds when he wasn't holding her. Her arms went around his neck. For a moment that felt like an eternity to him, his own arms stayed rigidly at his sides. His heart thundered.

If he kept his hands off her body, he was just kissing her. If he put his arms around her, he was lost. Restraint had never been his strong suit, yet now it was immense. It held him in a fierce grip…because he wanted so badly. And always, always, when he wanted, he turned away.

But what he wanted didn't usually pursue him, didn't generally hunt him down.

Her hands were in his hair now. Holding him, melding his mouth more firmly to hers. And she was pressing against him, and it seemed to him that he could feel every single part of her with equal intensity, all at once. The steady, relentless warmth of her. Her breasts pressed against his chest. Her thighs flush against his. He sensed rather than knew that she was standing on tiptoe.

His hands finally moved. He heard a groaning sound and realized it came from his own throat. His arms went around her waist. *He wanted.* He found himself with handfuls of her dress. *He needed.* His fist clenched and gathered the fabric at her hips, and he kissed her deeper, then he made a sound that might have been despair or rage. It didn't deter her. She didn't back off.

"Katie, what are you doing to me?"

She wasn't sure, but she knew she couldn't break their contact. It was as necessary as air. It was, perhaps, the first purely wonderful thing in her world. He pulled her dress all the way up, until it was pooled around her waist. And she knew then that she had been wrong that first day when he had tumbled her onto the bed—his hands *were* gentle. They cupped her bottom and she felt something growing inside her, trembling at first, then beginning to pound.

"Please touch me," she gasped. *"Please."*

Jake finally found his voice. "I've wanted to do this all day, ever since I saw you in those jeans, so tight, outlining every swell and curve." *But that didn't make it right.*

Heat spread up her chest to her neck, but it wasn't embarrassment. The way he said it only made everything pound inside her even more. "Then do it," she whispered.

His mouth came back to hers again, and there was a new urgency to his kiss. His hands moved, down to her thighs, up again, now sweetly, now dragging her into him. And even as she felt him grip her waist, even as she felt his thumbs slide under the elastic of her tights, she felt the hardness of him, too, pressing into her belly.

He wanted her. This wasn't just words, wasn't designed assurance. This was real. *One more good thing.* One more defiance against everything that was supposed to protect her, but had let her and her children down. She would take the one thing for herself that she wanted most of all. She wanted this man for as long as he would be here.

That was the precise moment when Jake felt her begin to tremble under his hands. It was the moment he forgot finesse. He forgot what it was to enjoy himself and give pleasure in return with happy nonchalance, that one part of himself always holding back, almost seeming to watch on. He craved. He ached. And he did it from the bottom of his soul.

He pulled her tights down a little too roughly and felt her gasp into his mouth. He was on a wild, desperate search for skin now, to feel the real heat of her, because maybe, just maybe, it might be the thing that would finally warm him. But she wore panties beneath the tights. There were a million barriers. Her dress kept trying to spill back down her hips unless he held it.

He finally let it fall. His hand fought with her apron. He found the tie at the back of her waist and he yanked at it. He was going to scare her and he knew it, but he couldn't seem to stop.

He wasn't scaring her. What Katya felt was a sweeping, incredible euphoria as she felt him unraveling, losing control. His mouth was hot and wet at her throat now. It slid to her jaw, then back again. She bent down and unlaced her shoes and when she stood again she felt the apron pool at her feet. Then his fingers were at the buttons on her back. He popped the first one easily, expertly, fumbled with the second, then he swore.

She reached to help him, but he was over the edge. She gasped again as he took the fabric in his hand and pulled. Buttons popped, scattering, and she felt the cool air kiss her back.

More barriers, he thought helplessly, as his fingers found her bra strap. Never in his life had he encountered a woman with so damned many clothes. The man he had been only an hour before would have laughed, would have enjoyed it. Now he was frenzied.

She was trying to help him. Their hands collided. She pulled out of the long, demure sleeves. His fingers caught the front of her collar and dragged the top of her dress down to her waist.

She thought she felt him make a sound in his throat. It was almost inaudible, a murmur against her mouth. Something shot through her, something liquid and almost debilitating, because his hand came back to skim the side of her breast. No, she decided, no. It didn't skim. It searched. And she wanted more. She wanted to feel his hand there fully.

But his hand stopped moving. Only his thumb moved along the ridges of her ribs. It felt better, warmer, made things squirm inside her, but...

More, she thought. *More.*

He finally found the hook at the back of her bra and tore it free. He flung it in the general direction of his coat, then bent to lift her in his arms. He carried her to the bed and remembered at the last moment to lay her upon it gently. Her eyes were wide and wondering as they flew over his face. What was she looking for? he asked himself. Would she find it? He found himself praying that she would, then he bent over her and claimed her mouth again.

Her hands were flung against the pillows, the quilt trapped beneath her, forgotten now. She used only her mouth to kiss him back. Something about that made him realize that he wasn't the one giving at all. It was her. She was giving herself to him, and all the sweet and pure simplicity that was her heart.

That made him all that much more determined to give something back.

He was kneeling over her. He eased down against her side, afraid to lay his full weight upon her, afraid to hurt her. His mouth followed her hairline, though she kept turning her face into his, searching for his lips with her own. His hand moved up her ribs to her breast. She gave a little cry.

It died in her throat as the most incredible sensation shot

through her. This, yes, this was what she had wanted. She wanted his palms on her skin, on her sensitive skin, not just her ribs. She wanted his hand right where it was, cupping her, a delicious feeling, so intimate, so astounding and powerful. He had calluses on his fingers, and her skin felt a little chafed by them, but in the most incredible way. When he moved his thumb over her nipple, circling it, teasing it, it was more than she could bear. She held herself very still and concentrated on it, anticipating its next full circuit, waiting until his thumb came around again...*right there.*

She shuddered. Then it struck her that she was naked from the waist up, while he was still dressed. She waited for embarrassment, almost managed to stiffen herself against it, because for a heartbeat, maybe longer, she remembered that she was too thin, flat-chested, and Frank had always said that she was about as alluring as a fence post. Then that fled from her mind because Jacob's mouth followed his hands and he did things to her that Frank had never done.

His mouth slid. His tongue stroked. It was delightful, so good, but then he did something even better. She felt his teeth close gently over her nipple, and she cried out, her back arching off the bed as though some wanton, hidden woman inside her had come alive for the first time. And somehow her hands were in his hair, holding him against her. She felt his tongue and cried out again, mindless. His mouth left her breast abruptly and he returned for another kiss.

"Shhh," he whispered against her lips.

He did it with his last moment of clarity, of sense, the last remnant of his control. They had to be quiet. There were other people upstairs. Then she was wriggling against him, and he was lost.

He dragged at her dress again, trying to get it down over her hips. Then his mouth went back to her body, but not where she wanted it. She wanted him at her breast again, but this time his tongue touched her nipple only briefly, enough to make it spring up and ache for more. Then his mouth trailed down her ribs, warm and wet. His hands held her hips. His tongue slid along the elastic waist of her panties, then it touched her abdomen through the fabric.

This time she couldn't have stopped herself from crying out if lightning had come down from heaven and struck her into silence. His mouth closed over her through the cotton and the heat of his kiss flashed through her from that intimate point of contact. His mouth stayed, gentle, sweet, coaxing something from her.

No, not from her, she realized. *In* her. Urgency throbbed inside her now, and she found her hands in his hair again, holding him. She heard her own voice—was it *her* saying those things?—pleading, whispering, begging for more.

He had to draw a line, he thought again, had to fix on some point beyond which he would not go. Instead, he slid a finger beneath the elastic at her leg, sliding it along, down, down, savoring every tremor that rocked visibly through her with the anticipation. He looked up and saw that her eyes were huge, but she made no move to stop him.

Her reactions rained fire through his blood. Her soft cry filled his head, his soul. Her need weakened him and all his resolve.

His finger encountered the edge of soft curls, and her body bucked off the bed almost with a will of its own with just that hint of promise. He looked up into her face, her beautiful face. Her eyes were closed now.

"Okay?" he rasped and wondered what he would do if she said no.

"Please," she whispered huskily. "Again. More."

He let his fingers slide farther beneath the nylon. It would be okay, he told himself, perfectly okay, as long as he didn't take her panties off. He found the center of her and slid into heat. She cried out again and moved her hips against him instinctively. He stroked and watched her unravel. Her hands were back in his hair, clutching, then somehow he was using his mouth again, though he hadn't intended to, his tongue sliding along the edge of the nylon this time. He made a sound of frustration and eased the fabric aside. She groaned a little and opened to him without even seeming to realize she did it.

He touched his mouth to her over and over and felt her unravel even more beneath his touch.

His hand dragged at the nylon, pulling it down. He slid her panties as far as her thighs, and he told himself that was okay, too, because he could pull them right back up again. He combed his fingers through blond curls and found he needed to taste her, needed it as much as he had ever needed anything else in his life. So he used his tongue once more—gently, he'd be gentle—but then he found himself using more pressure because her responses were without guile, without shame.

She began pulling at his shirt.

"Lie back," he said roughly. "Just lie back and let me touch you." But it was as though she hadn't heard him.

Katya chose not to hear him. She would not be told what to do. Not now, not in this most priceless moment. She found the buttons of his shirt, freed one, then another. She gave a smile of pure feminine triumph when he groaned and stopped fighting her, stopped trying to push her hands away. And finally she got his shirt off his shoulders, finding skin. He shrugged the rest of the way out of it and let it fall off the side of the bed to the floor.

She had loved his body from the first time she had crept in on him while he was sleeping. Had she wanted this even then? Perhaps, but she had not ever dared to believe it might happen. She skimmed her palms over his chest almost fervishly. And his skin was smooth and warm. She let her thumbs find his nipples as he had done to her and gave a husky sigh of pleasure when they sprang up, too.

She wanted more. She found his belt, tugged, and his hand came down almost hard on hers again.

"No, baby, no," he murmured. "Leave well enough alone."

Was he saying they should *stop?*

She rooted for his mouth again, found it, pleaded with him silently. *Don't take this away. Don't make this be over.* His hand fell away from her wrist. She pulled at his belt again and this time he didn't stop her.

There had to be a line, he thought again, desperately, and

he struggled to find one, a point beyond which he *definitely* would not go. He felt as though he were sinking in quicksand, but warmth surrounded him and it was too seductive. When she began struggling to get his jeans off, he let her. As long as he kept his briefs on, that was okay. But he wanted to feel her against him, wanted skin to skin. So he finally pushed her panties the rest of the way down and gathered her to him even as she kicked them off.

She thought that perhaps this was what heaven would be like. The heat of his skin was everywhere, his arousal hard against her, and she was able to not think of anything at all in that moment except sensation. She did not think of Sam, of the little ones she'd been forced to send away. She did not think of Frank or Adam or Mariah. She had never believed that peace could be so volatile, that respite could ignite.

If she thought at all, it was of the *ordnung* she would defy, of taking something back for herself from the religion that would destroy her, and she was so very, very glad she had.

She wrapped her legs around him, holding him, and he murmured something against her neck, some kind of protest, but it wasn't clear anymore, even to him. He tried to remember why he had needed lines. He hadn't come in here to seduce her. He wasn't prepared. He didn't want to hurt her. And he wanted her too much.

He peeled his briefs away. Her skin tasted like honey and salvation. Her mouth was hope. Before he could start reminding himself of all the reasons he wouldn't, all the reasons he shouldn't, he heard himself murmur, "Please."

"Yes. Oh, yes."

"I can't—"

"We must."

"I didn't—"

"It doesn't matter."

So he let himself sink into her heat. It was too easy, too necessary. She sighed and melted around him. And he never wanted to go.

He hadn't come in here to seduce her. She had captivated

him. He wasn't prepared. He was much less worried about protecting himself than protecting her.

He didn't want to hurt her. But she moved against him, with him, and finally, this once, there was no pain for either of them.

He moved inside her, slowly at first, then harder and faster, still watching her face, watching a beautiful light build and dawn in her eyes. He felt heaven erupt. It was a place of raining stars. He stiffened against the urgent need to fall into them, into utter release. He needed to wait, needed to make it good for her, too. Then he felt the delicate spasm of her body, and he let himself go.

Chapter 15

There was no panic afterward, and that surprised him. There was no urgent necessity to get away fast now that ardor had faded. Probably because it hadn't, not entirely. His mouth still felt warm where it had touched her. His head was still filled with her scent. His blood still rushed, his heart still pounded.

He needed to talk about it. He was a man who had always avoided feeling too much. Now that it was happening, that he was feeling long after he should no longer be, he needed to tame it with words. Maybe lazy words, maybe cocky words, just…something. But in that moment, a fist began pounding on the door like a jackhammer.

"Damn it, Jake, open the door," Adam grated quietly. "Before I wake Mariah."

Panic was followed by fury, then resignation. Jake finally rolled to face Katya. "He gave us longer than I thought he would."

Her eyes were still luminous. Her skin was still dewy and flushed. She met his eyes evenly, as if she knew and understood everything in his soul.

The room got warmer. His blood rushed harder. His head hurt.

She did not look embarrassed. If it appalled her that his brother had virtually caught them in the act, it didn't show. There was a fierce frown between her eyes, but it was one of...anger, he realized.

She always surprised him.

"How *dare* he?" She sat up quick and fast. She was about to shout something in the direction of the door. Jake realized it just in time and clapped a hand over her mouth.

"Want me to punch him?" he asked in an undertone.

She looked at him over his hand and nodded. He took his hand away. And in spite of everything, he laughed quietly.

"Okay. I owe him one." He remembered the scene at the pond and corrected himself. "Make that two."

He got to his feet. Katya had one more precious moment to savor. She watched him scoop his jeans off the floor where they had fallen and step into them. There was something so masculine and titillating about the way he zipped, buckled, moved shirtless to the door. He raked his hair back with his fingers as he moved. She shivered in a needy way, as though she had never felt replete just moments ago. Then she briefly closed her eyes.

Oh, it was going to be hard this time. It was going to be so hard to let this little bit of heaven go.

Jake only cracked the door. She scurried quickly off the foot of the bed, out of view, at the last possible moment, taking the quilt with her. She wrapped it around her shoulders. Then she realized what she had done, looked down at it and gasped.

Jake looked back at her, and his heart did something odd. It felt almost as though it rolled over. "What?" he demanded. "What the hell is it about that thing?"

She seemed to go pale. "I don't believe you want to know."

"Try me." He closed the door again, and Adam started pounding on it harder. "Just a minute!" he shouted at him.

"The circles," she whispered. "They're...wedding rings."

"Okay." His voice was even, but his heart skipped a beat.

"Wait a minute. I read something about that pattern somewhere."

"It's magic. Oh, Jacob, I'm so sorry. I *told* you to put it somewhere else!"

He stared at her a moment, then his heart steadied. Magic. He laughed a little, surprising both of them. "It's okay, Katie."

"No. No, it's not. You don't understand!"

"I don't have to. I don't believe in magic."

"But there's a *spell* on it! A powerful one. Oh, Jacob, it's centuries old, and it's always been used for bundling—"

"For *what?*" Impossibly, in spite of everything, he was having a hard time keeping a straight face. One look at hers told him he had to.

"Bundling," she whispered. "It's an old Amish custom. It just means sleeping together—*only* sleeping together—before two people marry."

He was beginning to understand. And he thought of a way to put her fears to rest. "Katie," he said quietly, "we didn't *only* sleep together. Honestly, we didn't sleep at all."

"But…"

Then the reason for her obvious fear hit him. He felt overwhelmed, touched in a place he had closed off from the world so long ago. She wasn't afraid for herself. She was afraid for him. She was afraid that that silly quilt was somehow going to take away his choices, force him into loving her, staying with her. And that was so purely selfless, it rocked him. But then, she was like that.

"Mariah had it," she went on, her voice breaking. "She and Adam—"

"I'm not Adam," he said gruffly, even as the pounding on the door started again. "Katie," he said carefully, "I can't marry you. That's not…my kind of thing."

If he feared he would hurt her with the words, he realized then that he should have known better. She rushed on without seeming to hear him.

"Mariah gave it to me to use because I didn't…I hardly brought anything when I ran from Frank. And we both thought it would be safe with me. Because I certainly wouldn't be bundling in it—"

"Katie," he broke in again, "we didn't bundle." It was just a damned quilt, he told himself. It was just fabric. He finally turned back for the door, not sure why it left him feeling so unsettled.

Katya watched him, feeling helpless and breathless, then she looked down again at the quilt around her shoulders. For a moment, she thought it entirely possible she might faint.

"She thinks I should hit you," she heard Jake say flatly. "I'm willing to oblige. Where the hell do you get off thinking this is any of your business?"

Then she heard Adam's voice come back, and everything inside her went painfully still. She forgot about the magic wedding-ring pattern.

"Sam's my business," Adam snapped. His voice was wire tight with control. "This settlement and what's happening to it are my business. There's a local cop downstairs at the door. He says a senior detective from the Atlantic County barracks in New Jersey is trying to get through to you. They've picked up Devon Mills. Letting you know that is *my business*."

Jake's blood instantly roared.

Gone was the lingering goodness, even the confusion, of a few moments ago. This was hot, fierce, furious. He wanted Devon Mills. He wanted to kill him with his bare hands. He wanted to fulfill his promise.

"Sam?" he bit out, already grabbing his shirt. "Do they have Sam?"

"No," Adam answered, and there was real pain in his voice. "He wasn't with them."

Katya cried out.

Jake was halfway into one sleeve. He let it dangle and went back to her. "Hey, easy." His voice changed. Even he heard it. It went soft, coaxing, gentle. "This is something, baby. He dropped Sam off somewhere, that's all. And I swear to you and your God that I'll pound the information out of him if he won't tell me willingly."

He let go of her shoulders and looked back at Adam. "I'll

need some more cash. My bank account is pushing empty. I need to rent a car to get over there."

Adam nodded and backed away from the door. "I'll meet you downstairs."

Jake finished dressing. Katya picked up her dress and slipped into it, then she stood rooted, her apron still dangling from her hand. She finally threw it away with a high-pitched sound of disbelief. "Why am I putting this on to just...just *wait?*" she cried.

"I don't know," Jake answered honestly, going to her again. He drew her into his arms. "As soon as I know anything, the minute I know anything, I'll get word to you somehow."

"Yes." She trembled. "I know you will. It will still seem like forever. I hate the waiting the most."

Jake made a strangled sound. That was the single thing that had had them tumbling onto that bed in the first place, he realized. It had nothing to do with yearning. Nothing to do with need. Not at first. Then, in the explosion of a heartbeat, everything had changed. He couldn't think about that now.

"We're closing in," he went on. "We've got him. It's just one more step to getting Sam."

His mind was already racing ahead. The fool had been stupid enough to go back to New Jersey. But then, he probably hadn't known that Adam was still here in the settlement, that Jake himself had made the trip up. He didn't know that he was tangling with the same two men who'd tracked him down the first time, last month.

"I've got to go," he said hoarsely. He closed his eyes, grazed his mouth over her hair. She reached up suddenly and caught his face in her hands. She kissed him hard.

"For luck," she said.

He stepped back from her unsteadily. *For luck.* For things to be different this time. For him to win, finally win, finally do something.

He left the room without another word. Adam was downstairs pacing the kitchen. Coffee was on. Mariah was nowhere to be found. By Jake's best calculation, it was maybe four o'clock in the morning. Some cash was sitting on the table. Jake took it and shoved it into his wallet.

"I'm out of here," he said, turning for the door.

"Not so fast," Adam growled.

Jake shot him a warning look. "Not now. There's a kid missing—"

"You've already used that excuse—earlier, out by the pond. It won't fly this time."

"Sam's still out there." Jake's voice went threatening. "And we don't know where yet."

"Mills knows, and Mills is in custody. He's not going anywhere. At least not in the extra five minutes this will take. You're damned well going to stand still and listen to me, Jake. I mean it."

The rage came out of nowhere. It actually turned the edges of his vision red. Jake crossed back to his brother. This time he didn't lay a hand on him. He didn't dare. He didn't trust himself.

"This is none of your business," he said for what felt to him like the thousandth time. What the hell was wrong with his brother these days? "Back off. *Now.* She doesn't want you poking your nose into this, and neither do I."

"Are you coming back?" Adam countered.

"When? After I'm finished in Jersey?" But already his pulse had started to thrum. Already panic began cavorting in his stomach again. He could have dealt with any question but that.

"Or are you going to head straight on back to Texas?"

"My problem, my decision," Jake snapped.

"Not this time. I'll be damned if I'm going to stand by and watch you hurt this particular woman."

"It's none of your business!" Jake roared.

"Mine is the only sane head in this household!" Adam shouted back. "Even Mariah thinks I should butt out! But I know you, Jake. I'm the only person left in this world who does. And I know what you're going to do now. You're going to do the only thing you've ever been good at. You're going to run."

It hurt. It really hurt. Jake stepped back from his brother's words. "That's not true," he said finally.

"Isn't it?"

"I'm a damned good cop."

"The hell you are. If you were a damned good cop, you'd be *doing* something with all the knowledge you've gleaned over the years. You wouldn't be horsing around in a low-paying job, turning down most every promotion, turning down the FBI and God knows who else has tried to hire you over the years. You'd take over ChildSearch."

"Don't start on that," Jake warned. "Don't you dare rake up the whole ChildSearch thing! You're just looking for an easy way out there, bro. You've bitten off more than you can chew, supporting ChildSearch and two houses in Texas, and a new wife and a kid, and five more mouths to feed besides with Katie and her kids! You can't afford to run the whole damned show anymore, so you're looking for a way to back out without losing face!"

"You stupid damned fool," Adam snarled. "I've already listed the houses for sale. I want to give you ChildSearch because you *are* ChildSearch. You always have been."

Jake turned hard for the door again. "I don't have time for this now."

"Then make time for this! Either one or two things just happened upstairs. Either that meant nothing to you, not a damned thing, and she was just a port in a storm—in which case, you won't come back. Or it *did* mean something to you, it meant *a lot* to you, and that scares the hell out of you so you *still* won't come back. You'll run. Again."

Jake's face hardened. "We still haven't cleared up the question of where you get off thinking this is your business," he said with careful control.

"Because I care about both of you," Adam said more quietly. "Especially you. You're it, Jake. You're my family. My blood. The only blood I've got left, except Bo. And I've come to learn lately that that means a lot."

A shifting pain hit Jake's chest. He'd thought that, too, before that cop had found him at Mariah's house and told him Adam was married.

"Tell you what, bro," he sneered. "Why don't you spare me this garbage and go upstairs and play house with your wife? *There's* your family."

"What's the matter, Jake? Are you ticked off because I found peace and you're too scared to take a grab at it?"

"Don't make me hit you."

"It seems to me that you were the one who said we were getting too old for that, just a few weeks ago in Texas."

Jake stared at him. "You're *trying* to make me lose it, aren't you?"

Adam didn't even hesitate. "Yeah, I am. Because I want to know why. I want to finally hear the truth. I want to know why you're going to do this to that really good woman upstairs, because maybe if I understand, I won't end up hating you for it."

"Because I'm no good for her."

The words slid out of him too easily. Jake realized he was closer to the edge than he'd thought. And his brother *had* shoved him right over.

Or maybe he'd been teetering there for a while.

Adam stared at him. He opened his mouth to argue, then something in Jake's eyes silenced him. He believed it, Adam realized, dumbfounded. *"Why?"* Adam asked at last.

"Ten minutes ago, you were trying to convince me of the same thing. I've got to go."

"Not yet."

"I've got to go to New Jersey."

"Don't run this time, damn it!" Jake had opened the back door. Adam leaned around him and slammed it shut again.

"This is going to come to blows, isn't it?" Jake asked levelly, without turning around. His voice was strained. It vibrated with the effort to keep his tone flat.

"Why?" Adam asked again.

Silenced stretched out, flattening the air with its weight.

"I can't believe you even have to ask me that," Jake answered finally. He kept speaking to the door. "Look around you, Adam. Open those love-struck eyes! Look at what we are! *Remember* what we are. We don't belong here. We're just a couple of poor kids from the wrong side of some Texas tracks, and we've lived with all the ugliness that went along with that every day of our lives. Now you think God's going to save you or something." He had thought the same thing upstairs. Briefly. Very briefly. He had to convince himself he knew better. "There are no happily-ever-afters in this world, bro," he finished. "Not for the likes of us."

"That's not true."

"Sure it is."

"I won't buy it. You're better than our beginnings. Hell, you're a man who regularly maxes out his own credit card trying to help kids he doesn't even know."

And in that moment, incongruously, Jake remembered what had happened to the missing ninety dollars from his checking account. He'd used it for a cash tip to pay off an informant in the Amber Calabrese case. A ChildSearch case.

That infuriated him. Because it made his brother right.

He turned back to Adam fast and hard. "Because I didn't do it the first time!" he shouted.

"What?" Adam asked blankly.

"I have to save those kids because I didn't do it the first time. Now will you let me get the hell out of here?"

"There was nothing you could have done," Adam said carefully.

Jake made a sound of disgust. "There was plenty I *should* have done. When I was eight and you were nine, I cringed in that bed with you, listening to our father beat the holy hell out of Mom. I didn't get up and go in there and *do something*. I could have created some kind of diversion, set the lawn on fire, something to take his attention off her, but I didn't. When Kimmie was six and I was fifteen, I stood there in the doorway of her bedroom and watched him bounce her off the walls, and when I tried to stop him, he laid me flat. He knocked me out cold. I helped a lot then, didn't I? Kimmie finally had to run off with a broken heart and a broken arm to save herself. And you have to ask me *why?* The only things I've ever saved in thirty-seven rotten years were the things I didn't let myself have, the things I didn't let myself love!''

Adam was shocked.

"No," Jake went on quietly, angrily. "I won't come back. Happy now? You wanted to hear me say it? There it is, bro. *I'm not coming back.* Trust me on this one—the best thing I can do for that woman is keep going. If I hang around here too long, sooner or later I'll let her down. I got lucky this time, bro—I had enough contacts to reel Mills in. But if I stay too long, I'll end up promising something I can't give her. At least now I have a chance to set the first screwup straight. At least now I have a chance to find her kid. And if I can do that, then yeah, I'll quit while I'm ahead.''

Adam finally found his voice. "Why you? Why not me? You blame yourself for cringing in that bed while Mom got hit. But that makes no sense. She chose to stay. She wouldn't leave. And I was there *with* you, Jake. Why are you pulling all this down on your own head? There were other responsible parties. Why not me? I was the oldest. *I* should have done something.''

Jake shook his head in disgust. "You were always the one with the heart. You *bled,* Adam. You felt too much, cared too much, and you always believed in miracles. Look at the whole business with Bo! He was gone for four years and you never gave up! I was the cocky one, the tough one." He paused. "I was the one who was always shooting my mouth off and saying I was going to do something. But *I never did.*''

"What could you have done, Jake? Come on, be reasonable.''

"I should have taken that goddamned shotgun down off the living-room wall and blasted him clear to hell with it," he snarled. "Man, don't you *see?* Don't you get it? I had a thousand opportunities, a thousand chances to make it right, and that shotgun just kept sitting up there, gathering dust.''

"Because you're not a killer!''

"No." He said it flatly. "I'm a coward.''

He turned away again. This time he opened the door. And Adam didn't slam it shut.

"You watch over her, Adam," he finished quietly. "*You* do it. You love it here. It's in your eyes. And I know that you love your wife. Hell, I've fought admitting it for days, but she's a fine lady. So stay with her. Take your chances that things can be different from what we've always known. You've got the heart for it. I don't. Just watch over Katie. Don't let that bastard of a husband come back to hurt her."

Jake went outside. He had stepped down off the porch and took two long strides, then he stopped to speak without looking back. "Just for the record, you were right the second time. What happened upstairs did mean something to me. It meant a lot to me, and yeah, that scares the hell out of me."

He began walking again.

Chapter 16

Katya crept soundlessly up the stairs. She met a sleepy Mariah on the landing. Her friend reached out for her.

"Katya, what's happened? I heard shouting and your face is *white*."

Katya stepped carefully past her without answering. She slipped into the bathroom, leaned weakly against the sink and promptly got sick. Finally, feeling shaky and empty, she slid down to sit on the floor.

As soon as she had known that Jacob and Adam weren't discussing Sam, she should have retreated. Or at the very least, she should have interrupted and made them aware of her presence. But she'd known somehow that if she had, the things that had been said would never have been spoken. There had been a raw intensity to their argument that had been too powerful to interfere with. It had been a private moment between them, one she had no place in.

So she should have gone away. But she had stood rooted. She had stayed and listened, and now, when she finally cried, she did it mostly for the boy Jacob had been.

I was the cocky one, the tough one. I was the one who was always shooting my mouth off. This time, she knew, *he'd* sold

himself short. Because a boy who was only cocky, only shooting off his mouth, would not have felt such pain at being
unable to do anything. He would not have chastised himself
over it for so very long. She'd lived ten years with a man who
was cocky and all talk with no substance. She certainly knew
the difference.

*You wanted to hear me say it? There it is, bro. I'm not
coming back. I'll quit while I'm ahead.* She cried out a little
without realizing it.

She had known that, of course. She had known from the
look in his eyes when the loving was over. And when they
had spoken about the quilt. There had been panic there, not
immediately, but flickering, then building. So, Katya thought,
it really was over this time.

She took in a shuddering breath of almost overwhelming
sorrow. And loss. Yes, there was the selfish ache of loss there
also. Because she had discovered something incredible in his
arms last night and she was never going to be able to reclaim
the feeling again. She'd found a dizzying feminine power
within herself. A vast reservoir capable of giving and receiving
pleasure. She'd discovered love.

She covered her face with her hands. Should she also feel
shame? she wondered. What she had done was so terribly
against the *ordnung*. She'd loved a man who was not her husband. She'd revelled in it, enjoyed, had needed it fiercely. That
shook her down to her core—but with awe, with wonder, not
regret. Jacob had been right. The quilt would not work its
magic on them. Because what they had done, what they had
shared, was so much more than what anyone else had ever
shared upon it before. Of that she was sure.

In any event, she would be punished for it. She would have
to let it all go, would have to put it behind her, and that would
hurt her as much, if not more, than anything had ever hurt her
before in her life. Still, it was necessary. She would have to
think clearly, not emotionally, if she was going to do the right
thing now. For Adam and Mariah. For her children. For
ChildSearch.

And for herself.

Hugging herself, shivering, she replayed in her mind the
conversation she had overheard. She smiled weakly. Yes, she

knew what she would have to do. She could no longer keep
relying on Adam and Mariah. If Adam had to continue supporting her and her family, he would not have any money left
to put into ChildSearch. And if she had learned one thing loud
and clear from Jacob in all these many days, it was that that
company meant something to him. It gave him something ir-
replaceable, something no one or nothing else could give. It
gave him a sense of self-value, of doing something for the
powerless and the lost, that he needed desperately. It was,
perhaps, the first thing he had done right in his whole life, she
realized, at least in his own mind. She knew differently. He
had also given her herself.

So she would use that precious gift and she would save
ChildSearch. And she would give her children a life, vistas,
opportunities in the process. She would leave the settlement
and start over.

When the sun finally began to creep up over the horizon,
Katya got to her feet again and went back to her room. She
felt shaky, strangely empty. And Jacob's words kept echoing.
*You've bitten off more than you can chew, supporting
ChildSearch and two houses in Texas, and a new wife and a
kid, and five more mouths to feed besides!* She groaned and
pressed her palms to her cheeks. No more. Mariah and Adam
did not even have a farm. They did not have chickens to provide eggs. They did not have cows to provide milk, a garden
to offer fresh vegetables. Adam had been actually purchasing
every morsel she and her children put in their mouths. If she
did not do something to rectify that, Adam's company would
fold.

No more. She was tired of relying upon a God who did not
answer her prayers. It was time she relied upon herself.
Enough. She ripped off her dress and flung it to the floor.
Then she grabbed it again because she didn't want to leave
Mariah anything to clean up. She wished more than anything
for the jeans and the sweater she had lost. Her purple Church
Sunday dress would have to do.

She left her hair down. She did not bother with an apron.
She found an old satchel in the closet and she stuffed it full
of one change of clothing for each of her children. Then she

carefully folded the wedding-ring quilt and laid it neatly upon her pillow.

There was one last thing she needed. The idea of taking money—more money—from Adam and Mariah made her head pound and her throat burn. But there was no help for it. When the house got quiet and she thought Adam and Mariah had left, she crept back downstairs. She took the grocery money Mariah kept in a little cookie jar on the kitchen counter. She found a notepad and a pencil and scribbled an explanation and a vow to someday, somehow, pay it back.

Two hundred dollars. Would it be enough? She wasn't sure. She had no choice anyway but to *make* it be enough. She had no way of getting more and she really didn't have to go very far. She thought briefly of waiting. Of planning. Of saving money. But she made no money to save, had no way of earning any here. And if she waited, this burning urgency she'd just discovered within her might fade again. It would be so easy to keep hiding behind Adam as she had been, too weak and too stupid to change.

She let herself out the back door. Then she hugged herself hard and marched toward the road, the little satchel slung over her shoulder.

Jake was firing on pure adrenaline. And caffeine. He'd had two cups of coffee before he'd even left the rental car place in Lancaster, another three on his drive to the other side of the Delaware River and into New Jersey.

"Where is he?" he demanded as soon as he stepped into the state police barracks in Toms River. Ernie was in the lobby and he turned to look at him sharply.

"Same place he's been since two this morning, pal. Right this way."

Jake's stomach rolled. *Two this morning.* They had maybe eighteen hours, then. The law said they could hold him for questioning for twenty-four. So they had eighteen hours in which to charge the bastard with something or set him free. To get information and a confession.

"I told my boss you were working in tandem with the Federal guys," Ernie said. "Back me up if they ask you."

"Sure." Then Jake swore. "A good lawyer will have any confession I get tossed right out of court. I don't have jurisdiction."

"So I'll go in with you. It'll be our word against his. We'll say you were just a bystander and *I* badgered the truth out of him."

"Good enough." Gray areas, Jake thought. They were necessary too damned often. *That* was why he hadn't moved up in the ranks with the Dallas P.D. He couldn't handle the politics, the focus of a spotlight that showed up every glaring and iffy procedure.

If you were a damned good cop...you wouldn't be horsing around in a low-paying job....

Damn Adam to hell, he thought angrily. Damn him for putting all these doubts in his mind.

"We didn't find a thing in his house," Ernie said. "No trace of where the kids have gone. Nothing except seventy thousand or so in cash stuck under a floorboard."

"The going rate for a healthy, Caucasian baby," Jake snarled, feeling sick.

"Maybe. Or at least a portion of it anyway. I suspect some has already gone up his nose in the form of cocaine. He was wired when we got him." They went down a hallway and stopped in front of a closed door. "You need to calm down, man," Ernie warned.

Jake looked at him sharply. "I'm calm."

"You look like you've been through the third world war. Alone. Without the rest of us grabbing guns to help out."

Jake scrubbed a hand over his unshaven jaw. "I haven't slept."

"Jake, I don't know what kind of a personal stake you've got in this and I don't have to know what it is, but you can't get too ugly with this guy. Not with all these people around to hear him holler."

Jake's smile was chilling. "No one will hear a blessed thing."

Ernie followed Jake inside the room.

Somehow, here, Jake finally felt the jolt. It hadn't happened in either Lancaster or on the drive here. Maybe he'd been numb then, he thought. Maybe he'd still been thinking about what had happened with Katie. *Dear God, he'd let himself fall in all the way.* He hadn't stopped. He hadn't drawn a line. And he was terrified.

Running again. Running.

Deal with Mills. Find Sam.

He just had to find her kid and go home, get out. It had turned into a pounding, driving urgency. But all he could feel in this room was the vast *difference* between her world and his own. Technology—a multiline phone, a fax machine, a coffeemaker, a bottled water dispenser—versus humanity, he thought. Justice walking a fine line versus the heartache of parents who had lost everything precious in spite of their strict and devout ways.

Katie.

Mills was seated at a long table in the center of the room. His eyes slid over Ernie and settled on Jake. Jake tried hard to take Ernie's warning to heart, to appear calm. But the menace in his eyes must have shown through because the guy shot to his feet and backed up fast.

"Who're you?" Mills demanded.

"I'm the guy who put your picture on the Internet so that Ernie could haul your sorry backside down here last month," Jake said harshly. "Remember that? You were telling us all about Linda Porter." That had been Jannel's real name.

Mills's eyes rolled a little. "Oh, man. Linda's guy."

"Nope. That was my brother. I've just been helping him out with a little problem some of his friends have developed over on the other side of the river."

"Yeah?" Mills watched him suspiciously.

"Yeah." Jake's hand flashed out. He caught Mills by the collar. The man squealed like a stuck pig as Jake lifted him off his feet and drove him back against the wall. He held him that way without flinching, the shorter man's feet dangling off the floor. He did not feel the strain in his muscles. Adrenaline and five cups of coffee did not let him feel anything at all.

Except panic, he thought. Except rage. And loss. He'd left her only hours ago, and already there was loss.

Got to find Sam. He *was* a damned good cop. And this time he would not fail.

"I'm sort of in a dangerous frame of mind right now, Mills.

You might want to bear that in mind. See, I had a fight with my brother earlier today and it dredged up a lot of things I'd really rather just forget. Things like a man I *should* have killed and didn't. I'd be just as glad to make amends by putting an end to you.''

Mills opened his mouth and closed it again. ''I want a lawyer.''

''Yeah? Think you can get one over here in the next ten seconds? That's about all you've got until I throttle you.''

''This ain't legal!''

''Neither's stealing kids, you bastard.'' He pushed him harder against the wall, then glared at him. ''There's one other thing I forgot to mention.''

''What?'' Mills gasped, obviously not sure if he should be hopeful or scared.

''That kid you just took? The most recent one. It just so happens that he's the son of a lady I care a lot about.''

Mills opted for scared. His face blanched. ''All right!'' he shouted.

Jake dropped him to his feet in disgust. ''Where's Sam Essler?''

''Who?''

''Don't push me, Mills. *Sam Essler.* The last kid you took.''

''I didn't say I took no kids.''

Jake shot a look at Ernie. ''I'm going to kill him.''

''Wait, wait!'' Mills shouted. ''You're like wanting a confession out of me or something, right?''

''He's so smart it's scary,'' Jake said to Ernie.

Mills was trying to circle around the table, trying to put it between them. Jake grabbed his collar and hauled him back. He shoved him hard into a chair.

''Sit down,'' he snarled. ''Here's the thing, Mills. One way or another, you're a dead man. You're either going to push me until I snap and you'll die here and now, or we'll play this whole thing out in court. That could take months, years. You know the FBI is in on this thing? You've got the attention of the big boys now, Mills. They *all* want you. Let's see, we've got murder one—I found Jannel's body, by the way. It was a good hiding place, but not good enough. I...''

Suddenly, treacherously, his mind went blank. He thought

of the way they had found Jannel. Of the way Katya had kissed him that first time he'd let himself touch her. The first time he'd crossed the line.

He tasted her again. He caught her scent again—it was as though she had just stepped into the room, the air stirring around her.

"What?" Mills demanded. "You what?"

Jake tried hard to focus on him. *He had to find Sam.* Nothing else mattered. But his mind stayed blank.

"They can't get me on murder one," the man went on. "You got a body. Big deal. Doesn't mean I killed her."

Jake shook his head to clear it. "Yeah, well, we've got a special forensics team working on what's left of her right now. If you did, we'll know it within a few hours. Personally, I'll put my money on a murder conviction."

Mills paled a little.

"Hey, now I remember where we were," Jake went on. "Besides murder one, you've got five charges of kidnapping across state lines hanging over your head. You know what that means, Mills? *Death penalty.* What with all of that, they'll hang you for sure."

"I ain't gonna confess. I'll take my chances. If I don't confess, you gotta get evidence."

"Oh, we've already *got* it. You left two kids at the pond last night, Mills. Two kids who can ID you, who saw you take Sam. They'll ID your car, too. Tell you what," he went on, straining for control, for patience. "You give me Sam and point me in the direction of the others and I'll put in a good word for you with the FBI."

"They'd listen to you?"

"Sure," Jake lied. *Got to find Sam.*

"You for real?"

"You'd better hope so. I'm all you've got. Where is Sam?"

"Hey, man, nobody got hurt or nothing. That's what you got to know right from the start. That's good, right? That's good for me, huh? I didn't hurt nobody."

Tell me. Jake's blood was pounding with urgency now. He was fresh out of games to play with this fool. "Five seconds, Mills. Then I'm walking out of here and you can take your chances with the FBI on your own."

"Okay! All right! I dropped him off already," Mills said.

Jake felt his blood pressure go up a notch.

"I got *clients*, see," Mills said proudly. "A whole waiting list. Got an agency here in Toms River. Private adoptions, that's what I call 'em. The kid last night went to some people in Dover."

Jake was shaking. "Who?"

"What do you mean, who? The kids I took."

"Who...in...Dover?"

"Chavers. Folks named Chavers. Hey, it's a good home. Rich folks. He'll have everything he ever wanted. Everything normal kids have. Everything that he couldn't get back in that crazy place I took him from." He looked at Ernie. "Weird place there, man, let me tell you."

"Yeah, he'd have everything but his mama," Jake snarled. *Just like me.*

Ernie was already half out the door. "I'm on it."

"Where?" Jake demanded. "Where in Dover?"

"Ur...Arlington Drive. Big white house."

Good enough. He could get the rest from the phone company.

His heart began roaring. He'd done it. For once in his life, he'd done something, finished something, fixed it.

"Hold on, Ernie, I'm right behind you," he shouted, and jogged from the little room.

He wasn't going to just get Sam. He was going to see this guy put away for life.

Damned if he wasn't a good cop.

Chapter 17

Katya stood with her nose pressed to the glass door of the bus station in Lancaster. Her palms were flush against the door. Despite the biting cold, they were damp with perspiration. There were so many people in there.

She pulled the door open and stepped just inside. She hovered there, her back pressed to the door now. After a long while, she realized that in spite of her odd dress, no one seemed to be paying her any attention at all. That made her feel braver. She crept a little farther into the terminal and spotted a long row of telephones across from the bus gates.

She hurried that way with fresh determination. She pushed a quarter into the slot of the first phone. With great care and precision, she pressed "O" for the operator as the deacons had said to do to ask for information.

A tinny voice answered. "Hello," Katya said breathlessly. "I need to call the policemen in Atlantic County, New Jersey, please."

There was a staticky sound. "One moment please. You need Information." And then, amazingly, the line was ringing again, though she had not put any more money in. In fact, her first quarter came plopping right back out with a merry ringing sound.

A new voice was speaking to her. "Information. What city please?"

"Atlantic County. New Jersey," she said again.

"That number is 606-555-1212."

She repeated it frantically to herself, disconnected, then fished for her quarter again. She pushed it back in and tapped out the new number. It was not the police.

"Information. Can I help you?" another mechanical voice asked.

She felt a thin line of perspiration trickle down between her shoulder blades. "Yes, I certainly hope so," she said. "I need to speak to the policeman."

"What police, ma'am?"

"The police in Atlantic County!"

"But what *city* there?"

Katya's mind raced wildly. She didn't think Jake had mentioned a city. Then she remembered something Adam had said. "Toms River!" she burst out, proud that she had remembered. And Jake's voice came back to her, giving her strength. *Do you know why Frank said that? To keep you under his thumb. To keep you his. Because if you believed in yourself, you might find it within yourself to fight him.*

Her thoughts were interrupted by a recording giving her yet another number. And the machine gave her her money back again. She grabbed it desperately and stuck it in the slot one more time. She called the newest number. This time the machine kept her quarter and a metallic voice asked for more. She dug frantically in her dress pocket and pushed in all the change she had.

"Toms River Police Department," a male voice finally said.

"Yes." Katya breathed again. "Oh, yes, thank you. My name is Katya Essler, and you're looking for my little boy."

"We are?"

"Yes, sir."

She heard him shouting to someone else, then the line went dead. *No, no, no!* But before she could react, before she could hang up, the man came back.

"You're sure you want Toms River, ma'am?" he asked.

"The thing is, we don't have any open kidnappings or missing children on the books," he explained. "Is this a recent case?"

"Yes. He was taken last night."

"Not here, he wasn't."

"Oh! No, I'm sorry. I wasn't clear. It happened in the settlement."

"The *settlement?*" His voice took on a wary tone. "And what settlement might that be?"

Suddenly, her eyes burned. Oh, God help her, maybe Frank was right. She could not survive out here. She could not even manage a phone call to tell Jacob she would come for Sam herself.

The man disconnected again. Had he hung up on her? She waited desperately. After all, he had come back before. After a moment or two, *music* began playing. She held the phone away and looked at it, amazed.

"Ma'am?"

She put the receiver back to her ear as soon as she heard his voice. "Yes!" she exclaimed breathlessly. "Yes, I'm here!"

"You want the state police, ma'am. A guy in the county barracks says they're involved with a kidnapping. You have the wrong number."

"Please, could you give that to me?" she asked. "The correct number?"

"I can take whatever information you have and send it over to them, if you like."

"That would be wonderful," she breathed, relieved. "There's a policeman there named Jacob Wallace. He's from Dallas. He's looking for my son. Please tell him I'm not at the settlement. If he would just please keep my baby safe when he finds him, I'll be there to collect him just as soon as I can get there. Tell him I'll come to your police station. In Toms River. We can meet there."

"But—"

"That's all," she finished more confidently. "Did you get all that?"

"Yes, ma'am."

"Sam will be safe with him. Sam is safer with him than

anywhere, until I can get there." She knew that with all her heart.

She hung up the phone, then got into line to buy a bus ticket to Berks County so she could collect her other children. Her heart was hammering. But it felt *good*, so very good, she realized. She was finally doing something, for herself, for Jacob, for everyone.

Jake heard Sam before he saw him, which was pretty amazing since Sam Essler did not make a sound.

A tense, white-lipped woman had opened the door to them at the house on Arlington Drive in Dover. Jake and Ernie O'Brien, four other troopers and two guys from the FBI's New Jersey office had made the drive in a convoy of three separate cars. Three more agents from the Dover field office had met them outside at the curb.

Jake had been absolutely convinced that for some obscure and ridiculous reason he would get here too late. Or that Mills had deliberately lied to him. They would get here and Sam wouldn't be here at all. Mills could have sent them on a wild-goose chase and meanwhile made arrangements—God only knew how, but Jake wasn't being rational—to put the boy into hiding.

But he felt him. He felt Sam. He felt him as soon as he stepped in the front door.

"Where?" he asked the woman hoarsely. "Where is he?"

"The first bedroom on your right," she said quietly. "That way." She didn't seem surprised by the arrival of so many lawmen. Nor did she seem to doubt what they had come for. Jake thought she was on the verge of crying.

One of the Fibbies began to read her her rights.

Under any other circumstances, Jake might have felt sorry for the woman. But he could think of nothing other than finding Sam. He jogged down the hallway and into the first room he came to. Sam was standing up in a crib. As soon as he saw him, the boy's eyes widened in recognition.

How does he recognize me so quickly, so easily? Sure, he'd given him a piggyback ride one night after dinner, but other than that, Jake had spent much more time with Sam's big brother, and that had been none too comfortable, either. He'd thought he'd kept himself removed, apart from Katya's kids.

Obviously, he hadn't. He felt a sinking sensation in his gut. Then he felt a glow.

"Wawa," Sam said.

Wawa? Water? *Wallace.*

The baby began jumping up and down in the crib. Jake crossed the room to get him out of the thing.

"I found you." *I made it all right this time. I did something.* He held the kid as tightly as he dared and he wasn't the least bit sure which of them was crying.

Two hours later, Jake prowled the FBI field office in Dover like a large cat confined to a cage. "Know anything yet?" he demanded.

The man at the desk looked up at him with impatience. His nameplate said Dave Winslow. "Detective Wallace," Winslow said with exaggerated care, "you've been pacing this office for the past thirty minutes. Have you noticed me pick up the telephone and speak into it? How is it that you expect me to know anything more than you do?"

Jake had had enough. He stopped moving to plant his palms on the man's desk. Winslow jumped. "You guys bungled this whole thing from start to finish," he snapped. "If it weren't for me, Mills would be home in Toms River, New Jersey, right now, counting out his money. You weren't even near to closing in on him. So let's be polite, okay? Do me a favor. Pick up the phone and call somebody in New Jersey. Find out if they've gotten it out of him yet where the other four kids are. Then find someone to inform me of the status of this situation so I don't *have* to pace."

It didn't turn out to be necessary. As Winslow glared at him, a door opened at the back of the office. Another man strode in.

Relief hit Jake squarely in the chest, driving out his breath. It was Lawrence Spina from D.C., a face he finally recognized.

Spina shook his hand. "Good work, Detective. Actually, it was excellent work. Sure you're not interested in a job with us?"

"No way," Jake said automatically. And his brother's voice came back to him. *You wouldn't be horsing around in a low-paying job...turning down the FBI...* He managed a quick, tense grin. "I don't do suits," he explained. "What are you doing here? What have you guys done with Sam?" They'd taken the baby from him outside the Chavers house. Jake was uncomfortably aware that they hadn't done so easily.

"I'm here because *you're* here," Spina said, "and you're not with the Bureau. I was called in to smooth the waters, so to speak. As for Sam, he's still with our doctor. Mills never mistreated him, for what it's worth."

Jake acknowledged that with a guttural sound.

"Of course, his mother will probably pitch a fit to know what he's been eating lately," Spina went on. Mills poured orange soda in his bottle in lieu of milk. "Sam has a bellyache and he wants his mama."

Jake winced. He wanted the boy's mama, too.

He couldn't think of her now. Not yet. Not now.

"Are you going to take him to her?" he asked carefully.

"Sure. There's a chopper waiting out in the parking lot—the same one that brought me in from D.C."

"Good." Jake cleared his throat, to no avail. "I need to say goodbye to him," he said hoarsely.

"Sure. They'll bring him out in a few minutes. Like I said, they're almost finished debriefing him."

"You can't *debrief* a kid who's not even two, for God's sake!"

Spina smiled, unperturbed. "We're Federal, Detective. We can certainly try."

At least he was honest. Jake gave him that. "Is he scared?"

Spina thought about it. Jake liked him a little better for that, too. "His eyes have pretty consistently remained the size of two moons. Other than that, he seems fine."

Jake breathed again. "Yeah, well, that's to be expected. What else? What's going on in New Jersey?" Ernie had gone back there, and he hadn't yet heard from him.

Spina looked at his watch. "Mills ought to be arraigned on the federal kidnapping charges any minute now. We're pushing that through fast so we can get a bond hearing and keep him in custody. As for the murder of that woman you found, we're going to have to wait for the forensics team to finish with her. We've got nothing with which to charge him on that right now. Nothing but conjecture."

Jake nodded. No surprise there. "What about the other kids?"

"All in the northeast. Mills didn't have to go far, what with all the childless couples waiting to adopt. Pittsburgh, Baltimore, Cleveland and New York."

Jake's heart stalled. "Where in New York?"

Spina looked uncomfortable. "City. As in Manhattan."

Jake closed his eyes. In *Manhattan?* He thought sickly that there might be some long-term scars there for that baby. Talk about culture shock. Then again, with any luck, the little one might just grow up believing it had all been a very strange nightmare.

"You're going to go get them?" Jake demanded.

"Yes. Our field officers in all locations have been notified and they're moving in."

"What about the people who…well, who bought them?"

Spina shook his head. "There can't be any across-the-board decisions on that. We'll have to take it on a case-by-case basis. It will depend on how much they knew of Mills's operation."

"They had to know," Jake snarled. "How the hell else was a healthy baby going to suddenly and easily fall into their laps?"

"Sure they knew, but they looked the other way in their desperation and pretended they didn't. We've been through Mills's 'office'—it's more or less a broom closet on the fifth floor of a high-rise. Fancy address, nothing there. He never let couples come to his place of business. He assured all of them that the mothers were unable to care for their babies, for one reason or another. He'd forged all the usual paperwork—hell, you can get forms in any legal supply store—so it looked as though the women had given up custody. But when something looks too good to be true—like being able to adopt a healthy baby after only a few weeks on a waiting list—it usually is."

Jake felt a surge of relief. At least they had Mills. He'd gotten Mills, and Sam and the others were going home. That was all that mattered.

The door swung open again. An agent came in carrying Sam. He looked very small.

Jake went to him. "You okay, buddy?" he asked, taking one small hand in his large one. Sam's other clutched a bottle filled with milk this time.

"Mama," Sam said.

Jake's heart stopped, then stuttered back to life. "Yeah. These men are going to take you back to her."

"Wawa?"

"What?" Jake was having trouble with his heart again.

"Wawa, too?"

"Oh." He stepped back from the baby fast, his throat tightening unaccountably. "You don't need me. You'll be fine."

Spina, damn him to hell, looked amused. "Got yourself into a bit of a personal mess this time, did you?"

"And now I'm getting out again," Jake said flatly.

"Whatever you say. You ready, Sam?"

Jake ruffled the boy's hair awkwardly. "Bye, kid."

Jake watched them go until he lost sight of them, until they had ducked under the whirring blades to climb up into the chopper waiting for them in the lot. Sam looked terrified. Jake's heart hurt. The phone rang briefly behind him. He barely heard it. He was having a ridiculously hard time swallowing.

He pulled the door open and hurried outside even as Dave Winslow shouted after him. He ignored him.

He just needed to get back to Dallas. That was all. Then he'd be fine.

Chapter 18

By the time Jake got to his apartment in southeast Dallas, it was past midnight. Thinking required a conscious effort he could not quite master, so he simply stood inside the front door, looking around.

The plants were dead, he observed. He'd left a towel thrown over the back of the sofa—presumably it was dry by now. He decided he wasn't hungry enough to see what the state of the refrigerator might be. Then again, he'd seriously like a beer.

He went to the kitchen. He'd been right about the refrigerator. An apple on the top shelf had gone soft. There was green stuff on the cheese. He took both and dropped them into the garbage disposal. The beer was good and cold. He returned to the living room with the bottle to open windows and let in some fresh air.

Dallas was damp and chilly on a February night, he thought, but at least it wasn't as frigid as Lancaster County.

Don't think about it.

Old routines, he decided. That was what he needed. Everything would be fine if he could fall into his old routines. Eventually, he would forget everything that had had him tangled up for weeks now. He would put it all behind him. He would stop feeling as though he had left some very pertinent piece of himself behind.

He swigged from the bottle and went to the answering machine. Twelve messages. Someone had missed him. He tried to grin and couldn't quite pull it off. He hit Play and listened.

"Jake. I thought you said you'd be back by now. It's Molly. Call me when you get in."

Molly, he thought, frowning. Ah, the blond in the spandex who had thrown a bon voyage party for him the night before he'd gone to Washington. He fast forwarded to the next message.

"Hey, Jake, this is Tina. I haven't heard from you in so long. Call, why don't you? We miss you."

Tina? *We?* He couldn't place her.

He scarcely heard the rest of the messages. He fixated on that second call, on the voice of a woman he didn't recognize, wondering desperately if she had mattered once and how long ago that might have been. Suddenly, he realized that the beer wasn't sitting well in his stomach at all. It was just that he hadn't eaten. He was tired.

He went back to the kitchen. He threw the beer bottle in the trash. He decided to take a shower. He stood in the steaming water longer than he had to, the hot water beating down on his skin. Then it began going cold. *Call it a day*, he told himself. He'd never looked back before. He wouldn't do it now.

She'd have Sam back by now. She'd be holding him, loving him—hell, she probably wouldn't take her hands off him. And she'd know he'd kept his promise.

So it was over. It was better this way, for both of them. They were really too different after all. Except...

He wondered if she'd think of him often and if she would smile when she did. He wondered if he had left her enough happiness in the end. Would she stay there? Would she remain forever trapped in the limbo of her marriage to that bastard who had hit her? Or would she finally get out?

He left the shower, toweled off and went into the bedroom. He dropped onto the bed, exhausted. And remembered the time she had crept in on him while he was sleeping. His body remembered and stirred even as he thought how hard it had been then to believe that she was really so sweet, so innocent, that she could think he was dying.

What the hell was wrong with him? *Stop thinking about her. Stop it now.* But even the scent of her seemed to linger in his head long after he should have left it behind.

That was when it hit him, what had happened, what he had done.

Suddenly, he couldn't seem to breathe for the warmth that enveloped him. His heart thundered. *Was he in love with her?* Every instinct he possessed leaped to deny it. No, he thought, no. He'd gone into the danger zone, certainly. Maybe he had begun to fall in love with her. But he hadn't fallen in all the way, had been able to stop himself, had walked away. Katya Essler would not leave a gaping hole in his life now that he had left her. He had never allowed that to happen. He would not start now.

Like hell.

From the first moment he had roused from unconsciousness to see her face above him, he had instinctively known that she would somehow undo everything he had come to accept about himself. That she was going to have a very big impact upon his life. From the first, something about her had scared him.

But…*love* her? He just needed to sleep, he decided. Given twenty-four hours, he would remember who Tina was. Maybe Molly would give him a welcome-home party. He'd go back to work. He'd be fine. No looking back. He never looked back.

With that decision, he fell hard and heavy into an exhausted sleep.

The ringing telephone jarred him awake almost immediately. At least, it felt like almost immediately. He blinked groggily in the direction of the window and realized it was morning.

He sat up and threw his legs over the side of the bed. He was careful to avoid bumping the coffee table in front of Adam and Mariah's sofa. When it wasn't there, his head began to clear. His heart jumped, sank, rioted, then something heavy and sad settled in.

He reached for the phone. "'Lo," he rasped, his voice still thick with sleep.

"Jake." Adam's voice was worried, maybe even scared.

Jake came instantly, fully awake. Something had gone wrong. "I saw him get on the helicopter, damn it!" he shouted. "I saw the bird take off!"

There was confused silence. "What are you talking about?"

"Sam!"

"You sent him back to the settlement?"

"Didn't he get home okay?"

"I don't know. I'm in New Jersey."

Jake felt his head fill with cobwebs of confusion. "Why?" he asked carefully.

"I'm trying to find Katya. She's disappeared."

The room spun. His blood began moving fiercely through his body. Hotly. And coldly, all at once. "Disappeared?" he repeated. He was moderately amazed at how level his voice came out. At how utterly reasonable it was. He sounded like the damned Rock of Gibraltar.

Somehow he knew that when the rock cracked, it was going to be too painful to contemplate. Already ugly words were resonating in his head. *Whatever she's done, wherever she's gone, somehow it's because of me...because of me...because of me...*

"She heard us fighting yesterday morning," Adam said.

"So?"

"So apparently she thought that if I didn't have to support her and her kids, I could continue funding ChildSearch."

"That's ridiculous," Jake snapped. And then a fissure spidered its way through the rock. And it hurt. He had said that. Yeah, it was ridiculous, but...

But she would take what she heard and she would heed it word for word.

"Katya wouldn't know that," he added. "She'd believe it." Just the way she had believed she'd killed him with the rolling pin. She'd done the right thing then, creeping into that room to check on him, no matter how scared she might have been. And she was doing the right thing now—at least as she perceived it.

He should have been used to it by now. But something giddy and terrifying was working its way up his throat.

"She left a note, and as soon as Mariah found it, I started looking for her. I've been one step behind her for about twenty-four hours now," Adam said, his voice a little amazed. "Apparently, she went to Berks County first to get her other kids. They were with her here."

"In Toms River?" Jake asked harshly. "You're in Toms River?"

"Yeah. She called ahead to the local police here. They sent word over to the state police barracks. She said to tell you to keep Sam here and she would come pick him up personally. When they got her message, the state guys called for you at the FBI office in Dover. It seems they just missed you."

Out of the blue, Jake remembered the ringing telephone when he'd escaped the FBI office. He remembered Winslow calling after him. His gut rolled. He'd been too intent on running to respond. What had he done?

"Then, early this morning, she showed up the way she said she would," Adam went on. "They called the state guys again. They found out Sam had been sent home. She's going to try to get back to Lancaster, Jake. They weren't aware of what kind of emergency it was, that she's not exactly equipped to be traipsing around on her own, or I guess they would have tried to keep her there."

"Well, good." Fine, he thought. Okay. It was a temporary snafu, but it would all work out okay. No reason for him to get involved. He was a thousand miles away, for God's sake.

But he was involved.

"Not good," Adam was saying. "She only took two hundred dollars and she's already worked her way clear across two states. She can't have much left. I was hoping like hell you'd heard from her."

The rock crumbled.

Laughter surged up from Jake's chest. It hurt. The reflex was so full, it hurt a lot. It made his eyes tear. "I'll be damned," he managed finally.

Adam's voice went sharp and angry. "I don't see anything humorous in this."

"Innocent little Katya. She's sure given you a run for your money, hasn't she?"

Adam was quiet a moment as he realized the truth of that. "I'll be damned," he agreed.

Jake sobered abruptly. His blood began roaring as the enormity of what she had done hit him at last.

How many times had he told her not to believe in him? She'd believed in him. She'd believed in her heart that he would find her son, that he would protect him and watch over him once he did. She had never doubted it, had believed enough to leave the settlement—the only place in the world she really knew—rather than wait there for Sam to return.

Jake almost reeled with the truth of what she had done. It was naive, certainly. It had been foolish in a lot of ways. And no one had ever believed in him so much.

It didn't matter that he hadn't really let her down. That he had done exactly what he'd said he would do. He'd found Sam. He'd sent him home. Safely. But that didn't matter, because she'd believed just a little bit too much. Now she was out there somewhere on her own. Without money.

Jake got to his feet, moving blindly around the bedroom, dragging the phone cord behind him.

"It's not your fault, Jake," Adam said into his ear. "Don't take this on your head, too."

Jake ignored him. "Go back to the settlement," he snapped, throwing clean clothes into yet another duffel bag. "Sam's there. Mariah's not going to know what the hell is going on. I can't be in two places at once, so *you* watch over the kid."

"You're coming back?"

"Yeah. I'll go to Jersey. I'm going to find her."

"Do you need money? Want me to wire some?"

"No. This is...mine." He zipped the duffel with a furious tug and hurled it into the living room, in the general direction of the front door. "My mess, my problem."

"I won't argue that. But this country requires United States currency, Jake."

"I said I'll take care of it!" Jake shouted, then closed his eyes and took a breath. She'd trusted him. He'd run. "I've got a CD I can cash in. I bought it in one of my rare responsible moods." He tried to laugh. Couldn't.

Adam was quiet for a long time. "Do you want my opinion on this?"

"Save it. I had enough of your opinions yesterday."

Adam told him anyway. "You've got to come to terms with what happened in the past so you can make it in one piece into tomorrow, Jake."

"I didn't ask for this," Jake growled. "Dammit, I didn't ask for any of this."

"No. But it's chasing you down all the same. She believes in you more than you believe in yourself. I don't know why, but she does, and that's what's scaring you, isn't it? Because somehow you've got to live up to it."

Adam hung up. Jake stared at the phone in his hand, his heart thundering. "I found her kid," he said to no one. His voice cracked. "I sent Sam home to Pennsylvania."

And then you ran back to Texas.

It hadn't been enough. He hadn't done enough. She'd always demanded everything of him without ever asking, without ever saying a word.

Chapter 19

Jake found a pay phone in the airport and called Ernie, tracking him down at home. "Have you seen her?" he asked as soon as his friend answered. "Has she come back to the police station?"

Ernie hesitated a moment with the bad news. "No. She'd have no reason to, Jake. She knows her little boy's been sent home. But if she does, we'll detain her." He paused. "Is this your personal stake, by any chance?" he asked.

"Yeah." And the ease with which he heard himself admit it made his heart kick. Then his mind raced on. *Think, damn it.* He had to think. "Can you bring the media in on this? Get a description of her on the air?"

"They'll probably comply. Sounds like good human interest."

"She's got three little kids with her," he went on, although Ernie already knew that. "That should make her easier to spot." *And she's as innocent as the dawn.* "And the kids, at least, are all in Amish dress." He wasn't sure if she still had the jeans with her or not. "Tell them she's got this incredible, long, white blond hair—I can't imagine she'd have it tucked up. She doesn't like it that way. And when it's down, she's beautiful. Hell, she's beautiful even when it's *not*."

"I'm sure that's just the kind of thing they'll want to put on the air," Ernie said dryly.

Get a grip. Jake warned himself. "Okay. Tell them she's about five feet tall and weighs a hundred pounds soaking wet."

"Got it," Ernie said.

"I'll call you again when I land in Philly. I owe you one, pal."

"You owe me several," Ernie corrected.

Jake hung up reluctantly, feeling as though he was severing some flimsy contact with her. He went to catch his flight.

Katya's feet hurt so badly it brought tears to her eyes. She couldn't ask the children to walk anymore. If she was in pain, she could only imagine what their small feet felt like. She'd offered to tote Levi on her back while she carried Delilah, and he'd looked at her as though she was crazy.

What had she done? She was in New Jersey, Sam was back in the settlement, and she had no money with which to get back to him. And the way things were looking, she wasn't even going to be able to find a place for the rest of them to sleep tonight. She straightened her shoulders painfully. It was harder now than it had been at dusk.

"There's one, Mama." Delilah hung on to her neck with one arm and pointed at a motel with the other. Katya looked that way.

The Lucky Clover. The name was emblazoned in brilliant red light on the front of the building. *Please be lucky for us,* she prayed. She wasn't sure what she would do if they were turned away here, too.

Her idea had seemed so brilliant at first, and it would certainly have worked in the settlement. She'd thought she could work in exchange for a room. It had seemed a reasonable arrangement. But here, in the *anner Satt Leit* world, people looked at her as though she was crazy when she made such a suggestion.

She staggered into the office of The Lucky Clover and decided to take a different tack this time. She was desperate. She set Delilah carefully on her feet.

A woman was standing behind the counter. That was good. It had always been her experience that women were kinder and more generous than men. This one had more hair than Katya had ever seen, even since she had been traipsing around *anner Satt Leit* cities. It was so black it looked blue, and it was a wild, huge swirl about her head. It looked stiff, as well. Her lips were as red as the sign outside. She looked up when Katya and her brood struggled inside and she cracked her gum at them.

"Help you?" she asked laconically.

"I'm looking for work," Katya pleaded. "Do you have work I could do?" She would ask about a room this time *after* she had ascertained that.

The woman blinked. "At nine o'clock at night?"

Was it that late already? "It's...very important."

The woman studied her. "Then yeah, sure. Come back first thing in the morning. About nine. Fill out an application. Have the guy on duty set it aside for me. Tell him Mona said to come in."

"An application," Katya repeated hollowly. "Mona."

"That's me." The woman's eyes narrowed. "I'm the manager. You're not from around here, are you?"

Katya shook her head. Her eyes burned. She would not cry. "No," she managed before she turned away.

"Hey," the woman said. "How come you're job hunting this late with all them kids?"

Katya looked at her. Her eyes filled even more in spite of all her determination. "We need a place to stay."

The woman scowled. "You got nowhere?"

Katya shook her head helplessly.

"Well, getting a job tonight ain't gonna fix that."

"I thought..." Katya began weakly, then she took a deep breath and brought her chin up. "I thought maybe I could work for a room."

The woman stared at her a moment longer. "Look, I got a vacancy," she said finally. "It's thirty-five bucks a night for a single person. I could pretend I don't see those kids."

"I don't *have* thirty-five dollars!" Katya wailed, then she steadied herself yet again. "But please, I could do thirty-five dollars worth of work for you. I can do many things. I can cook, clean, sew. I can even heal a little."

The woman stared at her, then she finally grinned. "Heal, huh? Well, this ain't no hospital, but some guy got shot up down the block not more'n two weeks ago. Look, I can give you some rooms to tidy up in the morning. You ain't gonna run out on me, are you?"

"No! Oh, no, certainly not."

"Didn't think so. Okay, here." She took a key from a pegboard behind her counter. "Number one twelve. And you want my advice, go in there and stay there. I can't believe you ain't been jumped yet. This is a lousy part of the city, you know."

"No, I didn't know that." Delilah had finally stopped crying. Katya took the extended key. "Thank you so very much," she said fervently. Her relief was so great she could hardly breathe. Her whole body felt weak.

She hurried out a little unsteadily before Mona could change her mind. The woman watched her go, then looked up at the ceiling. "That earn me a place in heaven, Mister? I sure hope so."

It was close to midnight when Jake's plane landed in Philadelphia. It seemed like a lifetime had passed since the last time he had flown in here. And he had been exhausted then, too. From the time he had laid eyes on this woman, shut-eye had been at a premium.

He found another pay phone and called Ernie back. "Well?" he asked without preamble.

"I think we got something."

Jake's heart soared. "What?" he demanded. "Tell me. What's she done?"

Ernie chuckled. "What any sensible woman would do with a bunch of kids, no money and no roof over her head. She went to a motel and offered to work for a room. Actually, she went to a lot of them. All but one turned her away."

Jake's head spun. It was so simple. So logical. So Katya.

"We put her all over the eleven o'clock news," Ernie explained, "and within minutes, the calls started coming in. She's at a place called The Lucky Clover."

"The address," Jake rasped. "Give me the address."

A moment later, he hung up and jogged off to find a rental car.

Katya dropped across the foot of the bed, just after one-thirty in the morning. The children took up most of the space. She curled into what little room they had left her and closed her eyes with a groan.

She was as tired as she had ever been in her life. No wonder that woman had agreed to help her, she thought. This room had been filthy. She'd cleaned it right away with water and the bar of soap she'd found in the bathroom and a couple of the towels, as much in a show of good faith as because she couldn't stand it. It had taken forever, but she felt better for doing it.

She closed her eyes and fell into a dreamless sleep. Almost immediately, someone began pounding at the door. She came awake groggily, then was instantly frightened. *The woman had changed her mind!* But surely she could change it back once she showed her just how clean this room was. She got to her feet, weaving a little on her way to the door. She was exhausted.

She quickly realized that she should have looked out the window first to see who was out there. What she found on the other side stunned her.

"Mrs. Essler, are you okay?" someone shouted.

"Why did you come to New Jersey rather than wait in your hometown?" someone else demanded.

They knew her name! How did they know her name? And there seemed like *thousands* of them out there. People holding glaring, impossibly white lights, and others thrusting strange black tubelike things at her. And everyone was shouting, yelling, jostling each other as they tried to get closer to her.

Katya reared back, terrified. And then she saw him.

Jacob! She would have run to him, but he came pushing through from the back of the crowd. His face was red, his eyes wild.

"What the hell do you think you're doing?" he shouted when he reached her. "Of all the stupid, idiotic stunts to pull!"

She was so startled she couldn't answer. He grabbed her by the shoulders and pushed her back inside the room. He turned to the people. He waved a hand over their heads.

"Thanks again, Ernie. I can take it from here."

He slammed the door. Katya stared at him. She was shaking now. "What have you done?" she whispered. "What are you *doing?*"

"Rescuing you. Somebody had to," he said roughly.

It hurt. It hurt so deeply, speared so completely through to her soul, that she almost lost her breath. *Rescuing you.* As though she was as helpless as Frank had always said, as though this man himself hadn't told her she was smart. *Somebody had to.* He had come for her only because no one else was available.

She backed away from him. "Go away," she said thinly.

"What?"

"I'm fine. Everything's fine. Go away."

"If everything's so fine, then where's Sam?" he demanded. Katya blanched. He cursed himself for the words as soon as they were out. "I sent him back to the settlement," he said more quietly.

"I know." She pulled away from him, but she was trembling. "I'll get there somehow." No matter that she didn't know how. No matter that she wanted Sam *now,* right now, and it would take her days—oh, God, maybe even *weeks*—to earn her keep here and save up enough money to get home besides.

She did not want his help. *Rescuing you. Somebody had to.* She could not bear it.

"How?" Jake shouted. "Damn it, you're over your head here, Katie!"

Her chin came up, though she could feel it tremble. She *wasn't* helpless. And if he was going to try to tell her she was, then he could just, well... "Go to hell!" she burst out. She felt the blood rush to her face as soon as she said it.

"Huh?" Jacob's jaw dropped.

"I've gotten a job," she said, drawing herself up.

Jake felt wonder, amazement and something like pure terror wash through him. Not that she had found work. Ernie had told him that, after a fashion. *She didn't need him.* It drowned all the staggering relief he had felt only a moment ago. ''A job,'' he repeated.

She clasped her hands together in front of her. On the bed, Levi stirred. ''Yes. And I'll thank you to keep your voice down, or you'll wake the children.''

''Wake the children,'' he echoed dazedly.

''Yes.''

''Woman, what the hell are you up to?'' he roared.

It was too much, he realized. It was simply too much. The stress of finding Sam, of needing to find Sam more than he'd ever needed anything before in his life. Then the emotional hell of escaping her only to find out that she was running loose in New Jersey without a dime to her name. It was the nagging certainty he'd had since flying back here that she might survive all this better than he would.

And she had. Apparently, she had.

''Sam's back in the settlement!'' he went on irrationally. ''You've got to go back there!''

''Yes,'' she answered stiffly, coldly. ''They told me that when I went to see the police.'' Then something inside her cracked. ''Oh, Jacob, why couldn't you have just kept him here with you! Everything would have worked fine if you'd just *kept* him with you!''

It went clear through to his heart. ''I found him!'' he shouted. ''What more do you want from me? Beyond that, he's not my job!'' And he heard Adam's voice. Or maybe it was just the voice of his conscience. *Of course not, Jake. That would require a little effort.*

''He's not a job, Jacob,'' she gasped. ''He's a *child.*''

''Damn it, you are *not* going to make me feel guilty about this!'' He began pacing. ''Where did you get off dumping him on me in the first place?''

''Dumping him?'' she cried.

''Mama?'' Delilah whispered from the bed.

''Shut up, Jacob,'' Katya hissed. ''Shut *up.*'' Then her voice softened, but not to speak to him. ''Go back to sleep, baby,'' she said more kindly to her daughter. Then she grabbed his hand and dragged him to the bathroom.

He flinched when she shut the door behind them, a five-foot-tall hellion with fire in her eyes. Making him feel small.

He raked a hand through his hair. "Look, we need to get you out of here," he said more reasonably.

"No."

"*What?*"

"I've got to clean rooms in the morning. To pay for this one tonight."

"I'll pay for the room!"

"No…you…won't, Jacob. I don't want charity. *No more!*"

She was going to cry. But they were tears of fury. He realized it with a feeling of bemusement. "Katie…" he began.

"You don't understand!" she burst out.

Yeah, he thought. Yeah, he did. "Katie, feeding you and the kids isn't going to prevent Adam from keeping Child-Search. And I can at least afford this lousy room."

"That doesn't matter!"

"Then what's the point here?" He was getting exasperated. He was getting a headache. He wanted to hold her. He shoved his hands into his jeans pockets instead. "What's the point?" he asked again. "What don't I understand?"

"I believed you!" she wailed.

His jaw tightened. "No. You didn't. Because I told you I wasn't a hero. So what did you do? You ran off into the sunset, trusting me to do the right thing for your kid!" And he should have, damn it, he should have. He had fallen a step or two short. Again.

Her chin came up. "It wasn't your fault or your responsibility that I decided to leave," she went on more strongly.

He stared at her.

"The important thing is that I can't go back to the settlement," she went on. "Not to stay. The important thing is that I don't *want* to stay there anymore. I'll get Sam, but then I'll leave again. You told me I was smart. That's what I believed! And…" She drew herself up. "I did it. I got my children. I came here. I got a job. I took this room on good faith and I *will* pay for it. And I won't let you take that away from me.

I won't let anyone take it away from me. Nobody had to rush out and find me."

He kept staring at her. Ah, he thought, *now* he understood.

"I only wanted to get my children and start over," she admitted unsteadily. "Someplace where I could depend on *me*. Someplace where I could have a future. Someplace where the children can, too. I won't have them trapped by the *ordnung*, Jacob. It's not doing us—my particular family—any good. I've known that for so long, but oh, I was so terrified to admit it. But you made me strong."

"Katie, no—"

"I can't have Levi longing for more, quitting school at fourteen because he has to," she rushed on. "And I can't have my girls marrying for life to a man they may not love. Jacob, perhaps after what they've seen of Frank and me, they won't want to marry at all. But the *ordnung*, the settlement, would force them." She fell quiet a moment, shaking visibly now. "I *am* a good mother," she said fervently. "That's the best thing I do. And it's one thing to suffer myself, but to let them suffer, as well, because I'm too weak and too scared to save them, would just be *terrible!*"

Jake felt amazement shift through him. He was overwhelmed. And so proud, so impressed, that it hurt his heart. "I didn't do that, Katie."

"What?" Her emotion was spent now. She looked pale, confused.

"You were already saying that the night you clobbered me." She shook her head fretfully, but he remembered. "You were saying, *no, no, no more.*"

Her eyes widened slowly as she remembered, too.

"You didn't need me, Katie. You were just looking for a chance to show yourself."

He felt himself shaking, somewhere deep, somewhere in the area of his heart. He wondered if Adam knew how very much they had underestimated this woman. And then he heard himself speak, and he knew he was lost.

"Will you at least let me help?" he asked hoarsely.

"What?"

"I know you don't need it. You'd make it anyway, with or without me. But I want to help. I want to be there."

"How?" she asked warily.

He still heard his own words as though someone else were speaking them. And peace spread through his chest like something red gold and warm. He realized almost distantly that he wasn't shaking anymore. And when he went down on one knee in the cramped bathroom, he was only moderately surprised at himself. Yeah, he thought, he loved her.

"Marry me," he said quietly.

Katya felt herself reeling. "Jacob, you don't have to—"

He interrupted. "Katie, I'm real bad at doing things that I'm *expected* to. Let me try my hand at something I *want* to do." She stared at him. He rushed on. There was so much to tell her, to explain. "Adam wants to give me the company. That's why he said the things he said. And I'm…" *Say it.* "I'm afraid to take it. That's why *I* said the things I did. None of it really had anything to do with you. Not that part." He took another breath. "I'm going to do it."

Her eyes widened. "You are?"

His heart kicked. "And my first official move is to give you a job."

"A job?" she whispered.

"If you want one so badly, then you've got one. But for God's sake, not here, Katie. Not in *this* city." *Not alone. With me.* But, above all, he would be honest. "It's hard work. Long hours. Lousy pay. But I wouldn't expect you to be—to *do* what you did with Frank. To turn yourself over to me entirely. To have nothing of your own to fall back on. You could work. You could have money of your own. If you wanted it."

"I want it," she breathed. "A real job?"

He wanted to shout in frustration. He was asking her to marry him, and all she could think about was the job. But that came first, he realized. With her, it would have to. So he would give it to her. Maybe it was the one thing he would ever give her, had ever given her, that really mattered.

"There are going to have to be some across-the-board changes from the way Adam was running it," he said. "No more handouts. Everybody gets charged *something*. If they can only afford a dime, well, then, damn it, they'll have to pay the dime. And we're going to have to cut way back on expenses."

"I'll help," she whispered. "But I really can't *do* any-thing."

He felt a strong urge to laugh. "Baby, I think you can do just about anything you set your mind to. So...are you with me?"

She looked around the bathroom. "Yes, of course I'm here."

He laughed raggedly. And closed his eyes. "No, I meant...never mind." Because, he thought, in the end, it was just that easy for her either way.

He still didn't mean to touch her because she had never answered him. Not really. *Marry me.* The words still hurt in his throat, but it was a sweet kind of pain. But then, suddenly, she was in his arms.

"Jacob, I'm already married," she gasped. "But, oh, I do wish it could be different!"

"We'll get you a divorce," he said hoarsely. Was she say-ing yes? God, he thought, let her be saying yes.

She was shaking in his arms. "A divorce," she whispered. "Yes, yes, I could do that."

She was warm, smelling sweet, like wildflowers and green springtime and sunshine. And he held her tightly, as if she was his salvation, when all along he'd been fighting off the re-sponsibility of being hers.

"We can do it," he corrected. And he waited.

"I love you, Jacob."

He was dying. Slowly. By degrees. "I love you, Katie Yoder. Now for God's sake, will you please tell me you'll marry me?"

She looked up at him, blinking. "Of course."

Just like that, he thought, feeling the room tilt. "Of course," he repeated.

"We bundled."

"We *what?*" Then he remembered. And he managed to laugh. "Oh, the quilt. Better pass it on this time to someone who's already married."

Because, he realized, he was starting to believe in magic.

He took them all to a fast-food joint for breakfast, one in a significantly better part of town. The city was waking up. It was a weekday. People were rushing to work, to responsibilities, harried and preoccupied.

If he expected Katya or the kids to quail and cling to him at such a crowd of twentieth-century humanity, he was disappointed. Only Delilah clung a little tighter to her mother's neck as they got out of the car. Levi stuck his nose into the restaurant, then immediately whipped around again to play in the big jungle gym outside.

And that's when Jake knew, he suddenly knew, that Katya was right. This wasn't just about her. And it wasn't about him. These children had been secretly yearning for this for some time, as well. Maybe the settlement was right for Adam and Mariah. Maybe it was good for Sugar Joe Lapp. But Katya and her children had fallen all too helplessly through the cracks in its protective web, had landed outside its fold, living with all its restrictions and none of the good. No, not helplessly, Jake corrected himself. Never that. And knowing that made him realize anew how right this was.

They reached the settlement at noon. The sight of a bunch of black-clad boys racing across a field—without an adult—warmed him. The kids were back, safe. As he passed, they stopped to stare at the rental car, but it was with more curiosity—and maybe a little wariness—than fear.

He tracked Adam down at a half-finished barn off Angels' Cross Road. He did what he had done a lifetime ago, on the day he had agreed to find the children. He got out of the car and merely stood there after cautioning Katya and the kids to wait inside. Because this was something he had to do himself, without interference.

Horses looked up from grazing to eye him with vague curiosity, then they apparently decided he didn't measure up to the grass. A lot of the snow had melted, Jake realized. He thought it might be the first real forage they had seen in months and he couldn't blame them.

He scratched Goliath's ear as he passed him. The gelding snorted. "Same to you," he muttered.

Adam looked up sharply at the sound of his voice. He said something to the man working on the roof beside him. It was

Sugar Joe. Joe looked up, too, and waved. Moments later, all the men converged on Jacob. Amalie's father and Lizzie's father. All of them, slapping him on the back, shaking his hand, clutching their broad-brimmed black hats in work-roughened hands as they thanked him. Adam watched him levelly from behind the crowd.

"How's everything going?" he asked when the men dispersed. Jake had sent word ahead, via the police, that he had found Katya, that she was with him, and they were all heading back to get Sam. He hadn't mentioned that it would be a quick in-and-out visit.

Jake shrugged, still deliberately watching the barn. He pushed his hands into the pockets of his new black leather jacket. So much for his savings. He'd be damned if he was going to hang around up north any longer without a warm coat. And he'd be coming back this way once in a while from now on. He cleared his throat. "So where's Sam?" he finally asked.

"Home with Mariah." Adam paused. "You know, someone once told me that Bo was going to miss the hell out of his friends here if I took him back to Texas. Same thing goes for Katya's kids, Jake, if you're thinking to take them back to Dallas."

It wasn't a question. How the hell did Adam know? Panic kicked in briefly, then Jake was calm again. "Yeah, I am," he answered. "But they'll be fine. Bo wanted to stay here. Katya's kids don't."

Adam digested this with careful neutrality. "This place hasn't been all that kind to them."

"No," Jake said simply.

"Okay. Then what?"

Jake glanced at his brother out of the corner of his eye. Damned if he was going to make this easy on him after the way Adam kept poking his nose in where it wasn't wanted. "Are you waiting for me to tell you I'll do the honorable thing by her?" he asked.

Adam's jaw jutted. "Yeah."

So he'd wait a little longer, Jake thought, grinning to himself. "I'll take over the company," he answered.

It was enough of a surprise that Adam momentarily forgot about Katya. "What changed your mind?"

"A tiny little bit of a woman who's barely been out of this settlement in her whole life had the courage to traipse across two states to save it."

"You're doing it for her, then."

"Nope. I'm doing it *because* of her. There's a difference."

Adam took a deep breath. "You don't have to keep denying yourself the things you love, Jake. It serves no purpose."

"I hope to hell you're right." His grin twisted. "I guess we'll find out."

Adam stiffened. "That's not fair to her. If you're going to take her and her kids back to Texas, they deserve more than 'I hope' and 'I guess.'"

Jake smiled. Really smiled. "It's all she asks of me."

She'd said she'd marry him. But in the car, on the way back to the settlement, she'd told him she wouldn't do it until ChildSearch was on its feet. She had her share of convoluted reasons, most of which he saw the wisdom in. She wanted—finally—the chance to stand on her own two feet first, without anyone else being responsible for her. And she wanted him to be absolutely sure it was what he wanted. Given everything marriage had done to her, he was overwhelmed and deeply touched that she loved him enough to do it at all.

"I'll marry her, Adam," he said quietly. "But given that she gets a little testy when anybody tries to make her decisions for her, I'll do it on her terms." He turned away, then looked back at Adam's stunned face. "Six months, right?"

"Huh?"

"You'll fund the company for six months?"

Adam nodded bemusedly. "Uh, yeah. Then I'll sign it over to you."

"Good enough. You'll need to transfer three thousand dollars into the business account by Monday."

"Three? That's not going to be enough, Jake. Expenses always run four to five."

Jake grinned and turned away again. "They won't this month. I'm not a bleeding heart."

Adam watched him go back to the car. "Wanna bet?" he asked softly.

Epilogue

It turned out to be the longest six months in Jake's life. And the time passed in a blur.

It was exactly noon on a Sunday when Jake realized that ChildSearch was going to make it without Adam's input. The first month he had indeed run over his three-thousand-dollar estimate—but not quite by the two thousand that Adam had predicted. The second month he had run over by a thousand. The third month it was by nine hundred, the fourth by five hundred, and in the fifth month he had broken even.

This month—and it wasn't even quite over yet—he was sixty dollars in the black.

He sat at his desk in the back room and grinned like a fool. Then he heard an unmistakable scraping sound from the front room—the door, despite several sandings, didn't quite fit the jamb. Jake got to his feet and poked his head into the lobby, and, as always, his heart kicked. "How goes it?" he asked Katya.

Katya looked up from herding the children inside with a smile as wide as Texas. "Wonderful. You should come with us next time, Jacob."

His heart did something strange again. She had never asked him to accompany them to the small Baptist church she had found shortly after arriving here. But then, a lot of things would change now. He hoped. He glanced down at the ledger again with its sixty-dollar balance.

Levi scattered his thoughts. "I'm gonna play football!" he announced.

"Good for you," Jake managed.

"Apparently, there's a city league, um…" Katya's voice trailed off.

"Peewee," Jake supplied.

"Yes, that's it. One of the boys in his Sunday school class recruited him."

"Can you coach?" Levi asked.

Jake hesitated only a moment. Once, before he'd given up his dreams, he'd been a hell of a quarterback. "Sure."

Levi beamed. "Cool." And he raced up the stairs.

"You go, too," Katya said, "all the rest of you. Rachel, take Sam. He needs a nap. Play quietly and I'll be up at five o'clock."

Jake watched them go. This was odd, too. Different. She always went upstairs after church to settle the children herself. What was she up to?

Katya smiled privately as the children left. Jake had given them Adam's old apartment upstairs. He said it was just sitting empty. It was small and cramped, and it was the most wonderful place she had ever seen. It was *hers*. She insisted upon paying him two hundred dollars a month for it. In addition to ChildSearch, she had gotten a job helping out at a nursing home. It appalled her the way the *anner Satt Leit* sent their old ones away. No *grossdawdy* houses here, she thought ruefully.

In the beginning, she had been painfully uncomfortable in Jake's world, in spite of her desperation to start over, in spite of her resolve. After the first few weeks, she had come to actually *hate* Dallas with all its distractions, all the many things about it that tried to pull a family apart. It had been a constant headache for her to keep her children in line with so much temptation.

Then she had found the Baptist church. She had turned her back on her people mostly because they would not let her leave Frank, because they would not let her take care of herself, because they would not give her children options, dreams, a chance. But she loved them. She missed them, and she had known right away that whether she left them or not, she still needed the comfort of God in her world.

She'd found the church's loud, joyous style of singing a little odd at first, but she'd gradually come to enjoy it and now she sang with the best of them. And within the congregation, there were sick people she could visit, Sunday school classes she could teach, values she could impress upon her own youngsters. The pastor had even gotten her the job at the nursing home. And she was going to school. Sort of. For now she was studying at home to get something called a GED.

A high school diploma! From there, she thought, *anything* was possible. She could even go to nursing school. But for now, first, she wanted to marry Jacob.

After Katya watched the children pound their way upstairs, she moved to one of the two desks in the front room.

Jake watched her scowl at the computer monitor there. Diploma or not, he thought, she'd learned to make that thing hum. She was wearing an old-fashioned dress that she had gotten at a secondhand store, and he knew it was one of her favorites. Actually, he liked it, too. He thought it was probably vintage forties, narrow and slim with pale pink flowers and a flounce at the hem. It had a modest V neckline and a little bow there, lest any cleavage appear.

He loved her.

"I, uh…" he began.

She looked over her shoulder at him. "Yes, Jacob?"

"Katie, we need to…" Why was this so hard the second time around? he wondered. But he knew. Of course he knew.

She had been right in making them wait. The first time he had asked her, it had been torn from his heart amid all the hell of thinking he had lost her. This time it was something that he had worked long and hard toward for six months. This time it meant so much to him that he couldn't even get the question out for the terrible fear that she might have changed her mind.

She'd turned back to the monitor, to a list of all the kids they were currently looking for and the method they were using—milk cartons, the Web site—to find them. The list was seventy-two names long now, despite the fact that Jake charged every single parent.

She interrupted without looking up. "Oh, there's a new one here since yesterday. No, wait..." He waited. "She's twenty-seven years old!" A pause. She turned slowly to look at him. "It's your sister," she said softly.

He tried to look away. Her eyes held him. "Yeah."

"Oh, Jacob, that's *good*."

"I've got to say I'm sorry. You know, for that day I tried to save her and my father knocked me out."

"Oh, Jacob."

He finally managed to turn away from her. He went to look out the front windows at the sultry street where no one moved too fast or too busily. It was Sunday, this was a business district, and it got hot in Texas in the summer.

Katya looked at the list again, then back at him. "Perhaps she won't want to hear it. Your apology, I mean."

"That's a chance I've got to take."

"Perhaps she doesn't blame you."

"She's human, Katie. The only person I've ever met who never blames people is you."

"Oh, but I do," she answered quietly.

He turned back to her sharply. "Who do you blame?"

"For a long time, I hated Frank for not living up to his vows, for trapping me in a marriage that wasn't a marriage." As it had turned out, she couldn't divorce him here in the *anner Satt Leit* world, either. She couldn't do it because as far as these authorities were concerned, she had never been married to Frank in the first place. The Amish *never* trooped into Lancaster for such a thing as marriage licenses.

"That's forgivable, Katya," Jake said shortly. But then she threw him a curve ball.

"And sometimes I get just furious with myself," she added.

"Why?" He was stymied. As far as he could see, she had done everything she'd set out to do.

"For putting us into this...this limbo." It was a new word she had learned and she grinned at it. "I should have married you right away. What was I thinking? That my feelings would change?"

His head swam. "Or mine would."

"Did they?" She held her breath.

"Yes."

She felt like the air in the room was going to crush her chest.

"Now it's even more important to me," he added.

She stared at him. Slowly, one beat at a time, her heart started moving again. "But you don't touch me anymore."

"Well, there's a good reason." He could barely get it out. He was losing his voice.

"I thought you didn't want me any longer," she went on. She had caught him looking at her. Not often. Most often she just *felt* him studying her. But sometimes she turned quickly enough to catch him at it—and on those occasions the look of longing in his eyes had nearly buckled her knees.

"That's not true," he managed.

"Then what is your reason?"

"I can't...compromise you."

She stood from the chair. "How in the world would you do that?"

How? he thought. There had been ways, a lot of ways, just moments ago. "By taking something from you that your God meant to be given only in marriage. I know that's important to you, Katie."

"Is that what you think that I want?"

"It's not what you want, damn it!" he argued, his anger growing. "It's what you deserve. I'm being honorable." Possibly, he realized, for the first time in his life.

"You're being silly."

"Katya, for God's sake—" Then he broke off, the words shattering in his throat like glass, as the little flower at the top of her bodice fell away.

He wasn't even sure she had done it on purpose. Her fingers had moved so fast. From her side to that spot just above and between her breasts. Then the flower fell loose and her hand came away again. He stared, trying very, very hard to figure out how intentional it had been.

"Uh…" he began.

"Jacob, I really hate having other people make my decisions for me," she said softly.

"Yeah. I've figured that out," he agreed, his voice raw. "But I don't. I never do that."

"Yes, you do. You've *been* doing it."

The whole front of the dress was tiny hook-and-eye buttons from neck to hem. She reached up and popped one.

"Don't do that if you don't mean it."

Katya laughed.

Actually, it was a nervous reaction. She had planned this, more or less, since halfway through the sermon this morning. The pastor had been talking about giving. About going out of one's way and helping others out even when it hurt or it was inconvenient. So she would help Jacob along. He hadn't touched her, hadn't mentioned marrying her again, since they had come here. Now, she decided, she would urge him along. She was tired of waiting, and her regret that she had ever asked him to was weighing her down more with every passing day.

She popped another button. This one was right between her breasts. Her heart thundered. She watched him stare at her, his gaze sliding up, down, up, down, between the buttons and her face. She reached for the next one.

Jacob finally moved. He shot at her like a bullet and caught her hand. "You can't do this."

"Jacob, you're wrong. Here, in your world, I can do whatever I want."

"Within reason, for God's sake! There are two plate-glass windows over there facing onto a city street!"

"Don't yell. The children will hear you and come down-stairs."

"Well, they're another reason we shouldn't do this!"

"Chicken?" she asked. And she laughed.

"*Me?* Honey, I..." He lost his voice as she tugged her fingers out of his and quickly unlooped three more buttons. He grabbed the two gaping sides of her dress in both hands, holding them closed again.

And he knew he was at the end of whatever honor he possessed.

"Okay," he said. "Okay. We'll talk about this."

"We just did."

"Not to my satisfaction. We'll...uh, we'll—"

"Get married?"

"I never stopped wanting that!"

"You have an odd way of showing it."

She stepped back from him quickly. But his hands didn't release her dress in time, and the end result was that the pull on the fabric popped the next five or so buttons. A couple spattered on the floor. She laughed again at his look of horror, then her heart leaped as his eyes came slowly back to hers, and the laugh died in her throat.

His eyes were on fire.

She turned and hurried into his office in the back. She could hear him following her. She shrugged quickly so the dress dropped off her shoulders. She let it pool on the floor and stepped out of it. She was still decently covered—she wore a lacy slip and undergarments, even shoes with pretty little heels—but she heard his feet skid up short as he came into the office behind her.

She shimmied out of the slip, as well. Jake was having a ridiculously hard time breathing. He took another quick step into the room and closed the door behind him.

"Not here, Katie," he managed one last time. "Not now."

"I believe you said that the first time we made love, too."

And it hadn't stopped them then, either, he remembered. "Yeah, but—"

"This is perfect, Jacob. It's where we've worked together

and wanted each other for six months,'' she interrupted. ''It's where we've waited, to make sure this matters.''

''Five and a half months,'' He corrected inanely.

''It was forever,'' she breathed. ''So very *long*.''

Finally, he thought, something he couldn't argue with.

''Lock the door, Jacob.''

Jake stared at her a moment longer, his heart thundering. There was a lot to stare at. If she didn't spend a lot of money on her dresses, then he thought she had probably splurged a little on the lingerie. He had never imagined that anything so demure could be so sexy, how anything so simple could almost immobilize him with need.

Her bra was purely white, just a hint of lace at the top. No bikini panties—they came all the way up to her waist, but the legs were high cut. And her stockings—dear God, her stockings. They were the thigh-high kind, and he knew somehow that in the back of her mind, she was being practical—it was hot as blazes out there after all—but he wondered, too, if she knew what effect they would have on him.

A fist grabbed his throat and tightened as she stepped backward and lifted herself onto the desk with a little hop. She sat there neatly, prettily, waiting.

Waiting.

He needed to say the words again, he realized. They were halfway up his throat, but they lodged there, tangled with fear, though what she wanted was obvious. He opened his mouth, swallowed carefully, and she took her bra off.

There was only so much he could stand.

He threw the lock quickly and closed the last of the distance between them. He caught her hair in both hands. She always wore it down now, enticing him, almost as though to please him. He ground his mouth over hers. She gave a little cry and reached up to grab his wrists. His mouth left hers, went to her ear, her neck, her collarbone, with a hunger he had only barely dared to acknowledge all these months.

Katya was elated, then even that emotion washed out of her on a tide of something else, of something like sweet delirium.

So long. She was absolutely sure she had wanted this man since before she was born.

He dropped her hair. Her eyes flew open, then she felt his hands slide beneath her on her desk, and he lifted her against him. She wrapped her legs around him instinctively, though she knew he'd never let her fall.

"Jacob..."

"I never stopped wanting you," he rasped.

"I know."

"I wanted you too much."

"I know that, too."

"I love you. Marry me, Katie. Please. Now. This afternoon."

"Whenever you say, Jacob. Just not in the next half hour or so."

He felt something lift off his chest with the words and he could breathe again.

She felt her eyes burn with simple relief, with happiness.

His mouth was back at her neck again, then he lifted her higher. And all thought shattered in her mind as his mouth found her breasts and nuzzled there. And this time when she tilted her head back and sighed, he didn't stop her.

His tongue circled one nipple then the other, and she tangled her hands into his hair to hold him there, at the same time wanting so much more. Then he groaned and his mouth went back to her ear, to her hairline.

"This still isn't right," he managed. "Not here."

"It's what I want," she gasped.

He made a sound that might have been laughter. "Well, then, that settles it."

He eased her back down onto the desk. He leaned over her, claiming her mouth again, finding the waist of her panties. He slid them down and she shuddered and called out his name.

Not Jake. Jacob.

He tossed the swatch of nylon aside. Need was pounding in his blood now, hot and violent. He had to get his clothes off and didn't want to leave her lying there to do it. So he leaned over her again, kissing her, and he felt her fingers tangle in the buttons of his shirt. She pulled as he had inadvertently done to her dress, and the buttons flew.

He laughed aloud that time, and shrugged it off his shoulders. He tugged off his boots and slipped out of his jeans. She sat up to watch him hungrily.

He was overwhelmed, shaken, still, after all this time. That she could be so pure and so perfect...with everyone but him. Just him. He finished undressing as quickly as he could.

There was not, after all, any way he could draw this out, make it as incredible as it had been the first time, so sweet and giving. The office wouldn't allow it. But there would be a later, he realized. There would be a million laters. For now, there was only an urgency too big to be denied, for both of them.

He lifted her hips and slid into her without warning. He watched her eyes widen a little, then a smile twitched on her mouth. He eased her back onto the desk again—tried to. She'd have none of it, and he laughed again.

She twined her arms around his neck and held on, planting a frenzy of kisses over his chest as he moved inside her, with exquisite care at first, then more desperately. There was a thump on the ceiling upstairs and her legs tightened around him and he thought, *Got to yell up to those kids to be good,* but then he felt the first tremors rock through her and he was gone.

It was a long time before she leaned back onto the desk with a sigh. He leaned over her still, but his mouth was gentle now as it traced her jaw.

"Do you know..." she whispered.

"Hmmm?"

"I'm probably never going to be able to watch you sit here at this desk again without blushing."

"Good."

In the meantime, chaos was erupting upstairs.

He caught her hands and pulled her to her feet again. She came reluctantly. He couldn't resist running a finger beneath the top of her stockings.

"What's with these?" he asked, half-grinning.

"It's too hot out there to be trussed up like a sausage. And I don't have to be anymore."

He gave a bark of laughter. He'd known it.

"And I thought you'd like them."

"I do." He drew her into his arms. "Oh, yeah, I do."

The next crash from upstairs was far more ominous. Katya groaned.

"Would you mind listening for the phones, Jacob? I've got to stop their shenanigans before they crash right through the ceiling."

He stepped away from her. "I'll do it. I have something to hold over Levi's head."

She blinked in surprise. "What?"

"Spy school."

"*Spy* school?"

"It's a sort of program some of my old buddies on the D.P.D. put together for the inner-city kids. But I think he'd like it."

"It's a program to be a policeman?"

Well, Jake thought, it was mostly designed to show kids how easy it was to grow up on the right side of the law. To give them some incentive. Jake had retired from the department to run ChildSearch, but he was offering his help with the program. It taught kids about being a cop, too.

"Yeah," he answered and began dressing. He was halfway to the door when he stopped and looked back. "There's something I ought to tell you."

Her heart skittered. "What?"

"The way we do marriage, in my world, you can leave if you want to."

"I don't want to," she whispered. She couldn't believe she'd ever want to.

He crossed back and kissed her. He wondered if she could taste his relief. "Good. Because I'd have to follow, have to hunt you down and bring you back."

She smiled widely. "And you can find anybody, anywhere. You're so smart, Jacob."

"Don't you forget it."

She wouldn't. And she would spend the rest of her days making sure he didn't, either.

* * * * *

Watch for Saving Susannah, *the last book
in* The Wedding Ring *trilogy, coming in October 1998
from Silhouette Sensation®.*

COMING NEXT MONTH

CAPTIVE STAR Nora Roberts

The Stars of Mithra

All bounty hunter Jack Dakota was supposed to do was pick up pretty M.J. O'Leary, but someone had set them both up. M.J. wasn't talking— not even when Jack found a giant diamond in her bag. And now they were handcuffed together and on the run...

A MARRIAGE-MINDED MAN Linda Turner

Enter Single, Leave Wed! & Heartbreakers

Sam Kelly was a cynical cop and he was deeply suspicious when Jennifer Hart gave him the facts of a crime that hadn't yet been committed! The fact that he was attracted to her only made him more irritated and determined to find out her exact involvement.

BRANDON'S BRIDE Alicia Scott

Maximillian's Children

Brandon Ferringer was just in town for the summer, the fire-fighting season, but seeing him each evening it was inevitable that the sexual tension that was building between them would rage out of control. But she wanted forever and he was his father's son...

KNIGHT ERRANT Marilyn Pappano

Southern Knights

To protect Nicholas Carlucci, Lainie Farrell had to stick to him like glue, close enough to see his noble soul beneath his tough exterior. Close enough to know that now she, too, was in danger...

COMING NEXT MONTH FROM

 **SILHOUETTE®**

Intrigue
Danger, deception and desire

HER HERO Aimée Thurlo
FORGET ME NOT Cassie Miles
FLASHBACK Terri Herrington
HEART OF THE NIGHT Gayle Wilson

Special Edition
Satisfying romances packed with emotion

TENDERLY Cheryl Reavis
FINALLY A BRIDE Sherryl Woods
THE RANCH STUD Cathy Gillen Thacker
LITTLE BOY BLUE Suzannah Davis
DADDY'S HOME Pat Warren
HER CHILD'S FATHER Christine Flynn

Desire
Provocative, sensual love stories for the woman of today

THE COWBOY STEALS A LADY Anne McAllister
BRIDE OF THE BAD BOY Elizabeth Bevarly
THE EDUCATION OF JAKE FLYNN Leandra Logan
HER TORRID TEMPORARY MARRIAGE Sara Orwig
THE KIDNAPPED BRIDE Metsy Hingle
THREE-ALARM LOVE Carole Buck

EMILIE RICHARDS

THE WAY BACK HOME

As a teenager, Anna Fitzgerald fled an impossible
situation, only to discover that life on the streets was
worse. But she had survived. Now, as a woman,
she lived with the constant threat that the secrets of
her past would eventually destroy her new life.

1-55166-399-6
AVAILABLE IN PAPERBACK
FROM SEPTEMBER, 1998

4 FREE
books and a surprise gift!

We would like to take this opportunity to thank you for reading this Silhouette® book by offering you the chance to take FOUR more specially selected titles from the Sensation™ series absolutely FREE! We're also making this offer to introduce you to the benefits of the Reader Service™—

- ★ FREE home delivery
- ★ FREE gifts and competitions
- ★ FREE monthly newsletter
- ★ Books available before they're in the shops
- ★ Exclusive Reader Service discounts

Accepting these FREE books and gift places you under no obligation to buy; you may cancel at any time, even after receiving your free shipment. Simply complete your details below and return the entire page to the address below. *You don't even need a stamp!*

YES! Please send me 4 free Sensation books and a surprise gift. I understand that unless you hear from me, I will receive 4 superb new titles every month for just £2.50 each, postage and packing free. I am under no obligation to purchase any books and may cancel my subscription at any time. The free books and gift will be mine to keep in any case.

S8YE

Ms/Mrs/Miss/Mr...................................Initials ....
BLOCK CAPITALS PLEASE

Surname ....

Address ....

....

....Postcode.................................

Send this whole page to:
THE READER SERVICE, FREEPOST, CROYDON, CR9 3WZ
(Eire readers please send coupon to: P.O. BOX 4546, DUBLIN 24.)

Offer not valid to current Reader Service subscribers to this series. We reserve the right to refuse an application and applicants must be aged 18 years or over. Only one application per household. Terms and prices subject to change without notice. Offer expires 28th February 1999. You may be mailed with offers from other reputable companies as a result of this application. If you would prefer not to receive such offers, please tick box. ☐

Silhouette Sensation is a registered trademark used under license.

JAYNE ANN KRENTZ

A Woman's Touch

He was her boss—and her lover!
Life had turned complicated for Rebecca Wade when she
met Kyle Stockbridge. He *almost* had her believing he
loved her, until she realised she was in possession
of something he wanted.

"...one of the hottest writers in romance today."

—USA Today